DAYL THE
BOA CAFE

ALISON SHERLOCK

B

Boldwood

First published in Great Britain in 2026 by Boldwood Books Ltd.

Cover Design by Alice Moore Design Ltd

Cover Images: Shutterstock and iStock

A CIP catalogue record for this book is available from the British Library.

Paperback ISBN 978-1-83617-705-0

Large Print ISBN 978-1-83617-706-7

Hardback ISBN 978-1-83617-704-3

Trade Paperback ISBN 978-1-80656-371-5

Ebook ISBN 978-1-83617-707-4

Kindle ISBN 978-1-83617-708-1

Audio CD ISBN 978-1-83617-699-2

MP3 CD ISBN 978-1-83617-700-5

Digital audio download ISBN 978-1-83617-703-6

This book is printed on certified sustainable paper. Boldwood Books is dedicated to putting sustainability at the heart of our business. For more information please visit https://www.boldwoodbooks.com/about-us/sustainability/

Boldwood Books Ltd, 23 Bowerdean Street, London, SW6 3TN

www.boldwoodbooks.com

For romance author 'buddie' and friend Jennifer Bibby for helping me to start this book and for seeing it through to the end as well!

With love x

1

Hannah Jackson looked at the group of people running along the muddy track and grimaced.

'If I ever feel the need to do something crazy like a triathlon, just kill me because I'll have probably gone insane,' she declared.

Lily Wilson, one of Hannah's best friends, turned to smile at her. 'The only time I do exercise is when my mascara runs,' she joked.

Ben Jackson, Hannah's older brother, shook his head at them both. 'Could you try and be a little more supportive?' he asked. 'This is the inaugural Dragonfly Lake Triathlon, after all.'

'As long as we don't have to take part in it, I'm happy,' Hannah told him. 'But I can think of better things to do on Easter Sunday.'

Like baking, she added to herself. The hot cross buns she had already made had gone down a storm at the hotel and the next batch were still proving in the larder.

But with her brother's words still ringing in her ears, she tried to concentrate on the race. She hadn't been joking about how hard it was to compete in a triathlon. The race had started at 10 a.m. with a 1.5 km swim across Dragonfly Lake, followed by a 40 km bicycle ride around the local Cotswold country lanes. The competitors were now on the final part, the 10 km run, which was five circuits of the lake.

Hannah thought it sounded utterly exhausting and even the Easter weekend sunshine finally appearing after heavy rain earlier couldn't help those athletes struggling around the course who looked exhausted.

Nearby, a thick red ribbon had been strung across the rough track as a makeshift finish line, placed just in front of their family-run hotel. Not knowing what to expect from this first triathlon held by Maple Tree Lodge, the whole family were thrilled by the response of having so many local competitors enter, as well as a large crowd of spectators.

After all, it had only been six months ago that the hotel had been close to bankruptcy. An uptick in fortunes, thanks to Ben and Lily, who had renovated the hotel into a cosy country destination, had meant that bookings had continued to fly in each weekend. Although business was still a little slow, so the hotel was not at capacity as often as they had hoped.

Ben gave his sister a nudge with his elbow as he noticed Tom Addison of the *Cranbridge Times* nearby. 'Smile and look as if you're enjoying this, would you?' he muttered. 'The local press are here.'

Hannah suppressed a yawn. 'I'm being supportive by just being here,' she told him. 'I had to work late last night, remember?'

'How late was that, by the way?' asked Ben with a frown. 'Even I went to bed before you and that was gone midnight.'

Hannah shrugged her shoulders. 'You know what Saturday

nights are like. There was loads of clearing up to do after a big works party at the pub,' she replied. 'It took me ages to tidy up before I could leave.'

Hannah worked at the Rose and Crown in Aldwych town, ten miles away from Maple Tree Lodge where she lived with her family. The waitressing job was hard and not particularly enjoyable, thanks to a demanding manager which led to a high staff turnover. But it was a job for which she was grateful as it helped bring much-needed funds into the family.

'Wasn't there anyone else to help you?' asked Lily.

Hannah shook her head. 'Everyone else had left.'

'Apart from you, as usual,' said her brother in a pointed tone. 'They take advantage of you. I don't know why you don't just leave. There must be better places for work somewhere out there.'

Faye Jackson, on the other side of her son and daughter, suddenly said in a bright tone, 'Oh, look! There's only two laps of the lake to go!'

Hannah glanced at their mum with a grateful look of thanks for the distraction, soothed as always by Faye's gentle way of diverting any arguments from bubbling up.

Faye was quiet and steady like Hannah. Ben was more hot-blooded, taking after their late dad and their grandad Walter, who was sitting on a camping chair nearby, banging his hand down on the arm rest. 'Look at that guy elbowing his way through the pack!' shouted Walter. 'That's blatant cheating!'

'Walter,' said Lily, before hushing him. 'Think of the guests, please.'

'It's a race, isn't it?' muttered Walter.

As the athletes ran along the track on the other side of Dragonfly Lake and despite feeling weary after her late night, Hannah couldn't help but smile at the view, her favourite in the whole world.

The lake sparkled under the spring sunshine, gentle ripples glittered under a soft breeze that was sweeping across the water. Beyond the track that went around the lake where the athletes were running were the trees and large swathes of forest, all of which was owned by the Jackson family.

Beyond the lake and forest were the green rolling hills of the English countryside, dotted with fluffy white sheep and meadows full of yellow daffodils. The tiny new leaves on each tree and hedgerow were beginning to unfold each day now it was the first week in April. Spring was bursting into joyful life everywhere.

It was a magical setting. No wonder her great-great-grandfather had fallen in love with the place when he had first discovered it in 1918.

Once he had purchased the land, Henry Jackson had begun to build himself and his new war-time bride a home in which to bring up their family. Each generation of the Jackson family since had added more rooms and space to the lodge, using a mixture of the sandy-coloured brick that was characteristic within the Cotswolds area and the endless amount of timber that the family now owned, thanks to the surrounding woodland.

Hannah's great-great-grandfather had felled many trees to build the original lodge and the future generations had followed suit so that the outside walls of the hotel were layers of huge logs, giving the place a solid but warm look. Vast brick chimneys hugged the outside walls all the way up to the slate-tiled roof, where spires of smoke were trailing upwards into the blue sky.

Nowadays, it was a two-storey building with long wings that extended along the sandy bank of the lake. It was too large a building for just his parents, his wife and two children to live in, so Hannah's father Tony had decided to open up the place as a hotel in the early 1980s. He had altered the top floor to accommodate twenty guest bedrooms with en suites, leaving the family to sleep in private staff quarters at the end of the west wing.

What would their dad have made of their recent success, wondered Hannah, glancing up at the nearby hotel. She hoped he would be glad of the hotel being busier than she had ever known. After all, it had been a struggling business for many years, only becoming successful once Ben had taken over as hotel manager after their father's sudden passing a year ago.

She knew that Ben felt the weight of the success of the family-run hotel on his shoulders. Something he had been anxious to relieve their grandad of when he had moved back home a year ago when their father had died unexpectedly.

Things were definitely on the up for Maple Tree Lodge thanks to a major renovation but Hannah knew that the frequently unoccupied rooms during the week were still a worry for her big brother. Ben, helped by Lily's interior design skills, had helped steer the hotel into a booming business over the winter most weekends when every one of the hotel's twenty bedrooms had been occupied with guests. But during the week when the hotel became quieter, the lack of steady income played on everyone's minds.

But, despite their business worries, to Hannah and the rest of the family, it wasn't just a hotel. Maple Tree Lodge was their home as well.

'Come on, Alex!' shouted Walter as the group of athletes began to draw near on their penultimate lap of the lake.

'We should be fair to everyone taking part,' Faye reminded him in a hushed tone.

'Humph,' said Walter, his grey eyebrows fusing together in a frown. 'It's a competition, isn't it?'

Hannah's diminutive grandmother, Dotty, agreed with her

husband. 'Oh, clever Alex! Come on!' she yelled, before noting her daughter-in-law's look. 'What?' she asked Faye. 'Why can't we cheer him on?'

'Of course you can,' Ben told her in a quiet tone. 'He's my best friend and I want him to win.'

'Quite right,' added Jake, Ben's other best friend, who was standing nearby. 'I mean, it's not the Commonwealth Games yet. But everyone says he's going to win the gold there so why shouldn't he win this little race as well?'

'*Little* race?' Lily laughed. 'When was the last time you were in an endurance event?'

'Last weekend when I had that awful date,' replied Jake, making a face. 'If you'd had to put up with Annabel's inane line of conversation, you'd have been in run-away mode as well.'

Ben rolled his eyes. 'Don't tell me, another one to add to the pile of abandoned ex-girlfriends.'

'Too right,' muttered Jake, with a shudder.

Hannah smiled. Jake's lack of desire to have any kind of long-term relationship was legendary.

'Come on, Alex!' shouted Ben, as his best friend ran past them, in the lead.

Lily nudged him in the chest at his lack of diplomacy but she was smiling and clapping the rest of the pack at the same time.

'I've got the champagne ready,' said Frankie, their mum's best friend, joining them. Frankie had moved in after being widowed a few years ago. She now ran the bar in the hotel where her expertise with cocktails had made the snug, as the family referred to it, a success with the guests at the weekends. 'Alex will have to be careful when he opens the bottle. I'm not sure how long it was in the cellar for.'

'Alex might not be the winner,' Lily reminded her in a whispered tone.

'Rubbish!' replied Frankie, who wasn't known for her diplomacy. 'Of course he's going to win! Anyway, he's part of the family!'

Hannah nodded in agreement. It was true. As soon as Ben had brought his best friends Alex and Jake back from university to visit them after their graduation, both men had quickly become close to the Jackson family.

Two years older than Hannah, it was like having two extra older brothers. But where Jake was flirty and fun, Alex was the quieter, dependable one. From his personality, he was entirely suited to the steady life of an accountant. And yet, somewhat to Hannah's amazement, she found out that his free time was spent taking part in triathlons. Since then, apart from work he always appeared to be training with his father and now he was aiming to reach the highest of goals in four months' time.

Hannah looked across the lake to where Alex was out on his own at the front, still wearing the wetsuit, which showed off his athletic prowess. There were many admiring females in the crowd nearby and Hannah knew that Alex always attracted women wherever he went, with his handsome face and incredible athletic body. But she had always tried not to think of him like that. He was just Alex, lovely, reliable Alex who was always so kind and generous to her.

All the men in her family had been supportive, especially with her struggles with dyslexia growing up. Ben had tried to shield her from any school bullies but, as wonderful as her big brother was, he couldn't protect her from everyone.

From Sean, in particular.

He had been Hannah's first and only serious relationship. She'd had dates before the age of twenty-one but had never fallen in love with anyone before then. Never felt that swimmy feeling in her stomach until she met Sean at work one day.

He had arrived in the position of deputy chef at the restaurant in London where she was a junior pastry chef. As far as she was concerned, Sean had much more talent than she did and so she was flattered when he asked her out, amazed that he had even noticed her. He was dark in both looks and personality, which reflected his skills in running the kitchen in strict style. A lot of the other staff grumbled about him but Hannah had liked that he wasn't too silly compared to the other men his age.

At the time she had been living with Lily in a shared house with their two other best friends, Beth and Ella. But when Sean had asked her to move in with him, Hannah had jumped at the chance. In love for the first time ever, Hannah had envisaged romantic meals for two, lazy Sunday mornings in bed and giggling in front of the television at the latest comedy series.

But Sean didn't giggle, she began to realise as soon as she had moved in with him. In fact, he barely smiled. When he did, it made her nervous. As if he was testing her to find out whether she was telling the truth. He would deliberately pick fights and escalate arguments for no reason. Then she would be accused of deliberately making him cross. Over and over again, it was a familiar story that ran all the time. Before she knew it, Hannah was trapped in a spiral of anxiety, dread and fear.

The lack of trust he had in her was also wearing. He would repeatedly ask Hannah where she had been, whom she had spoken with. It was exhausting, draining and sometimes made her even question herself. But with so little dating experience, she wondered if perhaps Sean was right? Maybe it was all her fault that he shouldn't trust her.

Only seeing her friends and family intermittently had made Hannah question whether he might be the one at fault instead of her. They gently probed her about her sudden weight loss and haggard expression but she was able to put them off by lying that her change in appearance was only from working too hard in the restaurant.

She struggled on for a whole year, trying to hide her unhappiness from her friends and family, hoping that time would soothe her fears. She continued to forgive him even when Sean had ruined her own birthday dinner with another tantrum but made it up to her with a ring that he made her wear on her engagement finger, even though he hadn't proposed. He never took any blame, never saw any fault with his own behaviour, only hers. She had never felt more alone and began to withdraw into herself.

Eventually something had to give. It was only when he had lashed out one night over a spilt drink, pushing her over and accidentally breaking the necklace that Hannah had been wearing. It was her favourite piece of jewellery, a simple silver star pendant that Beth had given her three best friends at the end of their two-year tenancy in the London flat. It was a lovely necklace but more important had been the promise when the gift was given that the four friends would always look out for each other wherever they were in the world.

Sean had grabbed the necklace from the floor and thrown it into the kitchen bin, causing Hannah to cry. Then he had held her close, telling her that it was her fault that she had made him cross but he forgave her, like always.

It had been an escalation in his wretched behaviour, the first time that he had ever attacked her physically. Hannah decided in that moment, as he held her close, that it would be the last time as well. She was frightened as to what Sean might do next.

In the end, unable to sleep, she crept downstairs and retrieved the necklace from the rubbish bin. She cried as she clutched it in her hand, willing herself to feel the love from her friends and knowing that they would support her whatever the situation. Feeding from the strength they always gave her, she hid the necklace under a cushion for safekeeping until the morning.

Then, after Sean had left for work, she retrieved the pendant, quickly packed up her belongings and rushed back to Maple Tree Lodge, leaving both his ring and the relationship far behind her. She had remained living at home ever since.

She had received frantic phone calls and texts from Sean when he realised that Hannah had finally broken free of him. Too scared to talk to him in case he somehow talked her into meeting up, in the end she had blocked the number and tried to move on with her life.

She had told the family and her friends that the relationship had ended amicably, despite their concerns about the tears that she couldn't suppress in those early days. But Sean had been clever with his gaslighting, all the bullying had been behind closed doors, never in front of anyone else. She lied when she told everyone that she wasn't upset because it had only been a casual thing for her and Sean. Not the gut-wrenching love that she thought she had felt for him.

She knew now that it hadn't been true love, of course. Love wasn't cruel like that. Love didn't frighten or abuse. Love was what she had with her family, support, a cocoon away from the world. She was embarrassed that she had been taken in by him, that he had turned out to be just another bully. Already battling with a high-handed chef at her job, Sean had promised to protect her but instead he had been the biggest bully of them all.

Still hurting, Hannah hid herself away from the world, reluctant to even go out and socialise in those early months and years. She took menial jobs, such as stacking shelves in the local town supermarket where there were many people about and she felt relatively safe.

The family, along with her best friends Lily, Beth and Ella, had tried to gently prise her away from her home and get her back out into the outside world.

'You're such an amazing baker,' they would often tell her. 'You should do that for a living.'

But Hannah didn't believe them. She knew that she was OK and that her cakes were edible enough. But was she good enough to be a baker full time? Of course not. It was a ridiculous idea.

So she continued, reluctantly at their urging in recent months, to make cakes and biscuits for the hotel guests and carried on working as a waitress to bring in some extra money. Now that the hotel was turning a profit, however, her role had changed to include helping out with breakfast and even making desserts for dinner to help out their part-time chef Jason, who had taken over the weekend dinner service from their mum.

In the early days of the hotel's success, Ben had tried to urge Hannah to take over the dinner service instead of hiring an outside chef. But Hannah continued to decline his request, telling him that she wasn't good enough to be trusted with such responsibility.

'Come on, Alex!' urged Ben once more.

Hannah smiled at her elder brother. The complete opposite of her, Ben had never lacked confidence. Academically he had excelled, gaining good grades before becoming a gifted architect. He had given all that up when their father had passed away and, despite the stresses of the early days of the business, even the hotel was relatively successful now as well. Successful in love too now that he was with Lily. They appeared to be in blissful harmony as they ran the hotel together.

She knew things were still tight for the hotel in the tricky world of hospitality but Ben had always been likely to succeed where Hannah had so often struggled.

Only the kitchen was her safe zone. It was where her mum

was often to be found, making breakfasts for the guests. It was where her family gathered for meals. They were her strength, despite being one fewer around the table these days. She missed her dad terribly but it still felt as if she were connected to him being at home.

Baking was her go-to stress buster. She loved it. The flavours, the feeling of the cake batters and pastry that she made. It was the only time that she felt full of confidence.

'Coo, ain't this exciting?' said a familiar voice.

Hannah spun around to find that Frankie's godson Del had joined them. Del was the local coach and taxi driver, a nice guy who was always trying to be helpful around the local villages. It was just that his dubious ideas to help out his friends and himself had earned him the nickname Dodgy Del a long time ago. Trouble followed Del everywhere he went, despite his generous nature.

Although this time he appeared to have company with him, in the form of a plump black puppy.

'Del!' cooed Hannah, reaching out to stroke the young dog pulling at the lead beside him. 'You have a puppy!'

'Not mine,' he said, with a grimace. 'Tiny belongs to my old nan.'

'Is Gracie with you?' asked Faye, also stroking the soft black fur before looking around.

'Nah. She's worn out, bless her,' Del told them. 'I told her that a puppy would be too much for her. I don't know why she got him in the first place. Here, you can take him if you want. My arm's gone to sleep. He's quite strong.'

He immediately placed the end of the lead into Hannah's hand. She tried to relish holding the dog next to her but Tiny appeared to have other ideas and began to wriggle, desperate to stretch his legs.

'Keep an eye on him, would you?' said Del, glancing at his phone. 'I've got to take this call.'

Hannah looked up as Alex came around the corner, smiling and nodding at all the applause as he came home way ahead of everyone else to claim first prize, the competition trailing him by some yards. She was so pleased that he would win. How wonderful it would be to be that successful and happy in life, she thought wistfully. Despite having run hard, he made it look as effortless as always.

Alex caught her eye for a moment as he ran towards them and gave her wink.

She was so distracted at his wide smile that she didn't notice a couple of ducks sliding into a landing in the shallows of the lake on the other side of the track. But Tiny did.

Suddenly the lead was yanked in her hand and Tiny was off like a rocket, charging across the mud towards the water.

Desperately trying to hold on to the lead, Hannah was amazed at the dog's strength, despite his young age. Having no choice but to trail after him at a run, she found herself in the path of Alex, whose run had faltered as he headed towards the ribbon strung across the track for the finishing line.

Alex tried to dodge out of the way and was desperately trying to avoid them. Hannah thought that she had just about got away with it when Tiny became distracted at another dog's barking and abruptly changed course, almost doubling back on himself.

Hannah, still desperately hanging on to the lead, found herself heading back directly towards Alex and this time there was no chance to avoid him.

She hit him at speed with a clatter and she heard him cry out as they both went down onto the ground in a crumpled heap. Meanwhile Tiny had run off, the lead trailing behind him as he went, barking in happy delight as he wreaked havoc in the shallows of the lake.

To her horror, Hannah then saw a small group of athletes run past them as they lay sprawled on the ground. It appeared that Alex's hopes of winning the inaugural Dragonfly Lake Triathlon were well and truly over.

2

Alex Grant felt numb with shock as he lay sprawled on the ground next to Hannah. What had just happened?

One minute he had been comfortably in the lead of the Dragonfly Lake Triathlon, the next he was lying in the mud with his foot in agony. He sat up slowly, feeling the severe pain shooting up his lower leg and knew, without a shadow of a doubt, that at least one of the bones in his foot was broken.

One of his best friends, Ben, rushed up to them. 'Are you both OK?' he asked, helping his sister to stand up before looking down at Alex. 'Mate, I can't believe you didn't win! What a disaster! I thought you had it all wrapped up.'

Despite his own pain, Alex immediately looked at Hannah to check that she wasn't hurt. Mud was smeared down one side of her body but thankfully she appeared to be fine apart from that.

'I'm OK,' she muttered, slowly standing up. 'But I'm so sorry about the race, Alex,' she said, looking down at him with tears in her eyes. 'The puppy just ran off and I couldn't hold on to him!'

'It's not your fault,' snapped Ben. 'It's bloomin' Dodgy Del. Honestly!' He turned back to look down at Alex with a roll of his eyes. 'At least you can guarantee that this kind of thing won't happen in the Commonwealth Games!' He held out his hand. 'Come on then. Let's get you up.'

But as Alex stared up at his best friend, the reality began to sink in. The Commonwealth Games were only four months away. He tried to wiggle some of his toes once more and winced at the effort. The pain registered something in his brain. A broken bone would mean having to abandon his heavy training for at least two of those months for the healing to happen properly, leaving him vastly underprepared and unfit.

In that moment, he knew that pursuit of a gold medal was over. Everything that he and his dad had been working and training for the whole of his adult life was at an end. He didn't know whether to laugh or cry.

All he knew was that he had let his dad down and now they wouldn't win the biggest prize of them all. Because as long as he could remember, Alex had been pushed by his father, the relentless burden to win at all costs bred into him at a young age.

His father had been a winner himself many years ago. He had been a long-distance runner and the bronze medal that he had won at the World Athletics Championships still hung in his study next to his desk. But he wanted more. He wanted the top medal. However, when his own body wasn't able to continue with the pressure, he had projected his gold-medal ambitions onto his son.

From a young age, Alex had known that winning at school sports competitions had only been the beginning. It had continued into his university degree as well. His dad didn't care about Alex's academic career, nor his accountancy qualifications of which Alex was quite proud. Alex had worked for a large firm despite his dad wanting him to have his own company, thus being able to have even more time off work to train. But the pressure that Alex was under in his personal life was not something that he wanted transferred to his career, so for once, he had said no to his father, being content to turn up, do a good job and then go home to unwind. Not that he'd ever had much time to relax. Any free time, including vacation time, was filled with competitions and training.

He had always followed the sensible route away from the competitions which had meant a good, steady income and then using his savings prudently to invest which had resulted in him owning a couple of properties in London. One was rented out, the other Alex used as a base. He still made good money from his job and investments and yet he had no time to spend it. He felt as if he spent nearly all of his adult life travelling around the globe, not to relax or enjoy the sightseeing of the many different countries. But instead having to swim, bike and run over and over again. Different rivers and seas, different streets and circuits. They had all begun to merge over the years until he had felt ground down by the relentlessness of it all.

Now in his early thirties, he wanted to pursue his own dreams, to be his own man in charge of his destiny. He wanted to be settled, to have a home, a family, a life away from the training and competitions.

However, his parents had made many sacrifices on his behalf, giving up time where they could be relaxing on holiday for the constant training in order that Alex would be in top condition. So, despite his growing reticence, he had carried on trying to pursue that elusive gold medal.

In the past couple of years, however, Alex had begun to secretly long to stop. He had thought that perhaps the Commonwealth gold medal would put an end to his father's ambitions at last. But even that dream appeared to have been taken away from him, given the sharp pain in his foot at that moment.

He found Ben still looking down at him, reaching out a hand to help him up.

'I can't stand,' he told his best friend, shaking his head. 'I'm hurt.'

Ben looked horrified before glancing around at their other best friend, Jake, who had come to stand next to them.

'Can't say that wasn't the best thing I've ever seen,' said Jake, his handsome face lit up with humour in his usual relaxed style. 'That was so funny. Should have videoed it. Couldn't do it again, could you? Just for me?'

All around him, Alex saw some people in the crowd taking photos of him on their phones. He was too numb to be embarrassed. Too distraught to feel the mortification of failing so publicly and comically so close to the finishing line. All he knew was that he had failed.

'Maybe not so funny after all,' Ben told him, frowning. 'Alex is injured.'

Jake's wide smile immediately dropped. 'What is it?' he asked, his eyes sweeping over Alex. 'What hurts?'

'My foot,' replied Alex, glancing at his muddy trainer from where the severe pain was emanating. 'I think it's broken.'

His best friends exchanged horrified looks before stepping forward to link their arms around his torso.

'OK. Easy does it. On the count of three,' said Jake, before they slowly lifted him up to a standing position.

Alex tried to put some weight on his foot before immediately pulling up his leg once more to hover above the ground. 'Nope. It's too painful. I can't even stand on it.'

Jake swore. 'Looks like our celebratory drinks will have to wait,' he muttered.

Ben's mum Faye had also rushed over and was looking at him

in concern. 'Bring him inside,' she said in a hushed tone. 'We need to get some ice on that as soon as possible.'

With the help of his two best friends, Alex made slow progress towards Maple Tree Lodge on one leg. He lived in one of his own flats but had never felt any inclination to add any homely features to it, apart from a huge television and a decent sofa. It was just a base to him, not home. Any time spent at his parents' house resulted in talking competitions and training with his dad so it wasn't a relaxing place to be.

In fact, the only place he had ever thought of as a true home was Maple Tree Lodge. He had met Ben at university and instantly bonded with him in the student digs, along with Jake. The three of them had quickly become best friends and met up as often as their busy diaries allowed once they all left university.

All three of the men had settled in London for their respective careers. Ben had been an architect and Jake was a chef. So the three young men enjoyed the bright lights of the city together most weekends.

But it was only whenever they met at Ben's family home in Cranley that Alex suddenly found himself feeling settled and at home. Maple Tree Lodge was warm and welcoming, unlike his own empty soulless flat.

He glanced around the familiar entrance hall as his friends helped him inside. It was double height, full of warm oak wood and the decorative touches that made every guest feel instantly relaxed, such as aromatic candles and seasonal décor. On top of the long reception desk that weekend, there was a small white tree from which pastel coloured easter eggs had been hung as well as a couple of matching flower arrangements placed on nearby tables. Most of the decoration in the hotel was new, thanks to Lily's skills, but the peaceful environment had always been there. It was a stark contrast to his own family home where there had always been constant pressure from his dad. Here at Maple Tree Lodge, he could relax. He could step away from competing and just be himself. Not an athlete, just Alex.

But it wasn't just the peace which made Maple Tree Lodge so appealing to Alex. It was Hannah, Ben's younger sister.

The first time he had ever visited Maple Tree Lodge after graduating from university, he had been entranced by the place. But where the magic of the beautiful setting soothed his soul, it was Hannah who had left him speechless.

He could still remember the first time he had ever seen her. She had been in the large family kitchen, baking a cake for everyone when they had been introduced. He could still see the smudge of flour on her soft rosy cheek, her blue eyes stunning as they lit up with a smile for him. As she had walked over to greet him, her blonde hair had swung around her shoulders in soft waves. A wave of desire had hit him so strongly that he had almost fallen to his knees to worship her.

He found himself tongue-tied around Hannah that weekend, when he had never had any trouble talking to women before. He had enjoyed many dates at university but Hannah touched something else inside him. They had had a little conversation that weekend, despite her shyness, and he had left dreaming of a future where he could work up the courage to ask her out.

But someone else beat him to it, he found out on his next visit to Maple Tree Lodge a couple of months later. Faye, Hannah's mother, had been chatting away about how Hannah had moved in with her boyfriend Sean and Alex had had to stop himself sinking down into a chair in shock. Instead, he smiled and nodded, agreeing with Faye how lovely it was for her daughter. All the while, he felt his hopes and dreams dashed.

Trying to move on from his broken heart over Hannah, Alex had continued to date but had had only one significant relationship in those early years. He had asked out Claire from work almost immediately after his return from that fateful weekend at the hotel. It had begun as a knee-jerk reaction to Hannah moving in with Sean. But slowly, he had grown fond of Claire and begun to perhaps even see past his infatuation with Hannah. He had been young but he had thought that it might just be love and had proposed. Claire hadn't felt the same way though, and he had discovered a few weeks into their engagement that she had cheated on him. All trust was broken and Alex went back to casual dating, never wanting to trust anyone ever again.

In the meantime, Hannah's relationship with Sean had broken off after a year together and she had moved home. Initially Alex had let her mourn her failed romance but slowly over time, she seemed happy to settle at Maple Tree Lodge in her single life. As far as Alex knew, she had never dated anyone since.

His feelings for her grew stronger over time. Whenever they were together, he just wanted to be near to her. But, wary of upsetting his best friend, he only ever saw Hannah when they were all together at the hotel. However, with such a big family around they were never alone, there was never a chance to ask her out or declare his own feelings.

Even now, as his friends helped him into the kitchen, his concern for Hannah was greater than his own. She was in tears by the sink, held by Dotty, her grandmother.

'He'll be fine,' Dotty was saying as she looked up when they came in.

Hannah too looked up, her cheeks shiny with tears, her eyes filling with even more.

'Alex, it's all my fault that you're hurt,' she told him, her voice breaking with emotion.

'It's fine,' Alex replied quickly, anxious to quell her fears. 'Please don't be upset.'

But Hannah merely shook her head and her lips continued to tremble. Alex found that even worse than the actual pain he was already in.

His friends helped him to the huge oak table around which the family gathered for many meals and he gratefully sank down onto the nearest chair.

Faye crouched in front of Alex and, with immense care, she slowly and carefully began to slip off his trainer. Alex winced and tried not to cry out when his foot was released, such was the pain he was now in.

Faye looked at the foot which was already swelling and changing colour. She shook her head. 'It's not good. I think you'd better go to hospital,' she said softly. 'You need a doctor to look at this.'

Alex nodded. He had already known that it was serious and would need to be checked to see if it were broken.

'I'll take him,' said Jake, with a heavy sigh.

'Thanks,' said Ben, still staring at Alex. 'Sorry, mate. I need to stay here to take care of the guests.' The hotel had full occupancy due to many of the athletes staying over that weekend, one of the many reasons that Alex had been so keen to participate in the triathlon and ensure that the hotel's tentative prosperity continued.

As Alex carefully stood up, only putting his weight onto one leg, he glanced once more at Hannah who was still staring at him with an ashen face and shaking her head in misery.

'Don't worry about it,' he told her softly. He hated seeing her so upset.

'Absolutely,' added Ben, ever the supportive big brother. 'It was just an accident.'

'Yeah, he'll be running around as usual and making the rest of us look lazy before the weekend's over, I reckon,' said Jake, giving her a wink. But as he turned away from Hannah, Alex saw that Jake's serious eyes betrayed his jovial tone.

Ben looked at Alex and said, 'Well, mate, it looks like you might finally get that holiday that we've all been nagging you about for the past decade.'

As his friends took him by the shoulders once more to help him towards Jake's car, Alex was surprised to find that, despite everything, a tiny part of him was relieved when he thought about Ben's words. A holiday? He wasn't even sure what that was. He and his dad had declared many times that the Commonwealth Games were the big goal. And without that, the pressure was over at last. The shock that he was finally free from competing swept over him.

And yet he could feel himself thinking that, at last, it was at an end. He had even given up his accountancy job a month ago to focus on the Commonwealth Games. Suddenly he had no work and no triathlons either in his calendar.

At least perhaps he could get in a rhythm now, he found himself thinking. Have a normal life, whatever that was. Whatever happened from here on in, it was his own future at last. That dream of normality away from the competitions perhaps made the pain just a little bit more bearable, in spite of knowing with sure certainty how that decision was going to impact on his dad.

He was comfortably off for money in the meantime. But his soul? It felt empty a lot of the time. Away from the time when he was swimming, cycling and running, not much else happened in his life. Take away the triathlete and he wasn't sure what was left in its place.

Despite being on his way to hospital, Alex realised that now he had nothing but time on his hands, he might just have a chance to find out, he thought with a glance back towards Hannah before his friends helped him out of the room.

3

Hannah sighed. 'What a morning,' she said.

She couldn't believe that she had tripped over Alex and lost him the race. What must he think of her?

'For the last time, it wasn't your fault,' Lily told her, coming over to give her a hug. 'And you can't blame that little puppy either.'

'Nothing little about that enormous creature,' muttered Walter. 'More mountain bear than puppy. Tiny indeed. Humph!'

As the family began to drift out of the kitchen, only Hannah and Lily remained.

'Listen, I'd love to stay with you but we've got a hotel full of guests that need taking care of so I've got to get going,' said Lily, biting her lip as she looked at her best friend. 'Are you going to be OK?'

Hannah nodded. 'I'll be fine. I'll do some baking.'

It was her automatic response to any stress. She had already made a chocolate and raspberry tiered cake for the guests. It was a simple sponge filled with cream and raspberries which she needed to finish decorating with chocolate shards and coloured chocolate eggs.

'I think we're nearly out of your biscuits in the lounge as well,' called out Lily as she went.

Hannah had already made some spiced Easter biscuits but wanted to bake some macarons as well as finishing off another batch of hot cross buns.

She began to bring out the ingredients and, although still worried about Alex, she could feel the tension begin to leave her. The kitchen was her favourite place in the home. The oak cupboards were weathered from many years of use. Open shelves were packed with all the dishes and bowls ever needed. The aroma of home cooking mingled with the fresh scent of the herbs in terracotta pots along the windowsill. A huge oak wardrobe acted as a pantry, stuffed full of every conceivable ingredient.

Baking was the one class in school that she hadn't struggled with. She could lose herself in the feel of the food under her fingers, despite getting a few recipes wrong thanks to her dyslexia. Nowadays baking soothed her stress and anxieties and she no longer needed recipes most of the time. She followed her heart once she had memorised all the numbers and weights of the ingredients and it came to her naturally, creating magic when she could at Maple Tree Lodge.

It was a talent that she had inherited from her mum but she truly enjoyed baking. The kitchen was where they all gathered. Where her mum was. Her strength. The beating heart of their home. And it still felt as if she were connected to her dad in there as well.

She glanced over at the long oak table where they often gathered for meals. Her mum had placed a vase full of sprigs of apple blossoms and pink tulips on the table.

Through the open doorway, she could see that Lily had

added some touches of spring colour and Easter decorations around the reception and lounge as well. Lily had been an interior designer and her taste was impeccable. Hannah would love to bottle the confidence that her three best friends exuded.

Fifteen years ago, it was Ben that had pushed her to move into London to try her hand at making a career out of her baking. But where he had been so successful in the capital, Hannah hadn't. She found the city streets too busy, too hard and noisy. Only by meeting her friends almost immediately had it become bearable.

It had been a random house share in a very undesirable area of London. However, it had turned out to be the most amazing piece of luck she ever had. She shared the house with three other women of the same age: Lily, Beth and Ella. All four women were fresh out of college and starting what they hoped were going to be successful careers. At that time, Lily was working as an apprentice designer. Beth was an aspiring astronomer working at the Royal Observatory in Greenwich and Ella was a social media assistant in Canary Wharf.

The time sharing a house with her future best friends had been the best and happiest four years that Hannah had known. To have true, close friends that she loved and could depend on meant the world to her. Before she had met Sean and trusted him with her heart, stupidly thinking that he was the one.

To her delight, Lily had met and fallen in love with Ben when she had helped with the hotel renovations over the past winter and had smoothly moved on to helping out both on reception and helping manage the hotel as well. But she always tried to sneak in any interior design wherever she could, giving the hotel seasonal décor updates.

Hannah felt much the same way with her cakes and became twitchy if she couldn't bake. The job in the pub gave her no outlet for her baking so she always enjoyed being in the kitchen at home and trying out new combinations of flavours.

As she washed her hands in the sink, she glanced outside the window to where her grandparents' cottage was. They had moved into the small single storey home a few years ago but still ate most of their meals in the family kitchen. All around in the forest, the fruit trees had exploded into colour and were now a mass of frothy blossoms of pink and white. Confetti sprinkled the air in the shape of petals as they wafted down to the forest floor.

She had a brief memory of Sean putting the ring on her finger and immediately a dull ache hit her deep inside. The shadow of their relationship hung low over her, even a decade later. She quickly dismissed him from her mind with a shake of her head. Weddings and happy ever afters were for everyone else. Her brother and best friend were a happy couple and she would enjoy watching their relationship instead. Romance was for other people like Lily and Ben, never for her. Her heart would stay firmly protected, away from any more pain.

Half hour later, the macarons were cooling on a wire tray, ready to be filled. Hannah then moved on to decorating the chocolate cake.

'Mmm,' said Ben, sniffing the air as he came into the kitchen. 'Are those ready to be eaten?'

'No!' called out Hannah, as her brother reached out to take a macaron.

'Too late,' he told her, swiftly stuffing the treat into his mouth. 'Oh! Hot. But good.'

'Any news from the hospital?' asked Hannah, putting a block of chocolate back in the larder. Despite baking keeping her calm, she couldn't help but worry about Alex.

Ben swallowed before replying. 'He's just had the X-ray results. Two small bones broken in his foot.'

Hannah sank down onto one of the stools next to the kitchen island. 'Oh, no. I was hoping it wouldn't be this bad.'

Ben nodded. 'Yeah. Me too, sis.'

'What about the Commonwealth Games?' asked Hannah. After all, it was all Alex had talked about, aimed for, for so long.

'I don't know,' said Ben, with a shrug of his shoulders and looking downcast. 'But given that it's going to be at least six weeks to recover, even if the breaks are clean it's going to be pretty tight for him to be ready and fit in time. I'm not sure he's going to make it.'

'Poor Alex,' said Hannah.

She looked down at the completed chocolate cake, her mind racing on other bakes. She immediately reached out to grab a jar of pecan nuts on the counter. 'I know,' she decided out loud. 'I'll make his favourites.'

'And what are those?' asked Ben, looking surprised.

'Maple pecan plaits,' she told him. 'He loves those.'

'Well, if your baking can't cheer him up I'm not sure what will,' said Ben.

'It really is the least I can do,' she replied. 'Considering what happened.'

'Listen,' began Ben.

But Hannah held up her hand. 'I know. It's not my fault. But let me at least do this for him.'

Her brother nodded. 'Still, at least the race was a good turnout, despite how it finished.'

'It was, wasn't it?' Hannah knew how tight things still were for the hotel so any successes were to be celebrated.

'There'll be a big write-up in the local newspaper as well which will be great publicity. I was going to suggest we make it a monthly race thing but that just seems cruel at this moment,' carried on Ben, with a frown. 'I'll have to leave that idea for a while. I don't want to upset Alex any further. But now that we're into the summer months, it's going to be impossible to hold the light festival to bring in new people from the local areas.'

The light festival had been Dotty's idea over the winter, in which floating lanterns had been placed on the lake in a show each weekend, in time to music played over speakers on the beach. It had rapidly gained in popularity, so much so that the hotel had become full each weekend that it had been held.

But now that April had arrived and the clocks had jumped forward, the lighter evenings meant that it wouldn't be possible to hold it over the coming months.

'We'll have to think of something else,' said Ben, still frowning. 'We need something to draw in the local community, I reckon.'

'You will,' Hannah told him.

As she began to make the puff pastry for the maple pecan plaits, she let her mind wander, trying to think up ideas that might bring in extra funds to the hotel that summer, but could think of nothing so carried on with her baking.

'Hope so,' muttered Ben before brightening up. 'But you know what always helps generate a good idea? Another one of these.'

He was already heading out of the kitchen with a second macaron before Hannah had a chance to lob a dishcloth at him.

4

On the way back from the hospital later that afternoon, Alex stared out of the window at the countryside, only responding to Jake's chatty conversation with the odd word or grunt of reply.

He knew Jake understood his muted responses. That was the thing about best friends. They knew all your faults and reactions, especially during the worst of times.

It had been a long wait of four hours at the hospital. Four hours since he had broken two small bones in his foot. Four hours of avoiding the texts and missed calls from his dad.

Alex had thought that he was finally going to get his gold medal that summer. That he would finally make his parents proud, but now that dream seemed impossible. He stared down at the large boot placed on his broken foot. The hospital had told him it would be six weeks before he could begin even light training. The more intense workouts would have to wait and that left him out of time for the Commonwealth Games. The dream of the gold medal was now out of the question.

He barely registered the journey until finally Maple Tree Lodge came into view as Jake drove into the car park. He instantly felt a sense of calm, despite his muddled upset thoughts.

Whenever he had finished a competition, this was where he came. It wasn't his official home and yet it was always the first place he thought to come to. He had planned to come home right after the Commonwealth Games in July, perhaps even take a bit of time over August to spend time with the family and his friends. Now time was all he had, stretching out in front of him.

He huffed out a sigh. He had trained so hard this past year, perhaps harder than he had ever done before. He had sacrificed so much to be the fittest he had ever been. And now what? What came next in his life? He had no idea.

He thought back to when he had broken his first swimming record aged ten and that had lit the blue touchpaper for his dad's ambitions. A junior European cup had followed. At his first World Cup, he had crashed his bicycle and despite dislocating his shoulder had got back to training the following day. He had thrown up sometimes on the finishing line, his body pushed over its limit time and time again. He had been exhausted, crying on the ground on other occasions, having pushed on through various ailments and pain from his muscles. He had trained harder and harder in every spare moment out of work. Training for him wasn't fun, but it was a means to an end and that end had always been a gold medal. He had never given much thought as to what happened when that day arrived. And now it never would.

He glanced out of the windscreen to the glittering lake beyond the hotel car park. Well, perhaps swimming across Dragonfly Lake had been fun, as well as biking and running the forest trail around the lake. Here, training had never felt like hard work. He enjoyed being amongst nature, staying at Maple Tree Lodge with the family. Welcomed into the heart of the Jackson family with their generosity and kindness, they had always helped take him away to a better place mentally speaking. A calmer, happier place where he could just be Alex. Not a competitor, not racing towards a gold medal. At Maple Tree Lodge, he was just like Jake, one of Ben's best friends, and that was all with no judgement or pressure. It was their adopted home, his and Jake's. And they were truly grateful for it. Here he could relax before time inevitably dragged him back to the reality of the next competition. But what happened when there wasn't going to be another one, perhaps ever?

Jake got out of the car and went around the bonnet to hold the passenger door open for him.

'Come on,' he said. 'Let's get you inside to your adoring masses.'

The crutches were going to take a little getting used to, thought Alex as he manoeuvred them out of the car and slowly stood up. Thankfully the flat in London where he lived had a lift but there was the small matter that driving would also be impossible for a while. There were so many questions that needed to be answered about his future but right now he was just feeling tired and in pain.

As Alex and Jake slowly went across the car park towards the hotel, Ben came out of the front entrance and strode towards them. Alex braced himself. He loved his friend but he wasn't sure he was strong enough to face any teasing, despite their long friendship.

But Ben merely stepped forward to give him a hug. Over his shoulder, Alex turned to look at Jake. If anyone was going to make a joke about his situation, it would be Jake. But there was no quip this time. No funny drawled sarcasm. Just support and strength from both of them as his friends gave him a gentle slap on the back.

In friendly silence, they headed inside across the large entrance hall and into the kitchen where he found all the family gathered to greet him.

Normally, the arrival of either of Ben's best friends would cause a ripple of good cheer and greetings. But this time, the atmosphere in the kitchen was much more muted.

Faye rushed up to him first, murmuring reassuring words in his ear. She was soft and gentle and reminded him of his own mother.

Dotty was next and Alex had to smile as she had to reach up on tiptoes to give Alex a kiss on his cheek. Even then, he had to bend down to reach the diminutive grandmother. She gave his arm a squeeze before stepping back to let Walter come forward.

The grey-haired man stepped forward and gave him a firm nod.

'Don't let the buggers grind you down,' said Walter.

Alex smiled at him in thanks.

Then there was Frankie, Faye's oldest friend.

'You know what I do when I'm sad?' she said. 'Pour myself a drink. So what'll it be?'

There was a resounding 'No!' around the kitchen. Frankie's cocktails were legendary and sometimes extremely strong. Thankfully she kept them a little milder but equally delicious when she was bartender in the snug each evening.

'What?' said Frankie, with a shrug at the chorus of negativity she had just received. 'I was talking for medicinal purposes, of course!'

Faye smiled but shook her head at her best friend. 'How about a coffee or a cup of tea instead?' she asked.

Alex nodded. 'Thanks. Tea would be great.'

Finally he looked across at Hannah as she walked towards

him. She was studying him with those deep blue eyes, as if she could feel the pain that was just bubbling under the surface.

He was surprised but pleased when she came across to give him a hug.

She didn't say anything reassuring. What could she say that would make any difference? But the extra squeeze she gave him before stepping back made all the difference and he felt better, despite the whole wretched day.

As she stepped back, she pointed at the pastries on the cooling rack.

'They're your favourite,' she told him. 'Maple pecan plaits.'

'You remembered?' he said, surprised and pleased that she knew him so well.

'Just in case the hospital food was bad,' she told him with a soft smile.

'It was,' he replied. 'Truly dreadful.'

'Sit down and I'll bring them over,' she said.

Jake was already making jokes about the pretty nurse who had helped them at the hospital. Alex rolled his eyes. He knew that Jake's revolving door on his love life was in direct response to the wretched divorce that his parents had suffered, and ensured that everyone else had suffered as well. He was a loyal friend though, and for that Alex was grateful.

Ben, on the other hand, was happy and settled after a difficult year when he had lost his dad so quickly. Ben was happy, both in love and in life too.

How Alex longed for that happiness, he thought. Even Jake's love life had made him envious in his more lonely moments. But it was Alex's decision not to get too involved with anyone, despite encouragement from both of his best friends. As an athlete constantly training and competing, having a long-term relationship had been near-on impossible and the spectre of Claire's cheating had made him suspicious of getting close to anyone new.

As the family fussed over him, Alex checked his phone once more and grimaced as he saw there was another missed call. At some point he would have to face his dad and tell him the worst of news.

Later, he told himself, as Hannah brought over the pastries with a soft smile. She placed one on a plate and handed it over to him.

There was still so much that needed to be decided upon. He needed to think about where he was going to work and earn a living. His foot ached inside the boot and he desperately needed a shower. He had always done the right thing by his family, worked hard and yet he was still utterly exhausted. His whole future was a mystery to him in that moment.

For now though, as the Jackson family chatted around the table, he was happy to sit with them where there was no pressure to be anything but himself.

5

After he'd eaten a couple of the pastries that she'd made for him, Alex had left the kitchen to go and have a shower. Despite his assurances that he was fine, Hannah was still worried about him.

'Was he OK at the hospital?' she asked Jake. 'He's pretty quiet.'

'Can't blame the lad for that,' said Walter from the head of the table. 'It's been a bit of a shock for him breaking his foot and all that.'

'I think he's in a lot of pain but not letting on,' said Jake, reaching out to give Hannah's hand a reassuring squeeze. 'Don't fret. We'll dose him up on painkillers and he'll be back to his old self very soon.'

'Poor Alex,' said Dotty, shaking her head. 'And he was so close to winning as well.'

'He must feel so disappointed,' said Faye, coming to stand next to the table.

'Disappointed is a bit of an understatement, Mum,' Ben told her. 'More like devastated, I reckon.'

Lily, who had been scrolling through her phone, looked up

with a grimace. 'And he's trending at number one on the local news as well,' she said.

Ben frowned. 'What are they saying?' he asked.

'That the triathlon was a success and the hotel is heavily mentioned.' Despite the good news, however, Lily looked downcast. 'But the comments online about Alex aren't funny. People can be very mean.'

'What can we do?' asked Hannah, feeling upset.

She hated the thought of Alex being ridiculed. He was always so kind and generous to everyone that it was awful to think of him mocked for an accident that wasn't of his making.

'I'm thinking of inviting him to stay here for the week or as long as he needs, especially in these early days,' Ben told them.

'Good idea,' said Faye, nodding her head as she basted the roast lamb before putting it back in the oven. 'He'll need taking care of and I don't like to think of him struggling in that flat all by himself.'

'Shame about all those online trolls though,' said Walter, his grey eyebrows crossing into a frown. 'People have accidents and make mistakes. It only makes them human.'

'Yeah, I know, Grandad,' said Ben. 'But in an instant world where everything can be quickly turned into a TikTok meme, it means it's out there forever.'

'I miss the good old days,' said Walter, shaking his head.

'You mean where the electricity used to cut off every other day and there were only three channels on the television?' replied Dotty, making a face at her husband.

Hannah smiled. Her grandmother had always had a positive way of looking at the world.

'Absolutely. Give me Netflix any time,' added Frankie with a grin as she came into the kitchen.

'At least the race was a success, despite everything else,' said Faye.

Everyone nodded. Hannah had been amazed when Ella had announced her idea for the triathlon. The last time the four best friends had got together in the spring, they had talked about getting much-needed publicity for the hotel to boost bookings. With Alex also staying that weekend, Ella had the bright idea to talk him into organising a triathlon whilst she handled the marketing.

Since her early days of being a lowly marketing assistant in Canary Wharf, Ella had since moved to Manchester and worked for a couple of start-up media companies. Hannah knew that her friend still longed to be her own boss though, despite her career success.

With Ella's normal efficiency, the triathlon had been quickly organised in time for Easter weekend. Alex had been advertised as the star athlete, of course. Not that it had done him any good, thought Hannah, biting her lip.

She still blamed herself, no matter what the family told her. If only she had held on to the lead a bit tighter, then Tiny wouldn't have run amok. She shook her head at herself and tried to dismiss her guilt as she headed into the lounge to check on the cakes she had made earlier.

Across the entrance hall, the lounge was a large room but felt comfortable despite its double-height ceiling. Thanks to Lily's excellent taste in interior design, it was filled with plump leather sofas, plaid-clad armchairs and cosy oak beams strung with fairy lights. A large fireplace on one side of the room, lit every day in the winter time, was currently filled with thick white candles and bordered by vases filled with fresh apricot-coloured tulips.

Through the door in the far wall was the snug, another newly decorated room which had been transformed into a popular bar, cosy but relaxing with yet more armchairs as well as a snooker table and an oak bar which sparkled with LED lighting, giving it a modern twist. The dark walls were both warming in the winter and cooling in the summer. It was a stylish but merry hub where both hotel guests and some locals enjoyed gathering in the evenings. But although in vastly contrasting styles of decoration, the lake was the bond that connected both rooms as they were both edged with huge windows and doors which led out to a veranda that ran the length of the rooms and hovered over the lake, giving that glorious view out across the water to the far side.

Lily had come up with the idea for a drinks and snacks honesty trolley for the hotel guests and Hannah was mollified to find that most of the cakes and biscuits she had made had already been eaten and hopefully enjoyed. It also provided a much-needed extra bit of income for the hotel, as she glanced inside the little tin left for donations and was pleased to find quite a bit of money in there.

Carrying the cash tin and the pile of used tea plates back to the kitchen, she found that most of the family had dispersed to finish various chores around the hotel before dinner but found her brother still at the dining table on his phone.

Ben sighed. 'Alex's wasn't the only bit of bad news today,' he told her with a grimace. 'Penny, the lady that was going to manage the Boathouse Café for me, has changed her mind already. She doesn't want to do it any more.'

Now that the hotel renovations were complete, Ben had fixed his sights on the rest of the land owned by Maple Tree Lodge to keep ahead with the business. There were plans to build some lodges around the lake for private accommodation to be rented out, as well as to utilise some of the older, empty barns as well.

But while the long wait for planning permission for the lodges continued, Ben's most promising idea was the old boathouse. He had come up with a plan to turn it into an extra catering venue for both guests and local visitors. It was certainly large enough and with the renovations already complete, he had applied for the temporary licence to run a café over the summer.

'Penny's quit the café already?' asked Hannah, amazed. 'It's not even ready to open yet!'

'Yeah,' replied Ben, blowing out a sigh. 'Talk about bad timing. The catering kitchen has just been installed and it's almost ready to go in a couple of weeks. We've already begun to advertise online that opening date will be the bank holiday weekend. That's not going to leave us a lot of time to find someone else.'

'Well, don't ask me to take over,' said Frankie, coming back into the kitchen and placing a few mugs into the dishwasher. 'I can hardly keep up with demand in the snug.' The hotel bar had become a huge success, especially at the weekends. 'Although what we're going to do come the summertime, I don't know,' she carried on. 'That veranda isn't very big and people will want to be outside, I'm sure.'

'That's why I thought the boathouse might be a good idea,' replied Ben, still looking downcast. 'It's got a great outside space.'

'Maybe we can put out a few rugs on the beach or something,' said Frankie with a shrug before walking out.

'Did Penny say why she had changed her mind?' asked Hannah.

'She said it was too isolated,' Ben told her. 'The commute would be too tricky.'

Hannah shook her head. 'She must be mad,' she said, with a smile. 'It's the isolation here that I love the most.'

It was true. The forest that hugged the land and hotel had always felt like a protective shield against the outside world for her. As soon as she had come home to live after her disastrous relationship with Sean had ended, she knew that she was safe. Secure. Loved. No wonder she had never wanted to leave it ever since.

Lily came into the kitchen. 'I need another coffee,' she said, coming to stand next to Ben. 'I'm dead on my feet this afternoon. Anyone else want one?'

But Ben was staring across the table at his sister with a strange look on his face. Lily followed his gaze, looking a little confused.

'What?' snapped Hannah, at her big brother, shuffling awkwardly under his gaze. She hated anyone looking at her for too long, uncomfortable under any kind of scrutiny.

'You could do it,' he said.

Hannah was baffled. 'Do what?' she asked.

'Run the Boathouse Café,' he told her.

Hannah immediately shook her head. 'No!' she told him. 'No, no, no!' She looked at her best friend for support but Lily was smiling instead.

'Oh, that's a brilliant idea!' she declared. 'Hannah, you'd be amazing! Just think…'

But Hannah didn't want to think about the responsibility. About serving her own cakes to strangers who were likely to be negative about them.

She would find other ways to help out the hotel and, along with her income from the pub, they would all muddle through somehow, wouldn't they?

She had only just begun to have the confidence to place her cakes on a tea trolley for the hotel guests in the lounge. But that was different. The hotel was still Ben and Lily's responsibility. They were in charge. Not her. Never her.

'I've got to sort out my clothes for work,' she said, walking out of the kitchen as quick as she could and leaving her brother and best friend behind to exchange worried looks.

6

After a much-needed shower, Alex sank gratefully onto the comfortable bed. The bedroom had been renovated by Lily and Ben about six months ago and was now a cosy but extremely stylish place to stay.

There were five bedrooms in the private family quarters at the end of the top-floor west wing. Away from the twenty guest bedrooms, there was space for Faye, Frankie, Hannah, Ben and, until a few months ago, Lily as well to have their own rooms. Since Lily had moved into Ben's room, the spare bedroom was left to be used by their friends whenever they stayed.

Alex and Jake were happy to share the room, despite its somewhat romantic theming, thanks to Lily's artistic skills. The room mirrored the guest bedrooms and so had a handcrafted four-poster bed made out of oak from the surrounding forest and thick expensive bed linen making it feel luxurious.

There was even some lavender spray on the bedside stand, filling the air with its romantic, relaxing scent. Not that Alex was feeling particularly relaxed. His foot was extremely painful and he had to keep the weight off for at least a few days, trying to rest as much as he could.

He was grateful to the Jackson family for offering the room to him for as long as he wanted, even after Jake left to head back to London the following day. By way of thanks for their many stays throughout the year which included free accommodation, Alex and Jake would try to repay the family wherever they could. Jake's skills as a chef were often utilised in the kitchen, mucking in to help cook the breakfasts, as well as finding them Jason, the part-time chef.

For his part, Alex had tried to help Ben with the accounts, even sorting out a large tax rebate on his dad's estate. From time to time, he had also given Walter a hand in the workshop whenever there was any heavy lifting to be done. Not that he would be much use for the foreseeable future, he thought to himself.

But he couldn't relax or even begin to think about his recovery until he had made the phone call that he had been putting off ever since his accident that morning.

He took a deep breath and then brought out his phone to video chat his parents.

After three rings, his dad answered.

'I've been trying to get hold of you all day,' his dad said, by way of greeting and looking cross. 'The flight to Sydney on Tuesday has been changed. It's three hours earlier so you'd better come here tomorrow night so we can get to the airport on time.'

Alex took a deep breath. 'Happy Easter to you too, Dad.' He paused before carrying on. 'How's Mum?'

'I'm fine, love,' said his mum somewhere in the background. 'Happy Easter.'

Alex braced himself before continuing. 'But I'm afraid I won't be able to make the flight on Tuesday, Dad.'

'What are you talking about?' his dad began. 'This has been

booked for weeks. Is this about staying with your friends? You know how important the training schedule is. We've got everything mapped out for the next sixteen weeks.'

'Well, the schedule is going to have to change.' Alex found himself gulping. 'I hurt myself this morning at the race.'

There was a short silence before his dad exploded. 'I knew it! I knew something would happen when you're dealing with amateurs. What were you thinking? I told you not to take part in that ridiculous fun run! You should have been training, not messing about with your mates in the mud.'

Alex held up his hand. 'Could you just listen to me for once?' he snapped, the pain in his foot making him more irritable than normal.

His dad's eyebrows went up in surprise but he didn't say anything.

Instead, it was his mum who spoke next. 'How did you hurt yourself?' she asked, her gentle tones as always trying to smooth things over between father and son.

'I tripped over near the finish line,' replied Alex. 'And this is the result.'

He spun the phone down to show his swollen ankle, the black and blue bruising beginning to show.

There was a deep intake of breath at the other end of the line.

'Twisted ankle?' asked his dad, sounding optimistic.

Alex almost laughed. 'I'm afraid it's a bit more serious than that,' he said. 'I've broken two bones in my foot.'

There was a shocked silence that followed.

'Broken?' whispered his mum, sounding tearful. 'Oh, no.'

Alex nodded. 'I'm afraid so. It's going to take at least six weeks to heal, according to the doctors at the hospital.'

Everything else was going to take a lot longer, he thought, looking at his dad on the screen.

His mum sighed softly and shook her head before she too looked at her husband.

They both knew that his father's quick temper was going to explode over them eventually. Better to get it over with.

His father finally lifted his head to stare at his son. They stared at each other in silence for a moment.

'Broken?' repeated his father at last.

Alex nodded.

There was a slight pause before his father spoke again. 'Well, that's something positive at least. Better than ligament damage, I reckon. Hopefully it won't take too long to repair and then we can get going again.'

Alex gave a start. 'Get going? On what?' he asked.

'On your training, of course.'

Alex's mouth fell open in shock. 'Dad, it's too late for the Commonwealth Games. We both know that. There won't be enough time to get fully fit in time.'

But to his amazement, his dad merely shrugged his shoulders. 'Listen, we can't deny that it's a massive setback but bones heal fast. So we'll have to be careful with the training but if we get the right intensity and build on what you've already got, I reckon this could be an amazing story for next summer. After all, it's the Olympic Games next year. Just imagine winning that gold...'

Alex couldn't believe it. After everything, his dad was still carrying on with the dream of a gold medal.

He finally found his voice. 'No, Dad. Just no.'

His dad looked at him in confusion. 'What are you talking about?'

'It's over,' Alex told him.

'People have come back from worse,' said his dad, frowning. 'Just think how good winning will feel after this!'

'I'm not carrying on,' said Alex.

His dad looked shocked. 'Of course you are.'

It was a statement, not a question. Alex couldn't believe it. His dad truly believed that he would carry on and on.

'When do you expect me to stop?' asked Alex. 'When do you think that this will be over?'

His dad looked bemused. 'When you've won, of course.'

Alex laughed but it was without humour. 'And what if I don't win?' he asked.

'Don't be ridiculous,' his dad snapped.

'I'm not,' replied Alex. 'I'm being realistic. I'm thirty-four, Dad. I'm not in my twenties any more. There are younger and better competitors than me coming through the sport every year.'

'Rubbish,' said his dad before huffing out a sigh. 'Listen, if you hadn't got distracted by your friends then you wouldn't have hurt yourself. But you just need to focus your mind more. Perhaps we can schedule some time to concentrate on your mental state as well as the physical side. That's where we went wrong.'

Alex stared at his dad for a while, briefly tempted by the lure of any Olympic medal. But in the end, his main thought was that he simply didn't want to train any more. He was always so very tired all the time. He wanted to rest. He had had enough.

And he knew that if he didn't put a stop to this now, it was never going to end.

'I'm finished, Dad,' he said slowly. 'I'm not competing ever again.'

'Yes, you are,' said his dad, with a firm nod. 'Of course you are.'

But Alex shook his head. 'No. I'm done.' He knew that it was finally the moment to put into words what he had felt for so very long. 'I want a normal life, Dad, without training schedules and competitions. I want a proper holiday, not a training camp. I want to have a home that I can live in all year round. I want a job that I can take my time with, not sporadic periods of work before jetting off again.' Alex found that now he had started, he couldn't stop himself from telling them everything. 'I want to run and swim for myself, for enjoyment, not to chase another record or medal. I want to be spontaneous with my life. I want a relationship, love and all the joy that could bring me.' He came to an abrupt stop and sighed. 'I'm tired, don't you get that?'

'It's just the pain talking,' snapped his dad. 'You were born a winner, son. You know that.'

'No, I don't know that,' said Alex, running a hand through his hair. 'All this time, I was hoping you could be proud of me trying my best, not the winning part.'

'The winning is the only important bit,' replied his dad. 'Take it from me. The failure will eat you up inside if you let it.'

'I'm not you, Dad!' Alex took a deep breath. 'In fact, funnily enough, I am like you because I've failed too. You failed and so have I. Neither of us ever achieved our dream. There! We're the same. Are you happy now?'

His dad stared at him for a moment before the call abruptly cut off. His dad had hung up.

Alex lay back on the bed, staring up at the ceiling with a sigh. All those times and years he had dreamt of saying the truth to his dad. He thought he would be relieved. But right at that moment, he just felt numb.

Perhaps, once the shock had faded for all of them then they would be proud of all they had achieved together. But right now he felt more exhausted than he had ever done before.

7

Hannah wearily came down the stairs the following morning and found Alex slowly making his own descent, at the very bottom.

'Morning,' she said, with a yawn.

'Morning,' he replied, wincing. He was clearly in pain as he struggled with the boot and crutches.

A few of the hotel guests glanced over at them, not that Hannah was surprised. As usual, Alex didn't just enter a space, he filled it with his presence and enormous muscles.

But where most people would only see his breadth of shoulder and powerful arms, Hannah knew him well enough to note the shadows under his eyes and the strain that he was trying so hard to hide.

'Busy night at the pub?' he asked.

Hannah nodded. 'Like always. How are you feeling?'

'Pretty sore,' he admitted, before giving her a soft smile. 'If you've slept half as badly as I did last night, we both need some caffeine this morning,' he told her.

It was true, thought Hannah. She had returned from the pub at 1 a.m. It had turned out to be her last shift. Before leaving, the manager told her that the pub had been shut down indefinitely due to finance problems and she had been let go from her waitressing job. She hadn't particularly enjoyed it but at least it had been a steady, if relatively small, income. Now what was she going to do?

'Are you in much pain?' asked Hannah.

Alex grimaced. 'I don't feel great, to be honest,' he replied.

'It's still early days,' she told him. 'Come into the kitchen.'

They found the normal family gathering as everyone went about their busy morning.

'Morning,' came the chorus of greetings.

The family fussed over Alex for a while longer until he had sunk down onto a chair in grateful relief before almost everyone began to disperse to start their duties for the day. Only Hannah, Ben, Alex and Jake remained behind.

Hannah made a fresh pot of coffee and took it over to the table, along with a plate of pastries.

'Here you are,' she said, placing them on the table. 'A breakfast special.'

The previous day she had made Alex's favourite blueberry muffins that she knew he liked.

'Great,' said Jake, instantly reaching out to grab one. 'I need to stock up on your delicious bakes before I leave for London later.'

'They're for Alex!' protested Hannah.

'He can't eat them all!' Jake told her. 'He'll get fat now he's not in training at the moment.' He shot Hannah a grin. 'Besides, you know I can't resist your pastries. It's the one thing that I can't make.'

As a chef, Jake's food was always amazing but he was always very supportive of Hannah's baking. Although Hannah knew that he was just biased because she was Ben's sister.

Hannah's brain, however, lingered on something that Jake

had just said. 'I suppose all your training will have to be put on hold for quite a while now,' she said to Alex.

As far back as she could remember, he had always been training for a competition. Any weekend he visited Maple Tree Lodge had been half spent running or cycling around the lake to keep up his fitness.

'Only for his six weeks' recuperation,' interjected Ben with a grin. 'Then he'll be off and gone again, as usual.'

But to Hannah's surprise, Alex shook his head. 'Actually, I think I'm done with the whole thing,' he told them, before reaching out to take one of the pastries.

There was a silence as Hannah, Ben and Jake exchanged shocked looks.

'You mean, you're done with training for the time being,' said Ben, assuming it was the pain in his foot making his friend misspeak.

'And who can blame you?' added Jake, nodding. 'You deserve a break, mate. Literally, as far as your foot is concerned.'

But Alex was still shaking his head at them. 'No. I mean I'm done. Finished. No more training. No more competitions. Ever.'

More shocked silence followed.

It was Hannah that finally spoke first. 'What will you do now?' she couldn't stop herself from asking.

Alex shrugged his shoulders. 'Live. Breathe.' He gave a heavy sigh. 'Relax, at last.'

'Well, you're in the right place for it,' said Jake, but he was still frowning at his friend.

Hannah looked once more at Alex with concern. He appeared almost in shock, hardly surprising given the way that he had lost his last race. Surely he didn't mean that he wouldn't ever compete again? Perhaps he did need a break after all, she thought.

'Well, I'd better get baking later then,' she said. 'Hopefully my cakes will help you heal faster.'

'I'm sure they will,' he replied with a soft smile.

As Lily came into the room, Ben exchanged a look with his girlfriend before turning back to Hannah.

'Speaking of baking,' he began, in what sounded like a well-rehearsed speech.

But Hannah immediately shook her head and walked out of the kitchen, giving the excuse that she had chores to do. If her brother found out that she had lost her job, he would be haranguing her once more about taking over the management of the Boathouse Café.

She knew he loved her but he was being totally ridiculous. Of course she couldn't run the café. She had no experience. None. She deliberately kept away from any kind of responsibility, knowing that it would be a total disaster. Despite knowing that things were still so tough business wise, it was better that way, no matter how much she wanted to help out her family.

8

Having walked out of the kitchen, Hannah went outside and around the side of the hotel to where the sandy shore was lapped by the lake. She loved the beach, as the family referred to it.

Plenty of happy memories on the beach came from her childhood. Playing on the sand with Ben. Seeing if the edges were really frozen on a cold winter's day. Their dad chasing them in and out of the cold water on a hot summer's afternoon after school.

Life had been a little harder this past year when he had died so unexpectedly. But slowly the family were beginning to find their way in the present without him with them every day.

Hannah paused briefly to look across the water. The lake was large at almost fifty acres. On that spring day, the deep cobalt of the sky was reflected in the almost still water. The air, however, was alive with the sound of birdsong and nature enjoying the rites of spring. Ducks skidded across the surface of the water as they came in to land. Baby coots flitted in and out of the reeds, scurrying along after their parents. And amongst the reeds, as the sun warmed the air as it became stronger day by day, the dragonflies rose into flight, their gossamer wings shiny under the sun's rays.

She turned to walk on along the shore and away from the hotel. The lake was a large oval, hugged by the green rolling hills of the English countryside all around them. The forest sounded alive as well, a woodpecker making holes in an old oak tree, squirrels flitting from branch to branch and the soft chirping of baby birds in their nests waiting to be fed.

The other side of the lake, away from the hotel, was empty of buildings, although a few spaces had been cleared amongst the trees where she knew that Ben had planned to place the new log cabins once they had been given planning permission.

The only other building along the shoreline of the lake was the boathouse. Walking along the path, she noted the newly covered furrows along the ground that reminded her that Ben had ensured that the new electrics and plumbing for the hotel had been extended to the boathouse as well. It also had a new roof and apparently new windows as well, although she had been too busy to look at the recently completed renovations yet.

She glanced over her shoulder but there was nobody else around. Well, perhaps she would just take a peek inside, she thought. Just to see the progress.

The path rose up a little as she walked along, leaving the lake a little way below. In front of her, the boathouse rose into view. It was built on the shoreline but with a huge veranda that ran the length of the boathouse, jutting out over the lake, hovering above the water like a dragonfly.

It had been built by her great-grandfather and, like the hotel, the boathouse was a mixture of local sandstone bricks and thick logs felled from the forest. It was a square building, built on thick wooden pillars that disappeared into the crystal-clear water of the lake.

Next to the pillars, underneath the main building, were three wooden docks, one of which housed a small rowing boat which was bobbing about in the water. On the far side of the boathouse was a short wooden jetty, next to a smaller patch of sand which led into the water.

Hannah reached the entrance and opened up the door to step inside. She hadn't been inside for a while and was somewhat amazed at the recent transformation.

Once it had been rotten and rickety but now the whole place felt secure and welcoming. She stepped straight into the huge main room of the boathouse, newly covered with oak floorboards which stretched all the way onto the huge veranda outside.

She gasped as she realised that instead of the small shutters that had once been in place, there was now a wall of glass dividing the room and the veranda. It made the light flood into what had once been a dark space and showed off the magnificent view of the lake beyond. She could just imagine the huge glass sliding doors flung open in the summer to let in the warm air.

The other main change was along the back wall where a large area had been separated by way of a long, high breakfast bar. Hannah walked past the bar and into the space which she could now see had been set up as a kitchen. She had overheard Jake advising Ben on which equipment would suit the small space and he appeared to have had great vision.

She marvelled at the sleek new fridges, freezers, dishwasher and double oven and ran her hand over the large stainless-steel hob. She spun around slowly, admiring the oak cupboards and shelves, which matched the floorboards, and she could see where all the new electrical sockets had been positioned, just waiting for the additional appliances to be installed. The double sink was also perfect and she could tell that someone had put real thought into the layout.

They had also had to put in a whole lot of money too, she thought, with a grimace. There had been a tax rebate once her dad's affairs had been put into order and seeing as how the hotel renovations for the main building were now complete, Ben had wanted to invest the money into the boathouse. At the time, Hannah had been unsure whether it would be money wisely spent but now she was in total agreement. It was stunning.

As she walked back out of the open kitchen, she couldn't help but admire Ben's vision to turn the ramshackle building into such a welcoming space. Someone, she wondered if perhaps it was Lily, had come up with the idea for a café. The hotel had a restaurant which was used whenever there were any guests for dinner at the weekend, as well as for breakfast every day of the week. For the rest of the day, however, there were no other catering options, apart from the drinks and cakes that they provided in the lounge on the honesty trolley. Of course, there was the snug, the newly renovated bar which Frankie ran in the evening, but that only had a few light snacks. But as she stared around, Hannah had to admit that the boathouse with its space and light would be an amazing setting for additional catering needs.

She saw a door near the entrance and opened it up, peeking around to see a staircase leading up into the roof area.

'Ben's original thought was that it could be used for storage up there.'

Hannah drew her head back to find Lily standing by the front door. 'But because of the sheer size up there, he changed the use to an apartment instead.'

Hannah closed the door. 'Great idea,' she murmured.

'It's got its own bathroom and enough space for a large bed and a sofa as well. He thought that Penny could move in there when she started to work here but it obviously wasn't meant to be.' Lily came into the room, giving her a sheepish look. 'Are you mad with me?'

'Of course not,' Hannah told her with a sigh. 'I just need you to work on Ben to let go of this ridiculous idea that I could run this place.'

'If that's what you really want,' replied Lily, sounding unsure.

Hannah raised her eyebrows at her friend. 'Of course it is.'

Lily shrugged her shoulders. 'I just thought that rather than working in that awful pub, you could be your own boss for a change. Wouldn't that be nice?'

'Nice? It just sounds like a lot of responsibility,' muttered Hannah in reply.

Lily walked over to take her friend by the shoulders. 'I know it's scary,' she told her. 'I understand and we would never force you to do anything that you wouldn't want to do.'

'Why do I feel as if there's a "but" coming somewhere soon?' said Hannah, raising her eyebrows.

Lily smiled. 'OK, just for you,' she replied. '*But* tell me you don't look around this space and see the potential. That you haven't dreamed of having your own place where you can serve your own delicious bakes instead of that microwaved rubbish at the pub.'

Hannah looked around at the room once more. Lily was right, of course. She stared around the empty space and at once she could just imagine a vintage-inspired tea room, with that magnificent view of the sparkling lake beyond. She could envision trays of sandwiches and cakes, mismatched china and even colourful cocktails.

Because where the reality was a large empty room, she could see chairs and tables. Fresh flowers on the bar. The chink of china and silverware. The buzz of conversation. Of people enjoying themselves. Of her baking in the kitchen and smiling at the customers. Of seeing that view out of the windows each and every day. Of being her own boss.

But it was a crazy idea, wasn't it? It was too much for her to expect to enjoy making a living from her favourite thing in the world.

So she shook her head at her best friend and told her that she had lots to do that morning. Lily looked at her with raised eyebrows but thankfully said nothing, merely giving her a reassuring squeeze of the arm.

Before they left the room, Hannah glanced around once more before dismissing her daydream. Dreams never came true anyway, did they, she reminded herself.

9

Back in the kitchen, Alex looked down at the blueberry muffin that Hannah had said she had baked just for him. He felt ridiculously pleased that she knew that it was another of his favourites.

The blueberries were a superfood, packed full of antioxidants, their sharpness contrasting with the rich cake and the sweet vanilla icing which he quickly wolfed down.

'Is that true?' asked Ben.

Alex finally looked up from his empty plate to his best friends who were both looking at him with concerned looks on their faces.

'You're really giving up competing?' carried on Ben, still frowning.

Alex nodded. 'That's right.'

Jake wiped his hands on a napkin and leant back in his chair. 'Listen, mate,' he said. 'We all get setbacks. And we both get it, we really do. But there's no need to make a rush decision today, is there?'

Ben nodded. 'He's right. You're exhausted and in a lot of pain. Take some time and rest up.'

Alex raised his eyebrows in surprise at his friends. 'You're both always nagging me to take it easy and so the moment I want to retire, you're telling me to carry on?'

Ben shook his head. 'No. If that's not what you want to do any more, then we've got your back like always. Just don't be too hasty, that's all we're saying.'

'Like Claire,' murmured Jake.

Alex shot a look at his friend. 'That wasn't impulsive. That was madness.'

Jake nodded. 'I agree. That woman was dreadful.'

Claire had been a knee-jerk reaction to finding out that Hannah had moved in with her boyfriend. Both failed relationships appeared to have cast long shadows over their future love lives. Hannah had never been on any more dates, as far as he knew. And Claire's cheating ways had caused him to put a wall up around his heart with regard to any future relationships.

'We all make mistakes,' said Alex, with a shrug. 'Look at your track record!'

Jake laughed. 'Yeah, but at least I didn't get engaged to any of the dreadful ones!'

Ben rolled his eyes. 'Away from Jake's questionable dating history and back to the question in hand,' he said. 'Have you spoken to your dad?'

'Yeah because he's not going to take this well,' added Jake with a grimace.

'Tell me something I don't know,' replied Alex. He leant back in his chair with a sigh. 'I spoke to him last night. As you can imagine, he was not exactly thrilled at the idea.'

After his dad had hung up on him, his mum had sent a text sending her love and advising him just to give his dad a bit of time. He hadn't heard from his dad since. But perhaps there was nothing left to say. Perhaps they both needed time and space away from each other.

He looked at his friends. 'Look, I know you're both a bit shocked but this has been coming for a while. I'm exhausted.'

'So this isn't a knee-jerk reaction to you messing up in front of everyone?' asked Jake.

Alex shook his head. 'No, but thanks for the reminder. I mean, I'm beyond embarrassed at what happened. I wish there was a pill you could take that could erase all bad memories. But I can't.'

Jake slapped him on the shoulder with his hand. 'Yeah. Time travel always sounds appealing.'

'But the truth is that I don't want to return to that life any more,' said Alex. 'I want more than just hours of isolation, training by myself on the open road. I want to enjoy eating whatever I like, whenever I like. I want to rest and relax and just stop.'

He sighed, wondering what on earth that would even be like.

'What about work?' asked Ben.

'I guess job hunting is next on the list,' said Alex.

He had given up his job at the accountancy firm in London a month previously, intending to concentrate on his training before the Commonwealth Games. Much good that did, he thought to himself. And yet that job hadn't given him much pleasure anyway. It had paid him highly over the years so that he was comfortable and yet it didn't fill his soul. And now that training for triathlons didn't do that either, he had no idea what to do.

'The truth is I have no clue what comes next,' said Alex. 'I know that I don't want to live in the city any more in a soulless empty flat. I don't want to train any more. I'm not sure I even want to be an accountant either.' He shrugged his shoulders. 'But beyond that I have no idea what happens to me next.'

There was a short silence whilst his friends exchanged glances.

'Listen,' said Ben eventually. 'Maybe you don't have to decide this minute. Why don't you stay with us for a while longer? Stay for a week, a month, however long you want. Just relax for once.'

'Ben's right,' added Jake. 'You need to rest up and let your bones mend. Then hopefully you'll feel stronger and more prepared for what comes next. Whatever that might be.'

'Thanks,' replied Alex, grateful for his friends' support when everything else was so uncertain.

'You'll just have to put up with my snoring a while longer when I next visit,' said Jake, before taking a last bite of his own pastry. 'Mmm. One day, I'll get your sister to give me this recipe. But then again,' he added, after swallowing, 'it still won't taste as good as this. I tell you, she could make a fortune in London.'

'Hannah hated London when she lived there,' Alex reminded him.

Jake nodded. 'The only good thing that happened to her there was to meet her friends.' He picked at the crumbs on his plate. 'Shame though. I tell you, talent like hers is few and far between.'

'Well, as it happens, there is a bit of a plan that I might need your help with,' said Ben. 'As you know, the Boathouse Café is pretty much finished apart from a lick of paint.'

'I've said all along it could be a great business,' said Jake, nodding his approval. 'I mean, look at the setting.'

'Exactly,' said Ben. 'If it can attract more bookings or even just local people wanting to walk around the lake then that would be great news for our meagre profits.'

'Or watching the light show,' added Jake.

'I thought that was finished now with summer on its way,' Alex reminded him.

'It is,' replied Ben. 'The light festivals have ended with the lighter evenings and later sunsets. So now what to draw people in over the summer? We need something new. Something different for the area.'

'Well, nobody else has a lake, do they?' said Jake.

'Exactly!' replied Ben. 'So we've got our temporary licence until the end of September.'

'So what do you need our help with?' asked Alex.

'My manager and baker has quit before she even began,' said Ben, with a grimace.

'I'd love to help you out, mate, but despite my amazing talents with food, I can't bake a cake to save my life,' said Jake.

Ben shook his head. 'Actually, it was more of your persuasion techniques that I'm interested in. Especially with women.'

Jake and Alex exchanged a surprised look.

'Don't look at me,' said Alex, laughing. 'That's your area of expertise.'

Jake grinned. 'Indeed it is.' He turned to look at Ben. 'So who's the lucky woman that I'm to woo?'

'Hannah,' Ben told them.

Jake gave a choking sound in his throat and Alex nearly fell off his chair in shock.

'Hannah!' spluttered Alex, feeling ill. The thought of watching Jake become romantically entangled with Hannah made his brain misfire.

'Let me clarify,' said Ben, with a grin. 'Keep your hands off my little sister. Any wooing is to be entirely mental.'

Alex looked at Jake in confusion.

'You're losing us,' said Jake, equally puzzled.

'I want her to run the Boathouse Café,' said Ben.

Although Alex was still trying to dismiss the idea of Jake and Hannah together from his mind, he spoke almost immediately.

'She'll never do it,' he replied. He knew her so well that her lack of confidence and shyness would mean that it was a step too far for her.

'That was her initial reaction, unfortunately,' said Ben, making a face. 'But I was hoping that with a bit of persuasion from my oldest friends, and if we all work on her together, then she might just make a go of it.'

Jake shrugged his shoulders. 'Don't think there's much hope, mate, to be honest. But yeah, I'll talk to her.'

They both looked at Alex, who nodded slowly. 'Sure,' he said. 'We can only try.'

He was still touched at Ben inviting him to stay on after the weekend and rest. After all, he had always loved staying at Maple Tree Lodge. Perhaps it would give him more time to plan his future. To think about building his own life away from the endless competitions.

Of course, he secretly hoped that perhaps he could ask Hannah out one day. He had waited for so long. Been so patient.

He had never let on to either of his best friends about his crush on Hannah. Thankfully, as the quiet one in the threesome, he was able to keep his feelings private. Or at least he had done so far.

However, Ben's warning to Jake about being hands off only served to remind Alex that his friend would never be happy with either of them dating his little sister.

But he could daydream, couldn't he?

10

Despite telling Lily that she had no interest in managing the Boathouse Café, Hannah couldn't stop herself from lingering in there for most of the morning.

She told herself it was because she was keeping out of both Ben and Lily's way. But the truth was that she had a good feeling about the space and found it a relaxing place to be.

Her mind reeled with the long list of reasons why she couldn't take up Ben and Lily's offer regarding running the café.

Could she really run a business? She didn't think so. And yet she could already envision how it would look and feel. But still, she didn't have the confidence. Surely she would fail?

It didn't smell of cakes or any kind of baking – yet, she reminded herself. Instead, the air was filled with the aroma of the large wooden logs that made up the sides of the building.

With the kitchen already fitted out, that just left the main room to be filled with chairs and tables, all of which would face that glorious view of the lake beyond the huge patio doors.

With the sun rays shining through and illuminating the oak floorboards, she was drawn towards the doors and, turning the key, stepped outside onto the newly renovated balcony. It was wide and large enough for many more tables and chairs.

All it needed was someone to serve up delicious teas, coffees and cakes. It was so tempting and yet totally beyond her reach. She leant on the balustrade, looking over the water which sparkled under the blue sky above, lost in her thoughts.

'If you're thinking of jumping in, I wouldn't.'

She spun around to find Alex hobbling towards her, making a slow and steady progress with his crutches across the floorboards.

'The water is at its coldest at the moment,' he added with a smile as he came to stand next to her. 'I can verify that after the race yesterday morning.'

He placed the crutches up against the balustrade and leant on the balcony next to her, looking out across the water.

'Thankfully it's much warmer up here,' he added.

Hannah nodded. 'Well, it is spring already.'

'And I haven't a single item in my calendar,' he replied.

'Well, you need time to recover before your next competition,' she told him, glancing down at his broken foot encased in the protective boot.

But Alex shook his head. 'No, I meant what I said in the kitchen. I truly am finished with competitions. Training. All of it.'

She could see the strain across his face as he spoke. He was always busy, she realised, thinking back over the years. Always on the go. Could he really tear himself away from all that success?

'Well, you deserve some time off,' she told him, thinking how rare it would be to see Alex relaxed and doing nothing. 'Will you go on holiday to recuperate somewhere?'

He shrugged his shoulders. 'Never really had a holiday, to be honest. If we went abroad, it was all about climate training or another competition. Now that that's over...' His voice trailed off as a frown crossed his face briefly before he looked at her once more. 'Well, I've never had much time off before now, I'm sorry to confess. What about you? What holidays do you dream of?'

'I've never had the money to travel.' She looked out across the lake, sparkling under the sun. 'Besides, if I'm honest, I'm happiest here.'

'Well, that sounds like a plan. Especially as your brother has invited me to stay for as long as I want whilst I recuperate,' he told her.

Hannah felt glad at the thought of seeing him every day. 'That's a brilliant idea,' she told him. 'There's worse places to spend a staycation and we'd all love to have you here for a while longer.'

He looked pleased. 'You wouldn't get fed up with me?' he asked, with a twinkle in his eye.

She shook her head. 'Of course not,' she replied.

And it was true. Alex was so easy to get along with. He never ruffled any feathers, just remained calm and steady.

'Well, then how can I say no?' he said, with a grin.

She laughed along with the joke, certain that he would only stay at Maple Tree Lodge for a short while before he got itchy feet to get out of there. Most people did. 'Well, wherever you recuperate I really do think it's a great idea for you to relax for a change.'

'Well, I can't take all the credit. It was your brother's idea,' replied Alex.

Hannah frowned when she thought back to Ben and Lily trying to persuade her to start her own business. 'He has the occasional decent thought,' she said, feeling irritated all of a sudden. 'But most of them miss their target, to be honest.'

Alex studied her for a moment. 'You're talking about being manager of the Boathouse Café?' he said.

She took a sharp breath. 'You know about their crazy idea then?' she asked, surprised.

He nodded. 'But perhaps it's not so crazy,' he began.

She turned away from him to look back across the water. 'Not you as well,' she muttered.

'You serve up cakes and pastries to the guests now,' she heard him say. 'What's the difference?'

She turned back to look at him. 'Because I'll be seeing them face to face,' she explained to him.

He looked confused. 'You serve customers in the pub, don't you?' he asked.

'Yes. But...' Her voice trailed off and she huffed out a sigh.

'But what?' he asked gently.

She wondered whether she could tell him the truth and then decided of course she could. It was Alex and she trusted him implicitly. 'But it's not my food when I'm at the pub,' she began. 'So it doesn't matter if it's rubbish or not. I'm just a waitress. But this?' She turned around to look back into the large room. 'I'll be setting myself up for everyone to complain when it all goes wrong.'

'Hannah,' said Alex gently. 'I've tasted your cakes. Trust me, nobody's going to complain.'

'I just don't think I'll be very good at being a manager either,' she told him, her lack of confidence bubbling to the surface. 'Besides, with my dyslexia, can you imagine what state the paperwork will be in?'

He nodded thoughtfully to himself. 'Well, maybe I can help you with that,' he told her.

'How?' she asked.

'If I'm staying around for a couple of weeks, I'll need something to do. I can help out in here and teach you how to run the accounts. Trust me, nobody wants to taste anything that I bake. But accounts? That I'm good at.'

'Yes, you are,' she told him.

'Brilliant,' he said, looking delighted. 'So you'll take on the business?'

She shook her head quickly. 'Oh, no,' she told him, laughing. 'Not a chance. But it'll be lovely to have you around for longer than the odd weekend.'

He studied her for a moment before breaking into a smile that lit up his handsome face. 'That's nice of you to say so,' he said.

Hannah laughed. 'Well, you are family,' she told him.

And it was true. He was a friend, not only to Ben but to everyone.

She hated to see him so hurt by everything that had happened to him. Was he really thinking about not carrying on competing in competitions?

It seemed as if they were both at a crossroads in their lives and didn't know what the future held for them yet.

11

Later that week, Alex was still mulling over his conversation with Hannah. She had seemed pleased that he was staying on at the hotel for a few weeks. And he was too, he realised, now that he had been able to spend a bit of time with the family over the past couple of days.

So despite the pain in his foot, he was feeling in a far more positive mood when he sat down with the family for lunch.

However, he had just finished his sandwich when there was a collective groan around the table. He looked up and saw a somewhat familiar face alongside an even more recognisable black puppy.

'Afternoon, all,' said Dodgy Del, coming into the kitchen with a wide grin.

Hannah immediately leapt up to fuss over Tiny.

Her brother's greeting wasn't quite so eager. 'Where have you been, Del?' asked Ben, frowning. 'I've been trying to call you on your mobile.'

'No can do,' replied Del, shaking his head. 'Dropped the thing last week and it broke. Why? What did you want?'

'Remember that paddleboard you dropped off as a prototype?' said Ben. 'It sank to the bottom of the lake as soon as I'd blown it up and placed it on the water.'

'No refunds,' said Del quickly. 'Can't think why it didn't work.'

'Because it had a great big hole in it,' said Ben, rolling his eyes. 'You can forget about us ordering any more from your so-called mate. I don't want to see the guests ending up in the water unexpectedly.'

Ben had mentioned to Alex only the previous night about hiring out paddleboards to guests that summer as a trial.

'Yeah, yeah,' said Del, with a heavy sigh. 'I'll get round to it. Look, it's been one of them weeks, OK?'

'Tell me about it,' said Alex in a pointed tone, glancing at his foot which was resting on a stool. Five days after the accident and the bruising was now a spectacular rainbow of colours.

Del looked at him with a start. 'Oh, yeah. I heard you got hurt. Sorry and all that, mate.' He gave Alex a shared grimace. 'Same thing happened to me at school.'

'I don't think I've ever seen you run anywhere except away from disgruntled customers,' said Walter.

'It was the egg and spoon race, OK?' replied Del. 'I was only six but I tripped over my own feet. Kids can be cruel, yeah? So I know where you're coming from, mate.'

Alex looked at him in bemusement. Dodgy Del obviously had the hide of a buffalo. 'Thanks,' he said. 'I think.'

At least someone could find humour in the situation, he thought.

Del hopped from one foot to another, looking fidgety.

'Is everything all right, Del?' asked Dotty. 'You look harassed.'

'Only from his unhappy customers,' said Ben, still looking disgruntled.

'Nah, it's not that,' said Del. 'It's this little fella.' He gestured at the dog which Hannah was now stroking. 'Nan can't deal with him. She keeps forgetting that she's ninety and lives in an upstairs flat! Anyway, I had to take him off her hands two days ago. She was that upset but she couldn't handle him. I've not had a moment to myself since.'

'Poor Tiny,' cooed Hannah as the dog looked up adoringly at her face and then gave her a gentle lick. 'What are you going to do with him, Del?'

'Find him a good home,' replied Del. He suddenly looked brighter, as if he had suddenly realised where he was. 'Hey! I know! This place is big enough!'

'No!' said Ben and Walter in unison.

Del immediately turned his laser vision onto Alex. 'Super things, dogs,' he carried on, going into what appeared to be a very rehearsed sales pitch. 'They're very good for the mental health, aren't they?'

'Unless they break your foot,' muttered Alex.

'Tiny didn't break it,' said Hannah, frowning. 'He just hadn't been trained properly and ran out because he was excited.'

'Exactly!' said Del, leaping on her words. 'Someone who's used to a rigid training schedule sounds perfect as a dog owner, I reckon.'

'How can I train him with a broken foot?' asked Alex, hoping that was the end of the matter.

'Well, he don't need much walking at his age, does he?' replied Del. 'Think how good he'd be when you're training for all those races.'

Alex shuffled in his seat, uncertain that he wanted the news that he had given up competitions to go any further than the family.

'He's so friendly,' cooed Hannah, giving the dog a cuddle.

'He's a smashing lad,' said Del, nodding and smiling at the appreciative audience. Lily, Faye and Dotty had all got up to fuss over him. 'But then again Labradors always are. Such family dogs, ain't they?'

'What age is he?' asked Faye, stroking the puppy's head.

'Nan didn't know,' replied Del. 'He's only a couple of months old, we reckon.'

'But he's enormous for three months! What are you feeding him?' asked Walter. 'Everything? He's a right porker.'

'Aww,' said Lily. 'Don't say that! He's cute.'

'All Labrador puppies are cute,' said Dotty with a frown. 'Is he a flat-coated retriever because Labradors don't normally have long fur like this?'

Del quickly nodded. 'Nan got him from some chap she met at bingo but that's what I thought, love.' He looked across at Alex. 'So? What do you think? Do you want him?'

'I can't, Del,' said Alex, shaking his head. 'I live in a flat in London. I'm only here for a week or two whilst I recover.'

'Well, you can stay here a bit longer, can't you?' asked Del. 'Best place I can think of to get yourself well.'

Ben looked at Alex. 'You know, for the first time in history, Del might just be right. It's been great having you here these past few days. Why don't you stay on for the full six weeks?'

The family immediately burst into excited chatter.

'Oh, that's a great idea,' said Faye. 'You'll be fighting fit by that time.'

'Didn't know he'd be having company though,' added Walter, with a smile.

'He needs cheering up, I reckon,' said Del, gently taking the dog from Hannah to plonk him into Alex's lap.

Suddenly Alex was holding a quite heavy puppy on his legs. Not that the dog seemed to mind. He merely looked up at him with big sorrowful dark eyes and panted, leaving a trail of drool across Alex's arm.

'He's lovely,' said Hannah, coming to crouch next to Alex to continue to fuss over the dog. 'Ever so sweet.'

Alex was still thinking that he couldn't possibly keep a dog but as he watched Hannah's reaction, he wondered if perhaps the dog was a way of bringing them closer. But he shook his head. That wasn't the right reason to have the responsibility of getting a dog, he reminded himself. Even though he had often pondered about getting one whenever he finally stopped competing.

Unfortunately, his hesitation was assumed by Del as an affirmation that he wanted the dog.

'Great!' declared Del. 'Glad he's going to a nice home. I'll get his stuff out of the car.'

'Wait a minute...' began Alex.

But Del had already left the room.

As the family gathered around, Alex became even more aware of the heavy puppy in his lap. He looked up at Ben. 'You could always keep the dog if I can't, couldn't you?'

'Not really,' said Ben, shaking his head. 'We've got enough on our plates as it is.'

'We would love to because he's so cute,' added Lily, reaching out to stroke the dog's soft fur. 'But like Ben said, we're rushed off our feet most days.'

'And what about the guests?' added Ben. 'What if someone's got allergies?'

'Besides, I'm not sure about this idea to stay here for the full six weeks,' carried on Alex, feeling awkward. 'It's too much of an imposition.'

'Rubbish,' muttered Walter. 'What's one more person around here?'

'Heartily agree, Grandad,' said Ben, with a nod.

'But what am I going to do about this puppy?' asked Alex.

'I wouldn't fight the inevitable,' Walter told him, coming over to also fuss over the dog. 'Once Del's got an idea in his thick head, there's no budging him.'

Alex shook his head but the dog in his arms was reminding him that he was also a little bit helpless and he found he couldn't help but want to protect the puppy.

Del came in, carrying a dog bed which was filled with a couple of feeding bowls, some squeaky toys and a lead.

'What do I feed him?' asked Alex, his mind racing as the full implication of taking on a puppy began to dawn on him.

'He's happy to eat whatever I like,' said Del. 'Last night he nicked half of my burger!'

'Del!' said Dotty, in a stern voice. 'He shouldn't be eating rubbish like that.'

'He didn't seem to mind,' replied Del. 'In fact, he really enjoyed it, I reckon.' He looked at Alex. 'Now, because you're helping out my family, I won't ask for payment for the lad. It's worth it just to see his happy face in his new home.'

Alex looked at Del in amazement that he had actually thought about asking for money for an unwanted dog!

'I haven't said I'll definitely have him yet,' said Alex, quickly. 'I mean, what about his medical records? Is he a pedigree?'

'Ain't got no papers,' said Del. 'But the man who gave it to Nan reckoned he's sound. Might need the vet to check him out.'

Alex looked down at the dog. 'He does seem awfully big for a retriever,' he said.

'Just puppy fat,' said Del before grabbing his phone out of his pocket and looking at the screen. 'Right. Gotta rush. I've got a text to pick up someone.'

'Wait a minute,' began Ben, rising up from the table. 'Didn't you say your phone wasn't working?'

'Must have suddenly fixed itself,' said Del quickly. 'Cheerio, everyone. Take care of Tiny for me!'

'What about my sunken paddleboard?' asked Ben.

But Del had already left the room.

Alex sighed and looked down at the dog in his arms who was beginning to fall asleep. This was a disaster, he thought. He couldn't keep a dog. His life had always been orderly and planned.

And yet the truth was that for the first time in his life, he didn't have a plan. He had always been sensible with his choices, taking time to decide on important matters. But Tiny wasn't a sensible decision. It was a crazy choice to make. But still Alex's heart reminded him how lonely he was most evenings by himself in the flat. He saw his friends and dated occasionally but it would perhaps be nice to have another living, breathing thing at home with him.

Anyway, he didn't particularly like the flat so he could always rent somewhere bigger when he and Tiny left for London.

As he looked down at the puppy now asleep on his arm, Alex's head reminded him that this was a ridiculous decision and that he should find a far more suitable owner as soon as he could.

But even with that thought, he couldn't stop himself smiling as he reached down to gently stroke the dog's silky head. Perhaps, he thought, just once, he might think with his heart instead.

12

Hannah came down the stairs the following morning to find Alex surrounded by overnight hotel guests, all crowding around to fuss over Tiny the dog.

Alex looked up as she came down the stairs and gave her a weary smile. He still looked tired, she thought. Still not quite his usual assured self after such a difficult week.

Thankfully all the attention from the guests had been taken away from the injured athlete and transferred to the black dog who was wagging his tail at the adoring crowd.

The puppy had already been a huge hit with the guests. There had been a couple of small accidents on the oak floorboards in the reception which everyone the previous evening had put down to excitement, despite Ben's muted grumbles.

Once Alex had finally dragged the puppy away, telling the crowd that it was time for Tiny's breakfast, he went into the kitchen with Hannah.

'Thanks for saving me,' he said. 'I'm not quite ready to be the centre of attention yet.'

'I know,' she murmured. 'But if you want to hide, having Tiny next to you isn't going to work.'

He gave a small laugh. 'I'm quickly finding that out. I'm also discovering that if I want to sleep, having Tiny next to me isn't a good idea either. We had to go outside twice last night. It took me ages to keep going up and down the stairs with my crutches.'

'I'll fix us both a coffee,' Hannah told him, going into the kitchen area whilst Alex went to sit down at the table.

Tiny immediately put his paws up on Alex's knees, desperate to climb on top of him for a cuddle.

'Just this one time,' he told the dog, lifting him up.

Hannah smiled. Perhaps the dog would bring a bit of comfort to him where nobody else's words seemed to help.

'Have you ever owned a dog before?' she asked.

Alex shook his head. 'Not growing up. Dad's too impatient for us to have any pets. And I was always too busy with the competitions.' He smiled down at the dog. 'Did always have a dream of owning one at some point though.'

She made them both a coffee and some toast before joining them at the table. Tiny was very interested in the toast so she moved her plate out of reach. Unfortunately, Alex was too slow and lost his marmalade on toast to the dog.

'I'll make you some more,' Hannah told him, getting up.

'Please don't worry,' said Alex. 'Besides, I've got an early vet's appointment. Your mum knows a great one in the next village apparently.'

'That's great but you must keep your strength up for your recovery,' Hannah told him, heading over to the toaster.

Ben came into the kitchen. 'Didn't get a wink of sleep until after 2 a.m.,' he said, yawning. 'Del's outdone himself this time with the dog.'

'You mean the howling?' asked Alex, with a grimace.

'I didn't hear anything,' lied Hannah, anxious to protect Alex from Ben's nagging.

But Alex was too honest to lie to his friend. 'Sorry,' he said. 'In the end, I had to bring him up from the kitchen and hustle him into my bedroom.'

'The rooms have only just been renovated,' said Ben with a frown.

'He didn't make a mess,' said Alex quickly. 'And I put one of my old sweatshirts on the bed so he didn't lie on the duvet.'

'Listen, are you seriously planning on keeping Tiny?' asked Ben. 'Because if not, I can be straight onto Del to get him to pick the dog up.'

Hannah placed the second round of toast on the table next to Alex and sat down.

'In all honesty, I'm not sure,' replied Alex. 'My lifestyle was just too hectic before to even dream about having a dog. But now?' He did a palms up. 'I guess I have the time but my living circumstances aren't great and like you said, living here in the hotel isn't the best place for him either. So maybe it's not fair.' He looked downhearted for a minute. 'I'll ask the vet to find out if there's a better owner out there for him.'

Hannah immediately felt upset. She felt that Alex really wanted the dog.

'I'm sure the puppy will settle down soon,' she said, shooting a glare at her brother for being so grumpy. 'And besides, like Alex said, Tiny didn't make a mess.'

Ben raised his eyebrows at her unexpectedly harsh tone.

Hannah shrugged her shoulders in response. 'I've always wanted a dog as well, remember,' she told him.

Ben smiled. 'Yeah, I remember all the begging to Mum and Dad every Christmas.'

'I must have always been naughty because Father Christmas left me off his good list,' she told Alex, with a wicked grin.

He seemed to choke a little on the coffee mug that had been lifted to his lips, perhaps at her small joke, she thought.

'Just let Tiny stay for a little while longer,' she begged her brother. 'I'm sure he'll be quieter tonight now he's got used to Alex.'

'It's all my fault,' said Alex. 'I should never have let Del talk me into keeping him.'

Ben shook his head. 'Not your fault, mate. Del has selective deafness so would never have listened to you anyway!'

Hannah reached out to stroke Tiny and sent up a prayer of hope that Alex might keep the dog. She thought it would be good for him. She also hoped that both Alex and Tiny would stay at Maple Tree Lodge for a while longer too. She found that she had got used to having both of them around for the past couple of days and didn't want to see either of them leave just yet.

13

After breakfast, Ben took Alex to a vet's surgery nearby.

Alex was still frustrated that he couldn't drive and once more felt the nuisance caused by the break in his foot. However, despite Tiny passing a successful health test, there wasn't any other good news to share with the family when they returned.

'This is unbelievable!' snapped Alex, storming into the kitchen on his crutches behind Ben. 'How do I get hold of him?'

'Who?' asked Faye, looking concerned. 'Whatever's the matter?'

'Dodgy Del, of course!' said Ben, rolling his eyes. 'Who else?'

'Sorry,' said Alex, looking at Faye with chagrin. 'I'm not cross with you.'

He sank down on a chair, still not quite believing what he had just heard at the vet's.

'What's Del done now?' asked Walter with a heavy sigh.

'The vet has told us that Tiny is most definitely not a Labrador retriever,' said Alex, still in disbelief. 'He is, in fact, a Newfoundland!'

A shocked gasp ran around the table, apart from Dotty who nodded and said, 'I thought so.'

Alex looked at her, aghast. 'You did?' he asked.

'Saw loads years ago in Canada,' Dotty told him. 'They make great rescue dogs.'

'Aren't they a large breed?' asked Hannah, frowning.

'Oh, yes,' said Dotty. 'Absolutely enormous!'

'The adults can weigh up to 80 kg! I mean they're giants!' Alex had immediately googled the breed as soon as they'd left the vets. 'I can't take on that responsibility,' he carried on, shaking his head. 'What will I do with a huge dog? I'm used to living in a flat!'

'Don't move into another flat then,' said Walter, with a grin.

Lily had been typing into her phone and looked up. 'It says here that Newfoundlands are a very bulky dog who can take up a lot of space in your house and the car too.'

Alex ran a hand through his hair. He had accepted the dog with no thought as to what size it might grow to. This was possibly all his fault.

'They can suffer from separation anxiety and destructiveness when left alone too much,' carried on Lily.

'I've had girlfriends like that,' said Ben, with a grin which he quickly dropped at Lily's raised eyebrows. 'Kidding. And present company excepted, of course.'

However, Alex had completely lost his sense of humour. He had thought the dog might just be a positive thing in his life but suddenly he had a giant breed to take care of.

'Newfoundlands can be stubborn, shed a lot of fur and can slobber and drool quite a bit as well,' carried on Lily.

Alex groaned. 'Is there any good news that you could tell me?' he asked, feeling quite desperate at that point.

'It says that they're a calm breed and that they love the water,' she told him.

'He's in the right place then,' said Walter, with a grin.

Alex, though, didn't smile, still mulling over the change in his well-intended plans.

'They love daily walks so that would fit in with your morning runs,' Lily told him. 'When you're all mended, that is. They're good at receiving training and they're good natured with everyone, especially children.'

But Alex still wasn't so sure and could only focus on the negative aspects of the breed. 'They suffer with separation anxiety? What happens when I want to go back to work?' Although he hadn't quite decided what he was going to do once his foot was fully mended. 'How am I going to get a sitter for Tiny when he's going to be an extra-large dog!'

'Perhaps Tiny needs a new name,' said Walter.

He and Ben stifled laughter together at the joke.

Alex sighed. 'You need to help me,' he said, looking around at the family. 'What am I going to do?'

'Listen, I think Tiny's a good idea,' Hannah told him. 'Like a fresh start. You did say you'd always wanted a dog.'

'Yes, but not one the size of a house!' said Alex.

'He's not that big yet,' she told him, leaning down to stroke the dog who was sleepy after his busy morning.

But even Hannah's gentle reassurance didn't make him feel better at that moment.

'*Yet* being the operative word,' said Alex. 'How am I going to cope with him? I'm still struggling to even walk at the moment.'

'I can help you with him,' Hannah told him. It was absolutely the wrong reason but the right thing for Alex to hear. 'I can walk him for you. Take him outside when your foot's hurting.'

'Anyway, you did say that you were going to take some additional time off,' added Ben.

'Quite right,' said Walter, nodding his head in agreement. 'You've been working or training ever since we've known you. Take some time for yourself.'

'To do what?' asked Alex.

'Absolutely nothing,' said Dotty. 'It's called relaxing.'

'Yeah, you should try it sometime,' said Ben, looking at his friend. 'They're not wrong, mate.'

'You could stay here for the whole summer,' said Hannah softly.

Alex looked across the table at Hannah, delighted that she wanted him around for that long, but he couldn't stop himself from shaking his head. 'I can't,' he told her before looking at everyone else. 'Tiny's already disrupted you all for one night. Are you and, more importantly your hotel guests, going to put up with the howling every night? If I keep Tiny, and I'm still saying that is a very large if, we still can't stay here. We need to be somewhere where there aren't any neighbours or hotel guests nearby.'

'We're hoping to have planning permission for the lodges but it's taking a bit longer than expected,' said Ben.

'There must be somewhere they can stay,' added Walter, frowning.

There was a short silence as everyone thought hard.

'I know just the place,' said Hannah suddenly.

Alex watched as her face lit up into a smile and was so distracted that for a moment he lost his focus.

'What do you mean?' he asked, still trying to hear what she was saying and not the shiny rose colour on her cheeks as he gazed at her.

'What about the upstairs apartment in the boathouse?' Hannah looked at Ben. 'What do you think?'

He nodded thoughtfully. 'It's plumbed in.'

'Detached,' added Hannah.

'It's a pretty big space up there,' said Ben.

'Away from the hotel guests at night,' added Lily.

'And the boathouse will be closed in the evenings so you get your privacy,' said Hannah with a final flourish.

Alex leaned back in his chair, nodding thoughtfully. Perhaps it might just work for the next month whilst he literally got back onto his feet. But beyond that? He wasn't sure.

'Excellent,' said Ben, with a nod. 'So that's decided. You and Tiny can stay here at Maple Tree Lodge for the summer.'

It sounded so tempting, to be in his favourite place all summer. But Alex immediately decided it had to be on his terms.

'That's a very generous offer but we need to decide up front how much rent I'll pay you for the apartment,' he said. 'If I decide to take it on, that is.'

Ben immediately shook his head. 'On the house, mate. You're family.'

But Alex wouldn't be deterred. 'Nope,' he replied. 'I insist on it, otherwise me and Tiny are out of here. I need to pay my way.'

His voice betrayed how fiercely independent he suddenly wanted to be. He had been leaning on his parents for so long but he was ready to stand on his own two feet at last. Even if they couldn't support his own weight at the moment, he added to himself ironically.

He looked his best friend in the eye and finally Ben slowly nodded. 'OK,' he said. 'We'll agree a fair rate. Deal.'

Alex found himself nodding as well. 'Great. Well, if you're sure. But look, what about Tiny making a mess in your brand-new apartment?'

'Oak floorboards,' Walter told him. 'Any more reasons that you can think of not to do this?'

Alex finally found himself smiling. 'I'm quickly running out of them.'

'Why don't we go and have a look?' asked Hannah.

And as Alex looked at her pretty face once more, he found he was all out of excuses.

14

Feeling a bit guilty that she might have pressured Alex to keep Tiny, Hannah decided to show him the apartment in the boathouse to at least see if he continued to agree with her. Ben came along for moral support and seemed pleased with her idea.

She found herself hoping that Alex stayed for the summer as the tentative plan was, at that moment. It would be lovely to have him around for a while longer. She had not been surprised when he had insisted on paying rent for the apartment. Alex was good and true, one of the few men she had met in her life that were.

'I think this might just be a cracking idea,' said Ben.

Alex still looked unsure and kept his eyes on the path as he manoeuvred his way along on crutches.

They'd left Tiny fast asleep with the rest of the family keeping an eye on the dog in the kitchen.

Once in the boathouse, Hannah led them up the staircase. Thankfully the stairs were wide and Alex was able to navigate them on his crutches with relative ease.

To her surprise, having not been up there before, it was a very large room, despite being in the eaves. The ceiling pointed up high into the roof, giving the illusion of an airy space and a huge porthole window brought in much-needed light as well as a great view of the lake.

'All you need is a bed and a few bits of furniture,' she said, slowly turning around and spotting a door. She opened it up and found a small bathroom with a walk-in shower. 'This is great. Perfect for you.'

They both looked at Alex, who was nodding thoughtfully. 'It is,' he agreed. 'Are you sure that the family won't mind me being up here for a while?'

'Of course not,' said Ben. 'We can get some furniture delivered here in a couple of days, I reckon.'

'I think it's a lovely idea you staying here.' Hannah spun around once more. 'And there's room for Tiny too.'

'Well, it seems as if I can't exactly say no, can I?' said Alex.

But his eyes were twinkling as he smiled at her.

She grinned back at him. 'I don't think you can actually,' she told him.

'Agreed,' said Ben, with a nod. 'Well, once the furniture is in, you and Tiny can move straight in.'

They went downstairs once more, Alex carefully on his crutches until they were in the large room that would be turned into a café.

Hannah wandered over to open up the large patio doors onto the veranda that ran the length of the boathouse to let in some cooler air.

'That's better,' she said, stifling a yawn. 'It's so lovely and warm in here it's making me feel sleepy.'

'You've got work tonight, haven't you?' asked Alex.

Hannah grimaced. She had been dreading telling anyone about her job, particularly Ben, but she found she couldn't lie to her family. After lying to her family about Sean, she had no more room for any other falsehoods.

'No,' she said slowly. 'There might be a problem with that.'

'Is it your bolshie boss?' asked Ben, looking concerned. 'Is he messing around with your hours again?'

'We should go down there and have a word with him,' added Alex, looking stern.

Despite his crutches, the size and width of Alex meant that he would be particularly threatening if he wanted to be.

She wasn't surprised to find Ben nodding in agreement, always ready to defend his younger sister.

She quickly shook her head. 'Please don't,' Hannah urged them. She hated the thought of a scene. 'Besides, you don't need to because the pub shut down. I'm out of a job.'

Ben stared at her and even Alex looked shocked.

'You are?' asked Alex.

Hannah nodded. 'So there's no need to go down there. Anyway, like everyone kept reminding me many times, it wasn't a great job.'

It was true, she thought. She was tired of the late hours and the manager who never seemed to appreciate how hard she worked. There had to be better places to work at in the area, although she still didn't relish the thought of working each evening. She'd have to find something that fitted in more with her helping out at the hotel.

Ben was still studying her. 'When did you intend to tell me?' he asked.

'I meant to say something over the past couple of days but it's been so busy.' She looked away so that she didn't make eye contact, despite feeling both Ben and Alex's eyes boring into the top of her head. Instead, she looked back around the room, enjoying the natural light flooding in.

But she couldn't put off Ben's reaction any longer. She stole a glance at her brother but instead of him looking upset and concerned for her, he was breaking into a smile.

She straightened up. 'Well, I'm glad to see that you're taking my unemployment so well,' she told him, feeling a little hurt. 'Embracing poverty and all that.'

'I'm all for new starts,' he replied, still smiling. 'As the past twelve months has testified. They haven't done me any harm.'

'Is that why you're smiling at my misfortune?' she asked, putting her hands on her hips.

'First, I would never enjoy you being upset,' he told her, his face becoming more serious. 'And second, I reckon that I have just the thing for all that free time you've got on your hands.'

'You mean helping Mum out for the breakfast rush? Way ahead of you, bro,' she replied. 'You know I'm happy to help wherever I can. And with Tiny too,' she added, with a smile at Alex.

But Ben was shaking his head. 'I'm talking about this place,' he said, gesturing at their surroundings. 'I still can't find anyone to run the Boathouse Café. Certainly not someone with your spectacular baking skills.'

'But...' she immediately began to protest.

'Listen,' he said, interrupting her to walk over to stand in front of her. 'I know you're worried. I'm worried too but not about your ability to bake. My worries are about how to keep our home from going under financially. We need some more income streams and I really think this could be a success. If we could get some outside customers, as well as the hotel guests to use the café, then it would all help towards keeping a roof over our family's heads. Do you really want our grandparents to be homeless at their age?'

The twinkle in his eye told her that he was joking but still, she knew that things weren't exactly secure for them all.

She glanced over to Alex. He gave her a sad smile. 'I think it's a great idea,' he told her. 'And at least you won't fail as spectacularly as I did,' he added before glancing down at his foot in its protective boot.

'I still might,' she told him.

But as she saw him wince in pain as he continued to stand nearby, she couldn't stop herself from trying to reassure him.

'You didn't fail,' she told him. 'You had an accident. Big difference.'

'So?' Ben let his question hang in the air.

She glanced once more at Alex, who gave her a reassuring nod. Surely if Alex thought it a good decision then perhaps it might just work out?

She still wasn't sure about any of the business side of things but felt trapped into a corner. And without a job to call her own, she was all out of excuses.

'Fine,' she muttered. 'I'll open the café for you.'

'Excellent!' said Ben, stepping forward to give her a hug.

But as she moved back, she told her brother, 'Just don't blame me when it all goes wrong.'

'That's the spirit,' said Ben, with a grin.

15

Before his injury, Alex had only ever intended to stay for a weekend.

However, now that he had been invited by the family to stay for a lot longer, possibly over the summer as well, he needed to collect some more belongings from his flat.

Unable to face the long train and tube journey on his crutches, he took Dodgy Del's taxi into London, leaving Tiny behind with the family.

He didn't take long in his flat, merely packing up a few more bags of clothes including some lighter summer wear as it would be the middle of May by the time his foot would be mended. Grabbing a couple of books on his bedside table that he had never had time to read, he briefly opened up his bedside drawer and stared down. It was the collection of medals that he had won and placed in there for safekeeping. He was pleased to see there were quite a few but never gold, that elusive medal had always remained just out of reach. He briefly thought about calling his dad before dismissing the thought, and pushed the drawer closed before asking Dodgy Del to help him down to the street with his bags.

Still in quite a bit of pain from his broken foot, Alex tried to rest up as much as he could over the next couple of days. He was enjoying the camaraderie of staying with the family. But he still wasn't sure how long he would stay with them, not wanting to overstay his welcome, however warm.

And yet he found himself tempted by the peace that Maple Tree Lodge might give him whilst he recuperated.

After the weekend, the number of rooms occupied went down to a minimum so he felt able to relax in the lounge without getting in the way of the guests.

But relaxing was a state of mind that he wasn't used to and after only half an hour on the sofa, he headed out onto the veranda. With time on his hands, he couldn't help but dwell on the last conversation he had had with his dad. He'd shared texts with his mum since then, mostly her checking that he wasn't in too much pain. But still, the guilt over his abrupt walking away from the competitions hung over him.

He was also bored. Having always either been working or training, with the odd date or meet-up with Ben and Jake included, he just wasn't used to sitting around.

Out in the fresh air, the spring sunshine shone down and he realised how warm it was now suddenly as the days began to get a little longer.

'Lovely spring day,' said Dotty, suddenly appearing next to him.

'It certainly is,' he replied.

'In fact, it looks almost perfect weather for my first swim of the year,' she said. 'Care to join me?'

He glanced at the water and it looked very inviting, he found himself thinking. But still he hesitated. Surely he was trying to get away from swimming, running and cycling?

'Give me a good reason why not?' said Dotty, who had always been somewhat gung-ho in her attitude to life. 'The water would be great therapy and as you've not got your leg in a cast, what have you got to lose?' She burst into a grin. 'Long as you don't try to make it into a triathlon, of course.'

Alex found that he couldn't find a single reason to refuse her and she took his silence as a positive response.

'Excellent,' said Dotty. 'I'll meet you on the beach in five minutes.'

Not wanting to upset her, Alex reluctantly headed upstairs to change into his swimming shorts.

He met Dotty outside on the sandy beach by the hotel.

'It's only April. It's going to be a bit chilly in there,' he warned her, with a shiver under his hoodie and tracksuit bottoms.

'Oh, I'm sure it is,' she replied, with a grin before whipping off the large towel that she had wrapped around herself to reveal a black swimming costume. 'But the cold's good for the circulation, isn't it? After all, how else can I keep myself looking so young?'

She smiled at him before beginning to head towards the water.

Suddenly more concerned about Dotty's safety than his own, Alex swiftly stripped down to his swimming shorts and slowly hobbled across the sand to join her in the shallows.

The water was icy cold and he took a sharp intake of breath as he adjusted to the freezing temperature.

'I'm normally wearing a wetsuit,' he said, with a shudder. 'But I couldn't get into it with my broken foot.'

'It's a pain, isn't it?' she said, with a sympathetic look. 'Literally, I imagine.'

He nodded, hobbling in a little further up to his knees and once more wincing at the cold temperature of the water.

'Let's get this over with,' he said. 'Ten minutes absolute maximum. It's too cold otherwise for the body to cope with.'

He was making adjustments for Dotty's almost eighty years but he wasn't sure that he wanted to be in the water for too much longer either.

'Spoilsport,' muttered Dotty.

But Alex could see the goosebumps on her arms before they both finally pushed forward into the deeper water and he let the water take his weight.

Once immersed in the water, Alex immediately began to feel in a much better mood. The swim had always been his favourite part of the race but normally he hadn't got the time to enjoy his surroundings. This time, though, he had no choice. His foot was too sore for him to strike out with his normal fast crawl so he merely used his arms and one leg to float around, enjoying the buoyancy.

Because he wasn't up against the clock, he was able to take his time and look around at the glorious setting. The lake sparkled all around him under the warm sunshine and the view of both the hotel and the boathouse was completely different from the water.

As Dotty swam nearby, Alex even had time to turn onto his back and float, staring up at the cobalt sky for a while.

In the end, he could feel the cold beginning to seep into his bones and managed to persuade Dotty to begin their return towards the beach.

On their way, they passed a pair of coots, trailed by their babies bobbing around in the water. It was quite magical, he thought, and decided to make the lake swim a permanent addition to his many days of recovery.

As they began to slowly walk out of the water, Alex was surprised to find Ben waiting for them both.

'Thought I was dreaming when I first saw you both heading into the water,' he said, holding out his grandmother's towel for her.

'Thank you,' she said, taking it and wrapping herself up. 'That was wonderful.'

She looked across at Alex, who was trying to dry himself off whilst not putting too much weight on his broken foot.

'Thanks. It was,' he said. 'A real tonic.'

'Told you so,' said Dotty, with a wink.

Ben was frowning as he looked at Alex, struggling to pick up his crutches. 'If this is going to be a more permanent fixture, I think we'd better add a couple of seats though.'

'Agreed,' she said, also looking with concern at Alex.

'Don't worry on my account,' said Alex. 'I'm hoping to get better day by day, not worse, I hope.'

'I was thinking more of Grandma, to be honest,' said Ben with a grin. 'She might want a gin and tonic in a deck chair afterwards.'

'Sounds marvellous,' Dotty told her grandson, her eyes gleaming.

As Alex joined in with their laughter, he looked back across the water once more. It really would be the perfect therapy whilst his foot healed, he thought, and decided there and then to make it a daily routine.

16

'When you invited us for the weekend, this wasn't quite what I had in mind,' said Ella with a sigh.

Hannah handed over a paintbrush. 'I know,' she told her. 'But we've got to get these last walls painted before opening.'

Hannah was pleased that they were all together at long last. It had been a busy few weeks and it was great that Beth and Ella had come to stay at Maple Tree Lodge.

'And as you were here anyway for Grandma's birthday party tonight, I figured we could utilise the time,' carried on Hannah.

'She does love a party,' conceded Ella. 'And one of Frankie's cocktails will go down very nicely after you're making us work when it's a Saturday.'

'It's so exciting,' said Beth, tying back her long dark hair into a headscarf. 'I can't believe you're going to have your very own café soon.'

Hannah glanced around at the many deliveries that had already arrived, including a few bottles of beer and wine, as well as water and cordials.

Hannah grimaced. 'It's not mine,' she said quickly. 'It's part of the hotel.'

Lily frowned at her. 'Except it's all your responsibility,' she told her. 'We've got enough on our plates.'

Hannah's insides clenched in fear. 'But still, if it all goes wrong then the hotel won't be affected,' she carried on.

'Why would it go wrong?' asked Ella, putting on a shower cap over her blonde hair which was tied up in a bun.

Everyone else paused to look at her with raised eyebrows.

'What?' said Ella, with a shrug. 'I've just had these highlights done and I don't want to get paint in them.'

Hannah watched as Ella tucked a loose strand of perfectly straight hair into her shower cap. Her make-up was immaculate and discreet as usual, even with a slick of lip gloss on she looked gorgeous.

'Very glamorous,' murmured Lily. 'Is that going on your blog?'

'Not on your life,' replied Ella. 'My blog is all about high-end expectations and looking your best.' She glanced down at the paintbrush she held in her beautifully manicured hands. 'No offence but DIY doesn't come close.'

Ella was always dressed conservatively. That morning, even to paint the café walls, she was dressed in a crisp white T-shirt and black jeans. Around her neck was the simple silver star pendant that Beth had given each of them.

Ella had started a blog which was slowly but surely drawing in more followers each week. It was just like Ella herself. Cool and fashionable with a hint of humour. Despite her fixation on looking perfect all the time, thankfully her friends knew that Ella was also huge hearted and would do anything for them.

However, Beth was frowning. 'Shouldn't your blog's message

be about what's on the inside?' she said. 'Isn't that even more important? Why can't you tell your followers about that?'

'Of course being bright and kind is important as well,' Ella told her. 'But you like to look good, don't you? Well, present time excluded.'

Whilst Hannah and Lily were dressed in old shorts and T-shirts that they didn't mind getting splattered with paint, Beth still retained the vintage style that she always wore.

Beth often scoured the charity shops in search of retro fashion and that day's style was no exception. She wore a pair of extremely short cut-off denim dungarees which showed off a fabulous pair of legs. Underneath, she wore a Breton-striped T-shirt and on her feet a pair of Dr Martens boots. Somehow, as usual, she managed to pull it off with her own unique style.

Her long dark hair was braided into two plaits and her dark eyes were lined with heavy eyeliner, as well as wearing deep pink lipstick.

However, beneath her kooky fashion and dreamy romantic personality lay the sharp intelligent mind of an astronomer. She was extremely bright and could often be found scouring the skies for stars.

Beth glanced down at her denim dungarees, which were decorated with patchwork flowers. 'Don't you like them?'

'You look like you've come to fix the boiler, not ensnare some hunky man,' Ella told her.

'Around here?' murmured Hannah. 'You'll be lucky.'

'Oh, I don't know,' said Ella, looking out across the lake. 'There are some here to be found if you look hard enough.'

They all followed her look to where Alex was making slow progress with Tiny on a lead on the opposite side of the lake. Hannah was pleased to see that he had moved down to only using one crutch which meant that he was hopefully beginning to slowly recover.

'Oooh,' cooed Beth, always desperate to find romance for all her friends. 'Am I sensing a crush?'

Hannah found herself a bit perplexed about the thought of Alex and Ella having a romance.

Ella looked at Beth with raised eyebrows. 'Not in the least. I mean, he's lovely and all that but *so* not my type.'

'What is your type?' asked Lily. 'Not that you ever seem to date anyone.'

'That's because my type is rich, available and eminently pliable,' said Ella. 'Unfortunately that dating pool is extremely small.'

Beth shook her head. 'That's cold,' she said, with a shudder. 'What about romance, love, the flutter you get from seeing the one that you can't stop thinking about?'

Her friends all exchanged a knowing grin.

'Who is he this time?' asked Hannah.

Where Ella was entirely cynical about love and relationships, Beth seemed to fall for every date she ever went on. And because she was so beautiful, she went on quite a few.

'Brad,' Beth told them, breaking into a beautiful smile.

'And where did you meet this Brad?' asked Lily.

'Online,' said Beth. 'We've gone out three times and it's going so well. I really think...'

'That he's the one,' chorused her friends, finishing her sentence for her.

A frown crossed her forehead. 'Look, I know I've said it before,' Beth told them.

'Every time,' murmured Lily.

'But this time it's different,' carried on Beth.

'Also said every time,' added Ella. But in the end, she did a palms up. 'Well, it's your heart to be broken all over again,' she said, heading over to hug her friend. 'Just try and be careful this time.'

Beth gave her friend a squeeze before stepping back. 'So once the walls are painted, what kind of vibe are you thinking in here?'

'A cheap one,' said Lily. 'We used up almost all the money on the renovations.'

Ella immediately shook her head. 'That won't sell,' she said. 'You need a gorgeous Instagrammable space which makes people desperate to come.'

'It's only my cakes,' muttered Hannah.

Lily turned to look at Hannah. 'And what do you mean "only"? Your cakes are amazing.'

Beth nodded. 'Exactly. So we've got pale blue walls. How do you want the rest of it to look? You know the feel of the place.'

Hannah shrugged and glanced at Lily. 'You're the interior designer.'

'And you're the client,' Lily told her, taking her by the shoulders. 'We know you're scared but we've got your back, remember?'

'And your sides and front too,' added Beth.

It was a familiar mantra between the four of them and helped ground some of Hannah's nerves that she at least had her friends' support.

'You must have daydreamed a little about having your own café one day,' said Lily. 'So, close your eyes and how do you imagine it looking?'

'Do I have to?' asked Hannah.

'We're not going to push you in the lake, if that's what you mean,' said Ella, her eyes gleaming. 'At least not yet.'

'Very funny,' said Lily, giving Ella a steely glare. 'She needs to relax. Hannah, trust us. Close your eyes and tell us how it looks when you imagine it.'

Still a little uncomfortable, Hannah did as she was told. With her eyes closed, Hannah found at first it was hard to drown out all the negative noise in her head. But gradually she relaxed and suddenly there it was.

'It's not how it looks, it's how it feels and sounds,' she murmured.

'Tell us,' said Lily in a soft tone.

'It's warm,' began Hannah. 'The sun is flooding through the open doors. It's bright and airy with the lake sparkling beyond the veranda. There's little vases of wildflowers on each table that rustle in a gentle breeze. The silver teaspoons clink against bone china cups. There's a ripple of "oohs" and "aahs" as the customers have a tray of decorated cakes delivered to each table.'

'How does it smell?' asked Lily softly.

'Roasted coffee beans, tealeaves steeped in teapots and scones still warm from the oven,' said Hannah.

'And how does it look?' murmured Lily.

'Oak tables to match the beams. Turquoise chairs that really pop out with a bright colour. The rest is all cool blues and white. Bright and clean. Patterned plates and cups, plus cute teapots. A long bar on top of which are glass domes full of my cakes.' Hannah stopped speaking and opened her eyes. 'My cakes,' she repeated, with a gulp.

'In your very own café,' said Lily with a smile. 'I love the sound of the turquoise chairs. It sounds amazing.'

'It does,' said Ella, nodding her approval.

'I'll be first in the queue on opening day,' said Beth.

'No discounts,' said Lily with a grin. 'Listen, I'll source the chairs. I know just the kind of thing that you mean. But I'll show you before I order them so you can tell me how close I've got to the real thing.'

Hannah stood in silence, still coming to terms that the café she had just described might just come true.

'It's so exciting,' said Beth, clapping her hands.

Lily nodded. 'If it looks like you've just described it to us then it'll be a huge success. And let's hope so because we're still not out of the woods profit-wise.' She looked out across the lake. 'Ben's still trying to get some new paddleboards off Dodgy Del. We were hoping to use the lake this summer to try and bring some more guests in.'

'That's a great idea,' said Ella. 'Paddleboarding is huge right now.'

'Anything on the water really,' said Lily.

'It's lovely being out on the water,' said Beth. 'Don't you remember when I spent three weeks in the Antarctic a couple of summers ago? Whales and penguins everywhere. So amazing.'

'Not sure we'll be able to rustle up any penguins around here,' Hannah told her.

But Beth still had a dreamy look on her face. 'The skies were amazing. So clear,' she carried on. 'And it was lovely to share it with someone.' Her look suddenly darkened. 'You know. Before he cheated on me.'

Ella shook her head. 'If I'd have gotten hold of him, I'd have fed him to the polar bears.'

'Me too,' added Lily.

Beth's soft heart needed protecting, thought Hannah. What if she fell for someone really bad, like Sean? She couldn't bear it if her friend was hurt so badly. It had been almost a decade since she had split up from Sean and she still wasn't sure her own heart had recovered.

'Anyway,' carried on Beth, as ever finding the positive

amongst her heartbreak. 'What about canoes or boats for two out on the lake? Can you imagine? A soft sunset. Serenaded by their partner as they drift across the water, he's saying poetry and words of love.'

'To the sound of the ducks and frogs,' added Lily in a wry tone.

But Beth was still dreamy eyed and just nodded. 'How lovely.'

'And if you can hear yourself above the croaking and quacking?' Ella rolled her eyes. 'Let me think, what else would be heard? The sound of a big splash as she falls in, screaming, oars drifting away. Wet, cold and miserable.'

Beth blinked back to life. 'You have no romance in your soul,' she said, with a sad shake of her head.

'Thank goodness!' said Ella, with a hearty nod. 'Apart from Lily here, the rest of us are right to keep that rubbish out of our hearts.'

Hannah glanced over through the window to where Alex was now watching Tiny play with a stick. 'He seems to be recovering day by day,' she said.

'But he's going to have to use that boot for at least another month,' said Lily.

'You know what this place needs marketing-wise?' asked Ella, with a wicked smile on her face. 'Alex cooking in just an apron!'

They all laughed, except Hannah, who found she was shaking her head.

'What?' said Ella, still laughing. 'You don't think he can bake?'

As her friends carried on laughing, Hannah realised that it wasn't the joke that made her uncomfortable. She just didn't want to think of Alex that way at all.

But she still stole one more glance across the lake before swiftly dismissing the thought of an undressed Alex and carried on decorating, her cheeks warm from what she hoped was the sun streaming through the windows.

17

Dotty's birthday party that evening was a lively affair. After the dinner service and with only a handful of hotel guests around, most of the family were able to join in with the celebrations. Especially when those guests headed out to a local pub and the family could relax.

'That leaves us a couple of hours by ourselves before they return,' said Lily, taking a martini glass full of a colourful cocktail from Frankie early in the evening. 'Cheers!'

Hannah was pleased that so many people had turned out to celebrate her grandmother's birthday. Even Jake had come along for the evening, although there was one person less than happy about that. Jake and Ella didn't get on and merely suffered each other's company with barbed comments.

'So are you going to join us swimming at some point?' asked Dotty.

Ella shook her head. 'I'm afraid not,' she replied.

'I'm not surprised,' interjected Jake. 'Your ancestors suffered so much with the dunking of the witches, I imagine.'

Ella scowled at him. 'And what's your excuse for not going

in?' asked Ella. 'It must be time for your monthly bath after so long.'

Jake merely laughed off her comments and went to stand next to Hannah. 'How your sweet nature ever got stuck with a friend like that is beyond me,' he said, before shooting Ella a grin.

Hannah rolled her eyes. 'Can you two just get along for one evening?' she told them.

'I doubt that very much,' said Jake, at the same time as Ella shook her head furiously.

Hannah smiled at them, thinking that it was a good job that Jake and Ella didn't stay at the hotel at the same time too often. She looked around, pleased to see that all of Dotty's friends were there. However, Mavis had brought a plus one.

'This is my great-niece Aimee,' she was saying to Alex and Dotty.

Hannah watched as Alex stood up from his stool to greet the pretty petite woman with the bright pink hair.

'So you must be the yoga instructor?' said Dotty. 'Mavis has told me how popular your classes are becoming.'

Aimee nodded. 'I'm so thankful,' she said, with a wide grin. 'Not that the village hall is anywhere near as beautiful as the surroundings here.'

Aimee then went on to ask Alex how long he was staying for and about his injury rehabilitation, recommending yoga for the stretching.

'That's a great idea,' said Alex.

Aimee was looking up at him as if she were worshipping a god. He was smiling down at her too, especially when Hannah overheard Aimee suggest a one-to-one yoga session to help with his stretching.

As if Alex didn't know all about stretching muscles, thought Hannah, suddenly feeling grumpy.

'What's the matter?' asked Beth. 'Are you worried about the café?'

'No,' replied Hannah quickly. 'I'm fine.'

'Look, I know you're fretting but it's going to be a great success,' said Ella, guessing why Hannah might be in a bad mood. 'You just need to create a buzz.'

Ella was now an influencer in her spare time and had a knack for generating publicity.

'Producing footfall is key,' she carried on. 'Social media. Local marketing. It needs to be memorable. Who's your target market?'

'Anyone with money in their wallet,' drawled Ben nearby, drawing an arm around Lily.

Hannah shot her big brother a glare but remained silent.

'You look like you're at a funeral, not a birthday party,' said Frankie from behind the bar to Hannah, raising an eyebrow at her. 'You need one of my specials.'

'Then what am I drinking?' asked Lily, staring down at her half-drunk cocktail.

'That was one of my normal ones,' Frankie told her. 'Hannah looks like she needs a pick-me-up.'

'I'm not miserable,' muttered Hannah.

'Tell that to your face,' joked Ben.

Hannah tried to force herself to be more cheerful but found that she couldn't stop glancing over at Alex and Aimee as they continued to chat.

'When I was in Nepal,' she could hear Aimee saying.

Hannah ground her teeth together in irritation. Aimee had pink hair and had travelled the world. Hannah had normal-coloured hair and hadn't gone any further than London and even that had been a step too far from her beloved Maple Tree Lodge.

She had never felt more of a country mouse in all of her life.

'I must ask her whether she can help me with my bad shoulders,' said Frankie. 'I need loosening up.'

Lily stared into her almost empty cocktail glass. 'Just have one of your own drinks,' she said, with a hiccup. 'That'll loosen anything up.'

'Even Hannah?' asked Frankie, pushing a cocktail across the bar top towards her.

'For the last time, I'm fine,' said Hannah, picking up the drink and taking a gulp. 'Wow,' she croaked. 'That's strong.'

'Told you it was one of my specials,' said Frankie with an evil grin. 'And it is supposed to be a party, after all.'

Hannah took another sip of the strong drink. Why was it bothering her so much that Alex and Aimee were chatting? Except Aimee was most definitely flirting and not just chatting, Hannah decided. She kept putting her hand on his arm, Hannah noted, with a frown.

For some reason, she couldn't bear the thought of them becoming even more than friends. So where did that leave her feelings for Alex? He was just lovely, handsome Alex. That was all, wasn't it?

After a couple more of Frankie's special cocktails, Hannah was feeling far more cheerful. Her grandmother's birthday deserved to be celebrated, after all.

The only blot on the evening was when she checked her phone and read a text from an unknown number. It turned out to be Sean. She stared at the words on the screen, ever so slightly out of focus after all the cocktails she had drunk. But she understood the pretext. He wanted her back.

The alcohol gave her the strength to delete the text and block his new number too.

'That'll show him,' she thought, stabbing at the phone a couple of times before she could finally get it right.

'You're not drunk texting, are you?' asked Beth, as she watched Hannah slip her phone back into her pocket. 'Believe me, that never works and I should know.'

'Wait!' said Lily, sloshing her drink about a bit after one too many cocktails. 'Who would Hannah be drunk texting? Who's getting a booty call?'

'A booty call?' said Ella, looking amazed. 'Who? What?'

'Nobody,' said Hannah, rolling her eyes. 'I'm single. Always single. Dull Hannah. Single Hannah. That's me.'

'Oh dear,' said Frankie, overhearing the conversation. 'We appear to have reached the morose part of getting drunk and that's never attractive.'

'I agree,' said Beth, removing the still half-full cocktail glass from Hannah's hand and downing it herself. 'There. No harm done.'

Excusing herself to go to the bathroom, Hannah was still feeling down. No amount of alcohol seemed to be numbing her senses.

She was just on her way to the downstairs washroom when she spotted Alex chatting with Aimee outside. Ever the gentleman, he was seeing her and her grandmother to their car.

Scowling, Hannah did an abrupt turn but stopped before going back into the snug. Everyone was being very judgemental that evening. She just needed to be alone. So instead, she went out of the back door and around the side of the hotel.

The fresh air hit her pretty hard but it was quite nice, she thought. If you liked being alone under a starry sky, that was. Always alone. Never with anyone. Why couldn't she be sparkly and fun like Aimee? Why was she always so dull?

She didn't even wild swim with her grandmother and she was almost eighty! Well, perhaps she should start now.

Feeling a little wobbly, she headed towards the beach.

18

Despite the ache inside his broken foot, Alex had enjoyed the party. He had missed so many parties when he had been training that it was nice to be able to join the family for once and not miss out.

Dotty had introduced her to many of her friends and he had had a very interesting discussion with Aimee about how yoga might help with his recovery. It was certainly something to consider, he decided.

Thankfully, with the painkillers he was still on for his foot, Alex had stayed on the zero-alcohol beer for the evening and wasn't suffering the consequences of many of the family and friends who were reeling under the influence of Frankie's strong cocktails.

Beginning to grow tired, from both Tiny's disruptive nights and the pain, Alex had offered to see Aimee and Mavis to their car before turning in for the evening.

However, he was just returning from the car park when he saw Hannah disappearing around the corner of the hotel.

Wondering where she could be going at that time of night,

and having noted how much Frankie's cocktails had been flowing, he decided to follow her and make sure that she was all right and not upset.

He quickly realised that she wasn't upset at all, given away by the fact that she was singing to herself as she staggered along the lakeside path away from the hotel. He could see now that she was actually pretty drunk. Perhaps she was going to the boathouse, he thought.

However, when she made a beeline for the beach, he quickly picked up as much speed as he could on one crutch. Lakes and alcohol were never a good combination, he reminded himself, wincing as he forced himself to move even faster.

But by the time he had reached the beach, Hannah was standing at the water's edge and had already stripped off her top and skirt.

'Hey,' he said, his voice coming out as a croak as he took in her curves, almost all on show apart from her underwear.

She spun around and beamed at him. 'Hey!' she replied. 'You found me.'

'I didn't know that we were playing hide and seek,' he told her. He tried not to stare at her skin, creamy pale in the moonlight. 'Aren't you cold?'

She shrugged her shoulders up and down in an exaggerated manner. She really was quite drunk, he realised.

'I'm a country girl,' she slurred. 'Born and raised. Of course I'm not cold.'

He could see the goosebumps on her arms even in the semi-darkness.

'Let's go back to the party,' he told her gently. 'Get you in the warm.'

But she shook her head. 'I need to do something exciting,' she told him.

'Well, you're about to open up your very own café, isn't that exciting enough?' he asked.

'Pah! Not really.' Hannah gave a heavy sigh. 'Me! Dull Hannah. Always such a goody-goody.'

He had never heard her speak like this before.

'So what are your plans this evening?' he asked. 'Skinny dipping?'

Her hand went up to her bra strap and for a split second, he thought she was going to take it off. At that point, his brain almost short circuited.

'Skinny dipping? Why not?' she slurred.

He automatically took a few steps forward with his crutch, anxious that she didn't venture into the water in her drunken state.

But as he neared her, he realised that Hannah was looking at him with a certain look in her eyes. He'd seen it in a few women over the years, those that he'd dated at the end of a promising evening, perhaps. But never ever in a million years had he dreamt that Hannah would look at him like she was at that moment.

He found himself gulping as she abruptly closed the gap between them, staring up at him with something akin to desire in her eyes.

She shook her head. 'Not skinny dipping,' she said, slurring her words as she put her hands on his chest.

He glanced down at them before looking back at her face. He had tried so long to put his feelings for her to one side. Tried so long to ignore the lips which were now dangerously close to his.

'No?' he said, his voice still a little croaky.

'Something better,' she replied, her eyes gleaming. 'Something more wicked.'

He took in a sharp breath. 'You need to go to bed,' he said.

And so do I, he told himself. Perhaps he was already there and dreaming.

Hannah giggled. 'You can't boss me around. I already have a big brother,' she told him.

'I don't want to be your big brother,' he muttered, his senses reeling from her perfume as she leaned in closer.

'Good,' she said. 'You can be something else instead.'

Then Hannah suddenly lifted her head and closed the gap between them.

As her lips met his, Alex gave a start. When she didn't move away, he leant back but she followed him and their lips remained together. It took every inch of his self-control not to sweep her into his arms and kiss her back, despite his heart pounding in his chest.

In a reflex moment, his arms twitched and he was brought back down to earth when he realised that he was still holding onto the crutch. What was he doing? He had to be the sensible one now.

Finally, he took her by the arms and pushed her away so that their bodies were no longer touching.

'Well,' he began, not knowing what to say.

Hannah had kissed him. Did she know what she was doing? What did this mean for them both?

She stared up at him for a long moment before turning away.

Hoping she wasn't upset, he followed her before he realised that she was being sick. If that was her reaction to their first ever kiss then perhaps they really didn't have a future after all, he thought as he went over to help her.

19

Hannah woke up in her bed, wondering why she was wearing only her underwear underneath the covers instead of her usual pyjamas.

When she moved her head, however, she was instantly greeted with a monumental headache and groaned as the hang-over swept over her.

Her grandmother's birthday party, she reminded herself. Frankie's infamous cocktails, of course. But there was something else, said her conscience, nagging at her. What was it?

She glanced over to where she saw the clothes she had been wearing the previous night folded up neatly on a chair. And when she looked down she saw someone had also placed a bucket next to the bed in case she had been ill.

Someone practical, she realised. Who?

And then she remembered stripping off in front of Alex on the beach. Was there anything worse? Presumably not as she realised that she was still wearing her underwear. So what? Then the memories came flooding back. She had kissed Alex. And then promptly been sick.

She groaned and drew the duvet over her head, praying for some kind of imminent death rather than having to face him.

What had she been thinking of? Kissing Alex? Of course, he was handsome, funny, kind, built like the athlete he was. But still, Alex?

She hadn't kissed anyone since Sean. Getting close to a man was complicated. Caused pain, as she knew only too well. Of course, Alex was nothing like Sean. He was better in every way. But the shame rushed over her all the same. She had leapt on him and kissed him. She didn't think she would ever recover from the embarrassment.

There was a knock on the door and as it opened, she prayed it wasn't Alex.

Thankfully it was her best friends, all looking equally hungover. As the hotel hadn't been full, Beth and Ella had slept in one of the guest bedrooms the previous evening. Not that it looked as if it had a particularly refreshing stay, given their grey faces.

'What did Frankie put in those cocktails?' asked Ella, sinking down onto the bed with a groan.

'Please don't mention the cocktails,' moaned Beth, clutching her head.

Lily placed a tray on the bed, laden with mugs full of coffee, glasses of water and a pile of toast.

'I'm not sure I can face food,' muttered Hannah.

'You were pretty bad,' said Ella, with a nod as she picked up a mug.

'Yeah, I haven't seen you that bad in, like, forever,' said Beth thoughtfully.

'Where did you disappear to?' asked Lily. 'One moment you were in the snug, the next you went off.'

'Alex said that you wanted a swim,' said Ella, shaking her head. 'Good job he was there to stop you.'

Hannah groaned and put her head in her hands.

'What?' asked Lily.

Hannah sighed. 'I may or may not have decided to go skinny dipping in my drunken state,' she told them.

Shocked laughter rang around the bed.

'Nooo!' said Ella, laughing. 'That's too funny!'

'No, it's not,' replied Hannah. 'It's mortifying.'

'So you stripped naked in front of Alex?' Beth's eyes were on stalks as she stared at her friend.

Hannah shook her head which made everything go a bit swimmy so she sank back against the pillows. 'Just down to my underwear,' she told them, trying to keep the duvet from showing that was all she was still wearing, but her friends were putting two and two together.

'Did you walk back through the hotel in your underwear?' asked Lily, shocked.

'From what I remember, Alex had to walk me back,' said Hannah, frowning. 'How utterly mortifying.'

'Rubbish,' Ella told her. 'So what? You should be thanking him. Alcohol and swimming never ends well.'

Hannah stayed silent.

'Unless there's something else,' said Lily, studying her with narrow eyes. 'There is, isn't there?'

'How would you know?' asked Hannah, feeling defensive.

'Because you're about as good an actor as your big brother, which is absolutely terrible,' said Lily, with a grin.

'So what gives?' asked Beth.

Hannah sighed. 'So I stripped off down to my underwear in front of him,' she began. 'And, like you said, he stopped me going into the lake.'

'Thank goodness,' added Ella, with a firm nod.

Hannah put her hands over her face and groaned. 'And then I kissed him,' she said, her words muffled against her palms.

There was a long silence before she peeped through her fingers where she found her three best friends grinning at her.

'It's not funny,' she told them.

'It kind of is,' said Ella, with a wide smile.

'A romantic kiss?' asked Beth, all starry eyed.

'Not really,' said Hannah, grimacing.

'What did Alex do?' asked Lily, getting to the point.

'Nothing,' said Hannah, feeling a dull pain. She felt rejected even though it had been the absolute right thing for Alex to do. 'He was the perfect gentleman.' Hannah frowned. 'Then it all gets a bit hazy. I'm pretty certain I threw up and then the next thing I remember is him helping me inside and up here. I'm so embarrassed!'

'It's Alex,' said Lily with a shrug. 'He'll be fine about it, I'm sure.'

'Yeah, he'll laugh it off,' added Beth. 'You just need to talk to him.'

Hannah grimaced. 'I'd rather just pretend that it never happened, to be honest.'

'He's one of Ben's oldest friends,' said Lily. 'He'll understand. We've all been drunk at one time.'

'Yeah, what's the problem?' asked Ella. 'You've known him for years.'

'What if he thinks that I'm awful?' said Hannah.

'He would never think that,' Lily told her.

Hannah shrugged off the duvet and shakily stood up. 'I'm going for a shower to drown my sorrows,' she told them.

As she stood under the powerful jets of water, she thought back to what her friends had been trying to tell her. Yes, Alex was lovely. After all, he was safe. Her brother's best friend. It was fine.

Why on earth had she kissed him? Was it because she actually liked him?

Yes, he was supremely fit. It worked well with the ladies, so she'd heard. Or rather, tried not to hear. She always knew where she was with him. Safe. Trustworthy... and yet suddenly she felt in unfamiliar territory, as if something had changed between them.

Of course it hadn't, she reminded herself, feeling cross. It was just one drunken kiss, that was all.

After all, they never flirted with each other. Besides, she wasn't sporty enough for him. Nor tall. Nor anything. She most definitely wasn't his type.

Aimee was absolutely his type on paper. She was everything that Hannah wasn't. Confident, athletic and far more suited to Alex than she could ever be.

Hannah decided there was no way she was interested in him. No way. Yes, she'd checked him out in his swimwear but she was allowed to look at him, wasn't she? After all, he was the most handsome guy she knew. She knew him so well. And he knew her too. Which was why nothing was going to happen, she told herself.

So why did she keep replaying the kiss in her mind and wondering what would have happened if she hadn't been drunk? Would he have kissed her back?

It didn't matter, she realised. Because she had seen how relationships worked out in the end. There was too much pain to take the risk.

So she would force herself to think of Alex as the friend he had always been. And that would be the end of it, wouldn't it?

20

Alex wandered into the empty café and walked across the floor, still feeling in somewhat of a daze.

He had planned that one day, he was going to take Hannah in his arms and kiss her. One day. That day had sure been a long time coming, ten years, in fact.

And yet, despite all his dreams, she had kissed him first. Then she had spent the day hiding from him and scurried from the room whenever he found her in one. So now she was running for the hills and the tentative closeness that they had built up had dissipated.

Or had it? He knew that everything had changed for them both with that kiss. And that Hannah would never do anything about it, despite whatever connection lay between them. There was no way that she was interested in him that way.

He would just have to continue being happy to be her friend. His heart lurched. He wanted to be so much more to her than friends.

He grabbed an alcohol-free beer from one of the delivery

boxes, making a note to replace it later. Then he went to stand by the open doors, looking out across the lake.

The sky was incredible, hues of blue streaked across the sky in every shade. And yet he couldn't see anything other than Hannah flinging her arms around him and lifting her head to kiss him.

Despite the future looking less than rosy, he couldn't help but smile to himself when he thought about their kiss.

'Are you going to stand there all day with a goofy grin on your face or are you going to offer me a beer as well?'

Alex spun around to find Jake sitting on the furthest corner of the balcony.

'What are you doing here?' he asked.

'Still waiting for that beer, apparently,' drawled Jake, nodding at the bottle.

Alex handed his friend his unopened drink before going inside to grab himself another from the box. Normally he would have been happy to see Jake but his mind was still preoccupied with Hannah.

He sat down at the table with Jake and they both raised a bottle at each other before silently taking a sip. The cold beer slid down his throat but it did nothing to settle his racing thoughts.

'I'd like to ask if it was a bad day at the office but considering the view I don't see how that's possible,' began Jake. 'I mean, I'm stuck in a kitchen with no windows day in, day out and here you are with all this.' His hand waved across the magnificent view as he paused before speaking again. 'So what's happened with Hannah?'

Alex gave a start. 'What do you mean?' he spluttered, almost dropping his bottle.

Jake raised an eyebrow at his friend. 'You really want to play this game? With me of all people? Me who knows you better than anyone?'

Alex looked at him nervously.

'Me, who's known you for far too many years,' carried on Jake. 'And for every single one of those years you've had a crush on Ben's little sister.'

Alex drew in a breath but didn't reply. Jake had teased him once about not asking Hannah to dance at the Dragonfly Dance earlier in the year but he hadn't realised that he had been so obvious in his feelings. Which made him question how much Hannah knew about them as well.

Jake raised an eyebrow at his friend. 'I've respected your feelings for a long time, you know, but we're all over thirty now and time's marching on. Mate, you've been mooning over her since we finished uni.'

'Does he know?' asked Alex, before taking a small sip of beer.

'Ben?' Jake thought for a moment and then shook his head. 'I don't think so. And why would it matter?'

'Because he's very protective of her.'

Jake nodded. 'And rightly so. She's sweet and lovely and if you were ever to hurt her, I'm not sure which one of us would drown you in the lake first.'

'I would never hurt her,' protested Alex. 'I couldn't.'

'I know.' Jake threw him a look. 'So what happened last night that you can't tell anyone but me?'

'She kissed me,' Alex told him, feeling the smile play on his lips at even admitting to such a thing.

'Well, go and kiss her back, you fool,' Jake told him, with a grin.

Alex's good mood faded abruptly. 'I can't,' he said. 'She was drunk and she's been avoiding me all day. I know she regrets it.'

'And what about you?' asked Jake. 'Any regrets?'

Alex hesitated.

'What's the matter?' asked Jake.

Alex shrugged. 'I guess it's a trust thing. For both of us.'

'Of course you can trust Hannah,' said Jake, frowning. 'She's not Claire!'

Alex took an intake of breath. 'I know,' he said, trying to convince himself. He had tried to convince himself that Hannah wouldn't take advantage of him. She wasn't Claire. She could be trusted, couldn't she? But the kiss had been so out of character.

'You know, I never told you,' began Jake.

'What?' asked Alex, filled with dread.

'Claire tried it on with me once.'

Alex wanted to be shocked but instead he found himself sighing and saying, 'I'm not surprised.'

'Well, I was!' said Jake. 'Nearly had heart failure.' He shook his head. 'What a dreadful woman.'

Alex nodded.

'Whereas Hannah is the complete opposite,' Jake reminded him.

'Which is why I'm pretty certain that she regrets her actions last night.'

'Are you sure?' asked Jake.

Alex shrugged his shoulders. 'I reckon so. You know how shy she is.'

'It's a trust thing for her too,' said Jake. 'She was always shy in those early days when we met her, don't you remember?'

Alex nodded, thinking back to the young woman that he had first seen and fallen for.

'Ben told me that she seemed to come out of her shell a little once she met the girls and they all lived in that house in London,' said Alex.

'But then she met the idiot...' Jake's voice trailed off as he scowled to himself.

'She would never tell me anything about Sean,' said Alex.

Jake nodded thoughtfully. 'Of course, you weren't here the weekend she came back after they'd broken up. You had a competition.'

When didn't I? thought Alex. But his mind was preoccupied with Hannah. 'What did she say?'

'Not much,' said Jake. 'Even to the family. She just suddenly appeared out of the blue with all of her possessions. But she was pretty wretched. I hugged her on the Sunday before I left and she was trembling. I think she was frightened.'

Alex took a deep breath. 'Of him? Sean? Do you think he hurt her?'

'Physically?' Jake's eyes flared with anger. 'I don't know. I hope not for his sake if I ever get hold of him.' He leant back in his seat. 'Mentally? Without a doubt, unfortunately.'

It had confirmed all of Alex's suspicions as to why Hannah had no confidence.

'Look,' carried on Jake, his tone a little softer. 'If you like her, why don't you just talk to her?'

Alex shrugged his shoulders. 'I don't know, mate. I'm probably not even her type. Nice guys finish last, don't they?'

'No,' replied Jake. 'They're just nice guys whom you want people you care about to be with. Not complete idiots or playboys like me.'

Alex dragged his hand through his hair. 'OK. Say you're right and I'm still not convinced. I don't even know what to say to her to get her to open up.'

'You'll work it out. It's a trust thing. But I reckon you know about bullying more than most.'

Alex grimaced. 'You're talking about Dad?'

Jake nodded. 'Love is complicated. Which is why I never get involved with anyone.'

It was true. Jake's love life was a revolving door of new girlfriends, none of whom he let get close to him.

'What about us here?' asked Alex.

Jake laughed. 'I'm just here for the free beer,' he said, holding up his bottle.

Alex knew it wasn't true. That Jake's scars from his parents' bitter divorce ran deep.

'So what are you going to do about that kiss?' asked Jake.

'Absolutely nothing,' said Alex.

Jake sighed and shook his head. 'On the plus side, at least it'll stop me from having to act all big brotherly on her behalf.'

Alex looked out across the lake and tried not to think about Hannah's soft lips pressing against his. He knew she had been drunk and would sincerely regret it. But, he had to admit, he had thought about pretty much nothing else since. His crush was alive and real once more. Or perhaps he had just buried it for so long, tried desperately to ignore his feelings for her.

But the kiss had shattered everything and he had no idea what happened next.

21

Hannah was tidying up in the kitchen with Lily after dinner but still feeling low, which she was putting down to her hangover.

'I'm shattered,' she told Lily. 'I'm going to have an early night tonight.'

'Me too,' said Lily, as she stacked the dishwasher. 'By the way, one of our guests was telling me how much she's enjoying the cakes on the honesty trolley. Everyone is looking forward to the Boathouse Café opening, isn't that great?'

Hannah nodded. 'Yup.'

Lily straightened up and looked at her friend. 'It'll be fine, you know.'

'I know.' And yet Hannah was too tired to summon up the effort to put a fake smile on her face. She blinked away the tears which suddenly appeared in her eyes. 'Thanks, bestie.'

'You're welcome,' replied Lily. 'Come here.'

Hannah found herself drawn into a hug and relished the strength of the squeeze that Lily gave her.

They had just stepped apart when she heard someone say, 'Is everything OK?'

They both turned around at the same time to find Alex standing in the doorway.

Hannah was still embarrassed about the kiss and had tried not to be alone with him all day. Thankfully her plan had mostly worked. But now she could feel the heat rising to her cheeks at having to face him.

'Tell Hannah she's amazing, won't you?' said Lily, switching on the dishwasher. 'Now where did I leave that thingamy…'

As Lily quickly walked out, Hannah had a feeling that she was deliberately leaving her alone with Alex.

'You know, Lily's right,' he said. 'You are amazing. I'll make a note to tell you every day, if you like.'

As always, he was being kind. But her flight mode kicked in and suddenly she couldn't face him and the reality of what she had done. How everything had changed between them.

'Well, I'm going to have an early night,' she said quickly, going to walk past him.

But Alex stepped across to block the doorway so she couldn't get past.

'You OK?' she heard him ask in a soft tone.

Hannah gulped. She couldn't meet his eyes. All she could think of was the memory of her leaping into his arms to kiss him the previous night. So instead she gazed down at their feet.

'I'm so sorry about last night,' she muttered. 'I hope I didn't upset you.'

'Of course not. Don't worry about it,' she heard him say. 'It was just Frankie's cocktails, as usual.'

Hannah found herself thinking that she wasn't entirely sure that it was.

Still staring at her trainers, she jumped when she suddenly felt him take her chin with his fingers and drag her face up to look into his.

He smiled at her. 'Maybe you just needed to let go some of your tension about opening the café,' he said.

'Maybe.' She couldn't stop her face from blushing but as she finally forced herself to look into his eyes, she saw nothing but sympathy. Or was there something else there, she found herself wondering.

'Well, anytime you feel that stress again, you can totally use me, if you like,' he carried on.

Was he flirting with her? Surely not. But for some reason, she found her breath catching in her chest as he let go of her chin to reach out to stroke a stray wisp of hair away from her face.

For a second they stared at each other. She so wanted to trust him. But Sean's text the previous evening still burned in her brain. Relationships were bad, she had trained herself to think. No matter how lovely Alex was.

'Don't worry,' Hannah found herself saying in an overly bright voice. 'I'm sure I won't get that stressed again so I'll leave you alone from now on, I promise.'

Alex's hand immediately dropped from holding her face.

'Especially if I don't indulge in one of Frankie's cocktails again,' she added, fixing a wide smile on her face.

'Of course,' he replied. 'They are pretty lethal, aren't they?'

But his smile didn't reach as far as his eyes, she noted. She hoped she wasn't upsetting him. Surely he didn't want to take things further than just friends?

At the sound of the door opening and Walter walking into the kitchen, Alex abruptly turned away, telling Hannah that he was taking Tiny out for a walk.

Still standing in the same position, Hannah puffed out a sigh, realising she'd been holding her breath whilst he had been so close to her. Since when did she have that kind of reaction to being around Alex?

She had told him that she would never do anything like that again to embarrass him. The kiss had ruined everything between them, she felt. Because, despite her telling him otherwise, all she wanted to do in that moment was kiss him again.

And yet she knew that could never happen. It was for the best, after all.

22

A few days later, Alex watched as Ben and Dodgy Del manoeuvred a mattress up the staircase to the apartment in the boathouse.

Having watched them carry up a few pieces of furniture, he felt completely hopeless and hated the feeling. All of his life he had been blessed with good health and an athletic body. But suddenly he was at a loss. He couldn't do everything that he wanted and he felt the frustration growing inside of him.

Even walking Tiny was challenging because although he was down to only one crutch now, he still had to be careful when moving around so he didn't further injure his foot.

The only time he felt like his old self was when he swam in the lake, a daily occurrence now that he had gotten used to it. He certainly enjoyed the feeling of being in the water and the weightlessness meant that he could briefly forget about his broken foot as well. He even found himself encouraging Tiny to join him, although he seemed a little reluctant to go any deeper than his paws.

And yet he couldn't deny that he was enjoying having a dog.

Tiny gave him the emotional support he needed when his foot ached and he felt helpless. Even that morning after breakfast, when he could feel himself getting frustrated and agitated as he sat in the lounge, suddenly Tiny was there next to him. With one bound of his ever-lengthening legs, he had leapt onto the sofa and snuggled into Alex. When the puppy's breathing steadied as he drifted into his morning nap, Alex couldn't help but feel calmer as he watched the rise and fall of the dog's black furry stomach.

The rest of the time, apart from the obedience training of Tiny, there wasn't much else for him to do at Maple Tree Lodge. Everyone else was busy with the hotel and keeping the guests happy.

He missed having a purpose, he found. Well, perhaps not the accountancy work but the daily routine and keeping his mind occupied. But with the family around during the day and Tiny with him each night, at least the old feelings of loneliness hadn't resurfaced.

With the delivery of the new furniture for the apartment, Alex, and more importantly, Tiny, had a place to sleep away from the guests. After the first night, Tiny had stayed up in Alex's guest bedroom which at least had stopped him howling the place down and disrupting everyone's good night's sleep.

Not that Alex had been sleeping very well in any case. The pain was, quite literally, a pain. But it was more the radio silence from his dad that caused his thoughts to race in the early dark hours of the morning. He was hurt and upset by the lack of contact and it weighed heavily on his mind.

Alex winced as he placed his weight onto his broken foot, having briefly forgotten about it for one blissful moment.

'Do you want to sit down?' asked Hannah, looking concerned.

That was one blessing of having an enforced stay here, he

thought. He got to see Hannah each and every day. The memory of her kissing him had kept him awake quite a few nights as well and yet he knew they could only be friends, as far as she was concerned. His dream of being anything more had dissolved and he was trying not to feel heartbroken.

'I just forget sometimes about the wretched break,' he said, with a sigh before shooting her a grin. 'Sorry. I'm grumpy when I'm in pain.'

'I'm not surprised,' she told him, before slowly unwrapping one of the new chairs for the café which had just been delivered. 'What do you think?'

He looked at the turquoise leather and nodded. 'Great colour.'

'That was my idea,' she replied. She looked around at the remainder of the tables and chairs still in their wrapping.

'It's coming together,' said Alex.

She nodded, biting her lip as her nerves bubbled to the surface.

Alex could see her lack of confidence getting in the way of her dreams and was anxious to reassure her. 'It's going to look great,' he told her. 'I'll be first in queue for a coffee and one of your amazing cakes.'

She looked over at him and smiled. 'You can get family discount as well.'

'Glad to hear it,' he told her. 'Especially as I'm not working at the moment.'

At the sound of scraping upstairs, it at least sounded as if the apartment would be liveable that evening.

He wondered how he would get along with sleeping there alone. Or at least with just him and Tiny.

But one glance at the wide-open glass doors which were flung open to the lake and he knew that he would be just fine.

It was the peace that had always soothed him whenever he had come here to visit Ben. On the tube, in the gym, on the busy crowded streets of the capital city, it was noise all around him all the time. Music from shops and cars, traffic, roadworks, people talking, shouting. But here, deep in the countryside and with the healing power of nature, he could breathe again.

'We're all done. Do you want to see it?' called out Ben from upstairs.

With Hannah following him, Alex slowly went upstairs. As he reached the top floor he was amazed by the transformation.

Where before it had been a large empty space with a separate kitchenette and bathroom, now it was full of furniture. There was a large bed, drawers and a wardrobe and beneath the large porthole window was a sofa, coffee table and television on the opposite wall.

Even Hannah sighed. 'What a lovely space,' she said, walking around the huge bed.

'We had to get a king-size mattress for you as you're ridiculously tall,' said Ben, with a grin.

Alex had to concede that the space was lovely. With the oak ceiling and floorboards, it felt cosy but the huge porthole window in the side of the room meant that light flooded in from across the lake and the views were incredible.

'It will be like sleeping above the lake,' said Hannah.

'I hope that's all the furniture you need because we haven't ordered anything else,' Ben told him.

'It's great,' Alex replied. 'More than adequate for my simple needs. I just feel bad that you've had to go to all this additional expense just for me.'

'It's fine,' Ben told him, with a wave of his hand. 'Lily had the idea that we could always rent the upstairs apartment after you move out for some extra cash. Not that we're in any kind of rush to get rid of you.'

'If he doesn't want it, I'll take it,' said Dodgy Del quickly. 'This place will be a babe magnet.'

Ben rolled his eyes. 'Yes, that was our intention all along, Del. Now, about those paddleboards?'

Del gave him a quick smile. 'On their way. Any day now. Is that the time? I've got to pick someone up.'

And with that, he disappeared quickly down the stairs.

Ben sighed before looking at Alex. 'Do you think you'll manage up here OK?'

'Absolutely,' said Alex, nodding. 'It's the nicest flat I've ever lived in.'

It was true. The feel of the place matched the warmth and cosiness of the hotel.

At the sound of the patter of paws, they all turned around to find Tiny making his way up the stairs. A smaller dog would have struggled but Tiny was growing bigger day by day, his coat already becoming shaggy and his legs longer.

His black face appeared at the top of the stairs and he wandered over to slump on Alex's good foot with a heavy sigh. Alex could already see a line of drool that was now strung across his trainer laces.

'What do you think, Tiny?' asked Hannah, bending down to stroke his head. 'Do you think you'll be happy up here? Because if Alex doesn't want to move in here, I definitely would!'

Alex looked around at the cosy apartment and allowed himself a brief daydream of what it would mean to live there with Hannah. To distract himself, he sank down onto the bed and picked up Tiny to sit next to him on the mattress.

'It's great,' he said. 'But we still need to sort out the rent, remember?'

Ben nodded. 'First thing is for you to get that foot mended. And when was the last time you had an actual holiday? Apart from our lads' week in Las Vegas.'

Hannah's eyes gleamed. 'Oooh, tell me more,' she said.

'Not on your life,' said Ben quickly, shaking his head. 'You know what they say about Vegas.'

'Awww,' moaned Hannah. 'I never get to hear the juicy gossip.'

'Good thing too,' Ben told her. 'We don't want to corrupt your innocent mind.' He turned to look at Alex. 'So, what do you say? Just you and Tiny, living the countryside dream out here. You could stay here for the summer. Sounds like a great idea to me.'

Alex looked down at the dog who was staring up at him in adoration with big black eyes. Although that could just be because lunchtime was nearly upon them, Alex reminded himself.

He had always dreamt of having a dog. And the thought of all that fresh air, without the strict training schedule, was extremely tempting. They could walk without thinking about records and setting a decent pace. He could relax and enjoy the tremendous view, for once. All the pressure had been taken away from him, even though he was still trying to work out what was left in its place instead.

Perhaps it could work. Perhaps taking the summer to take stock of all of his life might just be the break that he had been thinking of.

Finally, there was Hannah. He loved his friends and the Jackson family as a whole. They were like a second family to him. But the temptation of spending some quality time with Hannah every single day was the biggest reason of all that he could find, despite her only wanting to be friends. He glanced across and found her blue eyes staring into his and began to nod without even thinking about it.

'That's a yes?' asked Hannah tentatively. 'You'll stay for the summer?'

Alex carried on nodding as if in a dream. 'It's a yes.'

'Brilliant!' exclaimed Ben.

'That's wonderful news,' she said, looking delighted. Standing nearby, she smelled of fresh air, sugar from her baking and the soft flowery perfume that she always wore. His senses reeled for a second until he dragged himself back into the present.

'Looks like we're both starting again at the boathouse,' he told her.

'Sounds like it,' she said, breaking into a nervous smile.

And he found himself wondering just what the summer might bring both of them and their friendship.

23

Once the boathouse had been decorated, Hannah felt as if opening day in a week's time was charging towards her at full speed. The date had been set in stone because all the marketing that Ella had put together had stated the spring bank holiday as the opening weekend for the café.

Even with the fear deep inside, she was pleased with the turquoise touches that she had discussed with Lily. The pop of coloured tiles along the bar separating the kitchen and the main room was just right and tied in perfectly with the new chairs in the same colour. The rest of the room was cool and neutral pale blues and warm oak wood.

Once more, Hannah looked at the second-hand catering equipment that Ben had bought, with Jake's recommendation, that was. Although she had to admit that his taste was pretty similar to hers. The large ovens were more than capable of holding quite a few cakes at a time. The dishwasher was also a second-hand industrial unit and she loved the double butler sink which would make things far easier. Plus the fridge freezer was enormous, which should make the storage of all the ingredients plentiful.

Not that she was sure that anyone would actually come.

The idea was that the café would be opened as a tea room in the afternoons. Between 1 p.m. and 5 p.m. each day, it would be available for cream teas, as well as a few additional cakes and hot drinks.

Planning her own menu excited her. As the café only had a temporary licence for the summer, she had decided that it should be full of delicious sunny flavours. Raspberry and lemon pie. Bundt cake with icing and edible flowers decorations. A raspberry-topped Victoria sponge too would feature, as well as home-made scones and strawberry jam with clotted cream.

Everything was to be served on the pretty china which Dotty had hoarded over the years, the majority of which had been used to decorate the hotel. But there had been a number of leftover items which hadn't found a place, such as china cake stands, and so the boathouse was ideal for most of the tableware items. Dainty flowery china teapots would be used for the cream teas, along with different-patterned plates, cups and saucers.

Hannah had decided to order pastel-coloured paper napkins for the time being, as they could easily be recycled. But when the delivery came, she realised to her horror that she had made a mistake on the online order form.

'Are you expecting a bit of a rush?' teased Alex as he looked down at the large pallet of pale blue napkins that had just been delivered.

Hannah shook her head in dismay, feeling miserable. She thought that she had ordered a small amount as a trial but at least thirty boxes had arrived that morning.

She sighed heavily.

Alex's face dropped. 'What's the matter?' he asked.

Hannah sank down onto a nearby chair. 'This was a crazy idea,' she told him. 'I can't do this.'

'It was just a mistake,' he said, coming to sit opposite her.

'But I make so many,' she replied. 'I'll end up wasting so much money that we won't make any profit at all. I mean, look at it!' She picked up the delivery note placed on top of the pallet. 'It's random numbers,' she carried on. 'They all just look like squiggles to me.'

'Because of your dyslexia,' he reminded her.

She was surprised and turned her head to look at him. 'You know about that?' she asked.

He nodded. 'Ben mentioned it a long time ago.'

She sighed. 'I just get so muddled,' she told him. 'It's awful. Ben's so competent all the time and I'm... not.'

'Everyone has their different strengths,' he said.

'And weaknesses,' she said, with a grimace.

Alex shook his head. 'Just focus on the positive. I'm good with numbers but I can't bake a cake to save my life. Like I said. Everybody is good at something.'

'But Ben wanted me to run the business and do all the paperwork,' she told him, the anxiety rising inside. 'I'm just not sure I'm up to it.'

Alex studied her for a moment before speaking. 'Look, I know I'm supposed to be resting up but I need to keep using my brain as well. So let me help you.'

'What do you mean?' she asked.

He smiled at her. 'Think of me as your accountant and temporarily lame admin assistant,' he said. 'It's not like I've got anything else to do while this wretched foot is healing.'

She knew how frustrated he was at not being able to do anything whilst the bones were still broken.

'To be honest, I could do with the distraction at the moment. I'm feeling a bit lost.'

'Lost?' she asked him.

'I just feel at a crossroads,' he told her. 'As if everything has been turned upside down and I don't know where to begin again.'

He looked so downhearted and dejected that Hannah found herself reaching out to take his hand.

He gave a start as he glanced down at them entwined. But as the embarrassment swept across her cheeks in a rosy blush and she tried to pull it away, he enclosed her hand in his.

'My whole life was work, training and competitions,' he said, still looking down at their hands. 'I'm not sure what's left without all of that.'

Hannah gave up with her embarrassment and gave his hand a squeeze.

'What's left?' she repeated. 'A good-hearted man who we all care for.'

He looked up into her face and she realised that she'd never noticed the colour of his eyes before now. They were the brightest blue that she'd ever seen. She'd only ever noticed the kindness that they carried.

'Thank you,' he told her. 'I was feeling a bit low this morning.'

'Do you want a napkin to mop up any tears?' she said, with a small smile of irony. 'I've got a few spare.'

He laughed and their hands let go. 'See? If you can laugh at your mistakes, you're halfway there.'

She felt relieved that they seemed able to move on from her drunken kiss at last and that any awkwardness had finally dissipated.

He stood up and looked down at her. 'Come on.'

'Where are we going?' she asked.

'You're going to show me all your documentation,' he told her. 'And then I'll start to transform myself into your glamorous assistant.'

She knew that Alex was being so kind, as usual. But she felt much better knowing that she wasn't alone in the new business venture any more.

24

Alex found that he was grateful in the coming days for the distraction of helping Hannah with the paperwork for the café.

He was still suffering with some stiffness and swelling in his foot which the doctors had said could still take a few months to recede. However, spending time resting in the boathouse apartment was helping. He was enjoying waking up in the mornings to the view of the lake and found himself taking his time to relish a lie-in to stare out of the window at the glistening water.

But where his body was slowly starting to mend, it was his mind that couldn't quite cope with doing nothing but rest every day.

Tiny helped as a distraction, purely because he had had no training up until that point. But he seemed an intelligent and well-behaved dog, despite his lack of training, and so even that didn't take up too much of Alex's daily routine.

Each day, he began to walk without the protective boot on his foot, starting with a small distance to begin a gradual increase in weight bearing on the broken bones. Normally just heading to the beach for his morning swim and then back again was enough before the pain increased and he didn't want to push himself too soon. For the remainder of the day, he used the boot and tried to keep busy. If he rested for too long, he found that his mind ran through everything, every competition that he hadn't won, every missed opportunity.

So he was glad to concentrate on the health and safety forms that Hannah struggled to complete, as well as the stock orders. He knew that she was still embarrassed about the over-ordering of the napkins but Alex had arranged for half to be returned or sold on to other nearby establishments that could use them so they weren't out of pocket.

'Thank you for sorting it all out,' she said once more as she sat opposite him on the balcony one afternoon after setting out the new weatherproof wooden chairs and tables.

'You're welcome,' he replied. 'So are you looking forward to glasses and cutlery arriving tomorrow?'

She nodded, looking inside briefly before grimacing. 'Excited and terrified,' she admitted.

'You sound like Tiny when he sees a duck,' he said, trying to cheer her up.

He was pleased when she laughed, reaching down to stroke the dog who was growing by the day. Tiny was currently sprawled under the table and taking up most of the room. He seemed to be growing in both length and width and was certainly going to be an enormous dog, thought Alex.

He looked up to find Hannah studying him.

'You look tired,' she said. 'Are you in pain?'

'And there was me thinking I was hiding it so well,' he told her, with a soft smile.

'Look, why don't I take Tiny around the lake this afternoon to wear him out whilst you rest up?' she said, standing up. 'What do you think, Tiny? Shall we go for a walk?'

He immediately sprang up, yelping his bark in glee at his second favourite word after 'treat'.

'I should join you,' said Alex immediately.

But Hannah shook his head. 'Nope. You're going to rest,' she told him, in a firm voice.

But as she turned to leave, Alex found himself wishing that he had joined her. Soon he would be better, he promised himself. And perhaps when he felt more like himself, he might work up the courage to ask her out, hoping that she might have changed her mind about their kiss after all.

As he watched Hannah and Tiny head through the empty café interior, Alex spotted someone coming through the open front door of the café. He was shocked to see his father exchange a few words with Hannah before heading towards him.

His dad walked out onto the balcony and they looked at each other for a moment.

'Hi,' said Alex, sitting up a little straighter in the chair.

'The lady on the hotel reception said you were in here,' said his dad, before sweeping his eye over the foot which was resting on a chair. 'How are you?'

'Fine, thanks, Dad,' said Alex, bringing the foot down automatically onto the floor, feeling slightly ashamed of the injury and how it had occurred. 'I didn't know you had plans to visit.'

'Seeing as you're still hiding out here, I didn't have a choice,' said his dad, sitting down opposite him.

Alex caught the word 'hiding' but decided to ignore it. 'How's Mum?' he asked.

'You can see for yourself when you come home with me this afternoon,' replied his dad.

Alex gave a start. 'What are you talking about?' he asked, shocked.

'Are you done licking your wounds?' His dad looked impatient. 'It's been a fortnight.'

'A fortnight of pain and frustration,' Alex reminded him.

'Well, that'll be over before you know it. And then we can move on.'

Alex was startled. 'Move on?' he repeated.

His dad nodded. 'You know, the mark of a great athlete is to pick themselves up after failure. So I still reckon next year's Olympic Games should be our next goal.'

Alex was aghast. He had bared his soul to his parents two weeks ago and his dad had dismissed everything that he had told him.

Feeling cross, he shook his head. 'No,' he found himself saying.

His dad looked at him in surprise. 'What did you say?'

Alex took a deep breath. 'I said no, Dad. I meant what I said a couple of weeks ago.'

'No to what?' His dad looked frustrated. 'It'll take extra training, of course, to get your fitness levels back after so much time off but I reckon...'

But Alex didn't let him finish. 'I mean no to all of it.' He sighed. 'I'm done, Dad. Finished.'

His dad still looked confused. 'Look, we all get knock backs, son,' he began to say.

'It's not about that,' Alex told him. 'I don't want to do it any more. The endless competitions, the training, the travelling. I've really had enough.'

His dad looked irritated. 'I suppose this is the influence of your so-called friends here, is it?'

'They're actually my best friends,' Alex told him in defence.

'But yes, they support me which makes a nice change, to be honest.'

'What does that mean?'

'I mean that when I told them I wanted a life away from competing, they listened to me and wanted to help,' said Alex.

'So you're working here, are you?' asked his dad, frowning.

Alex shook his head. 'No, but they've invited me to stay for the summer and that's what I want to do. I may not have a job but I have a life here. With people who don't care about winning every second of every day. They like me for what I am. I just wish you felt the same way.'

The silence stretched out so Alex forced himself to carry on speaking the words that he'd carried inside for so long.

'Thank you for all you've done for me. The sacrifices and the training, I mean. I've tried my best to live up to your ideals but I have nothing more to give. I love you, Dad, but I want to be your son again, not your gold-medal project to live vicariously through me.' Alex gulped. 'Please respect my wishes. I'm ready for a new chapter in my life. I can't do it any more. I'm out.'

His dad looked at him. 'I see,' he said finally with a sigh as he stood up. 'Well, there's nothing left for me here then.'

'*I'm* here, Dad,' said Alex, feeling hurt.

He had always wanted to be closer to his dad, not feeling like a project but a son.

His dad hesitated before giving him a small nod. 'Yes. Well, I'd better get back in any case,' he said. 'Take care of yourself.'

After an awkward goodbye, his dad walked away.

Alex leaned back in his chair and puffed out a long sigh.

It was over at last. Who had he been competing for all this time? Had it been for himself or his obsessive father?

The truth was that he had never truly wanted it. Deep down. All he had wanted was to be close to his dad. And that had only been available to him through practice and the competitions. Something they could share.

Without that, was there a chance that they could have a relationship?

He hoped so. But he felt the tears pricking his eyes as his dad left the boathouse, feeling lower than he had ever imagined.

25

Hannah had begun her walk with Tiny when she realised that she had forgotten his treat bag. Being an oversized puppy meant that bribes were essential in case of any misbehaviour, especially where the wildfowl on the lake was concerned.

So she was just on her way back to the boathouse to grab them when she spotted Alex's dad coming the other way.

Surprised to see him again so quickly, she walked up to him, hoping that nothing was wrong.

'Hi again,' she said with a smile. 'Would you like me to bring you both a cup of tea? It's really no problem. I'm sure you've got lots to catch up on.'

Alex's dad looked a bit shocked. 'Oh, no, thank you,' he said quickly, with a frown. 'I've got to get going actually.'

Given his angry expression, Hannah guessed that their meeting hadn't gone very well. Alex had told her of his dad's dismay when he had said that he wanted to give up competing but she couldn't believe that he would take it that badly.

Alex's dad gave her a nod as if to take his leave of her and started to walk away.

But Hannah found herself saying, 'Please don't leave. Not so soon and not like this.'

His dad stopped and turned around, looking surprised at her.

'What I mean to say is that Alex is in a lot of pain at the moment,' she began, blushing furiously. 'So I'm sure he would want to see you, whatever he says.'

'He hasn't told me anything except his desire to give up competing,' snapped his dad. 'So what else is there to say to each other?'

His dad was looking upset but Hannah knew that she had to try to somehow bridge the gap that seemed to exist between them both. Because she cared for Alex, she realised.

'He's in pain,' she told him. 'And I think he's a little lost too. His whole world has been turned upside down with this injury. He needs support, not blame.'

His dad raised his eyebrows. 'This was all his own doing,' he replied. 'Alex chose to compete in that race. Against my advice, I have to add.'

'He came here to help his best friend and my family,' said Hannah. 'He knows that the hotel is still struggling and he wanted to support us by taking part in the triathlon. Don't you think that that's worth more than any medal? That his kindness and the way he values his friends is more important?'

'He doesn't have the luxury of time to help people out when he should be competing,' said his dad.

Hannah began to get a little cross. 'Your son is one of the kindest, most generous people that I've ever come across. Despite being in pain, he's been helping me out with the café paperwork because I've been struggling with it.'

'Perhaps you should look to your own family for support,' said his dad.

'We *do* support each other,' she told him. 'Because we're family. Could Alex say the same about you?'

His dad drew in a deep breath and Hannah wondered whether her loose tongue had gone too far in its temper.

'Athletes like Alex have different kinds of goals,' he replied after a short silence.

'But life isn't just about achieving goals,' she told him. 'It's about kindness, support and friendship.'

'But Alex is different,' said his dad. 'His athletic abilities are special. He has a gift. He should be using it, not wasting it in the middle of nowhere.'

'But it's the rest of him that's special too,' she told him. 'Not just his athleticism, don't you agree? Can't you see that?'

'I see a quitter,' snapped his dad. 'And that's no good to anyone.'

'Rubbish,' said Hannah. 'I suffer with dyslexia and he's been helping me out with the paperwork for the café, otherwise I would have been a quitter too. But let me tell you something,' she carried on, getting up a head of steam. 'If I *had* quit the café, my family would have been there for me every step of the way. Because that's what families do. Support each other.'

His dad went to speak but Hannah found that she couldn't stop talking now.

'We lost my dad last year,' she said. 'And I would give anything to have him here now with us. Do you know how lucky you are? My grandfather can't see his son any more. He doesn't have that choice. You do and you're still walking away from him.'

His dad huffed out a sigh. 'Look, it's complicated,' he said.

'No, it's not,' replied Hannah. 'Alex is a credit to you, not a failure. It's just a shame you can't see him in that way. Because he's amazing and one of the best men I've ever known. I'm so proud of him. You should be too.'

She turned on her heel and led Tiny away towards the boathouse. She was shaking with anger and found herself taking a few deep breaths along the way to calm herself down. She didn't want Alex to know that his dad had been so cruel.

And yet, when she went into the boathouse and walked onto the balcony, she realised that Alex was hurting anyway. He was standing at the railing but when he spun around to look at her, she realised that the pain in his eyes wasn't from his foot, it was from his soul.

So despite trying to keep him at arm's length since her drunken kiss, she couldn't stop herself from stepping forward to draw him into a hug.

'I'm so sorry it didn't work out with your dad,' she murmured against his broad chest.

He squeezed her a little closer and she felt him give a shaky sigh.

'We'll work it out,' she told him. 'We'll think of something to make him see it your way.'

She hated to see him upset, desperate to take his pain away from him.

Because she had meant every word she had told his father. He was good and decent and kind. And she was beginning to really care for him now.

26

Three weeks on from breaking his foot, Alex was beginning to feel a few small signs of recovery.

He could now walk slowly without any crutches, for which he was grateful. He found that he missed running and using his body so easily as he had done before the accident. The need to keep up his physical well-being, as well as his heart rate, was still quite strong after all the years of training. But he was pleased to be feeling stronger at last after a frustrating couple of weeks.

He briefly thought about the conversation with his dad before forcing his mind onto something else. He had spoken his mind and said what was long overdue, as far as he was concerned. He just hoped that he and his dad could repair their relationship in time.

But he also was pleased to have found a different type of exercise which he intended to keep up for the duration of his recuperation. Each morning before breakfast, and after taking Tiny out for a walk, he would go for a swim in the lake whilst Tiny lay on the beach watching him with sleepy eyes.

'Best rehabilitation I know,' Walter had said to him one evening.

And Alex was now inclined to agree.

Swimming had always been part of the triathlon to him, the first stage in a race. So to discover that he actually enjoyed the tranquillity of the water by himself was a surprise. After his swim, he always felt better, calmer and happier.

Twice Dotty had joined him and Alex was pleased that she too was enjoying swimming in the lake, even at eighty years of age, and yet he was worried as well. He voiced his concerns to Ben late one morning.

'I was thinking that we need to order some safety equipment for the lake,' he said to Ben and Walter.

'Health and safety gone mad,' muttered Walter, shaking his head.

For once, Alex felt the need to disagree with him. 'I worry that if anyone gets into trouble out there, there aren't even any lifebuoys, let alone a lifeguard out there to keep an eye on people.'

'A lifeguard?' Even Ben's eyebrows shot up in surprise.

'If you're serious about wanting to open up the lake for paddleboarders then you'll need to be safe,' Alex told him.

Ben leant back in his chair, nodding thoughtfully. 'I see.'

'If Dodgy Del ever comes through with the paddleboards,' Walter reminded him.

Ben rolled his eyes. 'Summer might be over by then,' he said, with a grimace. He then turned to look at his friend. 'You really think we should be thinking about this?'

'I do,' said Alex. 'I've seen experienced triathletes get cramp in the water, as well as other difficulties like getting tangled in the reeds, for example. Even if it's only for hotel guests and your grandmother, then I'd be far happier if they were safe.'

'Agreed,' said Ben, with a nod. 'So you know about the kind of things we need?'

'I can get everything ordered for you, if you like,' replied Alex.

'Great,' said Ben, standing up. 'Better to be safe than sorry. We're responsible for everyone whilst they stay here so that should cover everywhere, including the lake.'

So when Alex went out the following morning for his swim, he made a note whilst he was out in the middle of the water as to where the shallows were, as well as suitable places for lifebuoys.

In fact, he was out in the water for so long that by the time he joined Tiny on the beach after his swim, Hannah had joined him, looking concerned.

'You were out there much longer than usual,' she told him, holding out his towel.

'Thanks,' he said, taking it from her outstretched hand.

'Are you back training again?' she asked.

He shook his head. 'Just rehabilitation,' he said, wincing a little as he briefly put his weight on his foot before sitting on one of the three deck chairs that Walter had put out for Dotty on the sand.

To his surprise but pleasure, Hannah sat down next to him. Tiny, delighted to have double company, wagged his tail and immediately rolled over, waiting for someone lucky enough to rub his furry tummy.

Hannah smiled at the dog and reached forward to oblige. 'You've always been so focused,' she said. 'I wish I had even a tiny bit of that self-confidence.'

He looked at her. 'I'm not so sure about that,' he told her. 'It was certainly easier to feel that certainty about everything when I was training.'

'How so?' she asked.

He thought for a moment, trying to find the words to explain.

'I guess it was all about the preparation for the next race. I had to be meticulous in training, otherwise I'd just be making up numbers.' He shrugged his shoulders. 'It was hard work but it did make me feel energised. Enjoying what you do helps.'

His frown caused Hannah to look at him in concern. 'What is it?' she asked.

'The trouble is I didn't really enjoy it these last couple of years,' he told her. 'It went from enjoyment to pure ambition to win a medal. That sole dream clouded everything else in my life.'

'But you're an athlete,' she reminded him. 'It's easier for you.'

He sighed, trusting her with the truth. 'Do you want to know a secret?'

She waited patiently for him to carry on.

'Tiny did me a favour,' he told her. 'I was tired, done. I was competing for Dad, not for myself. I put his goals way above my own. I want to be selfish for a while.'

She smiled at that. 'You're the least selfish person I've ever met,' she told him.

He was glad of the compliment but felt the need to correct her. 'Thanks, but I still want the same things that most people want.'

'Like what?'

'I want to settle somewhere,' he replied.

'Well, there's worse places,' she told him, laughing before looking over at the boathouse nearby. 'I wish I could bottle your confidence and take it with me. I'm dreading running a café, to be honest.'

'You don't want to have your own place?' he asked.

She bit her lip. 'Actually, yes, I do,' she said softly. 'I'm just not sure that I'm ready for it.'

'You need to be single-minded and focused on what you

really want,' he told her. 'If that's the café then be brave and go for it.'

'And what about you?' she asked. 'What do you want right now?'

The silence stretched out as he looked at her. Now was his chance. To tell her how he felt. To even ask her out on a date.

But in his hesitation, they were both distracted by Tiny suddenly leaping up to greet Lily as she came down the path towards them. And as Hannah got up to chase after the dog, Alex realised that he had missed his moment once again.

27

'I haven't got time for this,' complained Hannah as she parked the car at the edge of Cranbridge village. 'The café opens in two days' time.'

'You told me everything was all set. Besides, there's always time for tea,' said Dotty, before climbing out of the car. 'And cakes,' she added, with a smile.

'You know, you keep telling me that *I'm* already pretty good at making cakes,' said Hannah. 'So why do we have to go out for them instead?'

'It's called sussing out the competition,' her grandmother told her before linking arms with her granddaughter and walking towards the centre of the village. 'Besides, it's good to get you away from the hotel occasionally. You're too young to hide yourself away all the time.'

Hannah couldn't disagree with her grandmother, especially with Cranbridge looking particularly beautiful that afternoon. Instead of a main street, there was a wide shallow river running down the middle of the village, with three ancient pedestrian stone bridges connecting either side over the clear, bubbling water. Hugging the river were a number of houses, all built in the familiar honey-coloured stone.

They walked past the Cranbridge Stores, a thriving corner shop which they had often used as it stocked local produce as well as pretty much everything else, and along Riverside Lane.

Hannah smiled at a few familiar faces but she didn't know half as many people as her grandmother and they had to stop quite a few times to chat to local villagers before they finally reached their destination.

'Nice day for it,' said Dotty, pushing open the garden gate. 'Shall we sit in the tea garden?'

At the end of the row of shops was a large walled garden which was full of colour and customers. Hannah couldn't blame them for choosing such a pretty place to sit and have a morning break. It was a lovely setting, with the river nearby and the water-mill slowly turning at the far end.

'This place used to be so awful and overgrown,' said Dotty, as they sat down at the only free table and chairs in the garden.

'It certainly isn't now,' replied Hannah, looking around at the beautifully cared for plants around them. The air was alive with the sound of bees as they buzzed from one brightly coloured flower to the next, searching for nectar.

Her eyes moved on to the small indoor café alongside the garden, which was also full of people. It was certainly very popular, especially on a bright and sunny afternoon in May when everyone was desperate for the warmer days of late spring.

'Hi,' said a waitress, coming to stand next to their table. 'Oh, hello, Dotty!'

'Hello, Molly,' replied Dotty. 'I don't know if you've met my granddaughter Hannah?'

'Nice to meet you,' said Molly, smiling down at Hannah.

'You've done wonders with the place,' said Dotty, before turning to Hannah. 'Molly owns the tea room.'

Hannah smiled. 'Yeah, I kind of got that, Grandma,' she said, holding up the menu on the table which said Molly's Tea Room.

Dotty looked back at Molly. 'How's business?' she asked.

'Busy,' said Molly. 'And I'm about to get even busier,' she added, holding her stomach where Hannah suddenly realised she had a small baby bump.

'Oh, congratulations,' they both said at the same time.

'Thanks,' replied Molly. 'Logan and I are over the moon.'

'And your mum too, I'm sure,' said Dotty.

Molly nodded. 'First grandchild so he or she is going to be spoilt rotten. So what would you both like?' asked Molly. 'Tea? Coffee? Pastries?'

'Coffee,' said Dotty. 'Definitely one of your delicious cakes, you choose for us. We're not fussy eaters. And a little information as well, if you don't mind.'

'Information?' Molly laughed. 'I don't think anyone's ever asked me for that before now.'

'My granddaughter here is opening up her own tea room in the old boathouse on the lake,' said Dotty.

Molly looked delighted. 'At Maple Tree Lodge?' she asked, to which Hannah nodded her reply. 'Oh, that's a fantastic idea. Location is everything, as you can see,' she carried on, waving her hand towards the river. 'I would say you're definitely going to be onto a winner.'

'I'm not so sure about that,' replied Hannah, her fears bubbling to the surface once more. 'I've never done anything like this before.'

Molly gave her a sympathetic look. 'I know all about being nervous,' she said. 'I was a bag of nerves before I opened up this place. But you know what? I knew my cakes were good. Beyond that I had no skills at all but at least I felt that if my cakes tasted great then hopefully everything else would follow.'

'That's what I keep telling her,' said Dotty.

'Any advice for me?' asked Hannah before grimacing. 'Although I feel kind of bad asking you because we're in the same line of business.'

'Oh, that doesn't matter,' Molly replied, with a smile. 'There's plenty of room in the area for all of our small businesses. Now, let me see. Definitely start with only a short menu of your favourite items. It will help with the stock control before you know how many customers you're getting in each day. Also if there's less choice then you won't have quite so many leftover cakes.' She laughed. 'However pleased your family will be to eat them!'

'We always enjoy her baking,' said Dotty, with a proud look.

'I'm sure. Now, what else?' said Molly. 'Staff are key. I was lucky with mine and now I've got a great set-up with someone that I can rely on. And she's become a really great friend as well. That helps.'

'I've told her that I'm happy to help out,' said Dotty. 'I haven't got much else to do these days.'

'That's great,' said Molly. 'Family support really helps. Oh and finally, get yourself an amazingly supportive partner,' she added, twirling the engagement ring around on her finger. 'That makes all the difference in the world.'

After thanking her and placing their orders, Hannah thought back once more to Sean and knew that he could never be described as being supportive. What would he think about her new venture? He'd probably tell her that she would be no good at it, she figured.

That made her all the more determined to prove him wrong.

She was stronger without him, she realised for the first time. And with that thought, she began to feel a little more brave about opening up her very own café.

28

When Molly brought out the coffees and cakes to their pretty table in the Cranbridge tea room, Hannah had to concede that they were truly delicious.

Her grandmother agreed.

'That was lovely,' said Dotty, leaning back in her chair. 'I must say, Molly has done well with the place. It's a real success.' She smiled. 'Although I like to think that I played my part.'

Hannah was surprised. 'How?' she asked.

'I helped out with the clearing of the garden when it first became a community shared scheme,' said Dotty. 'They asked for volunteers and, you know me, I can never sit still.'

It was true, thought Hannah. Her grandmother was almost eighty years old and yet was still a powerhouse of energy. For most of the time, in any case.

The death of her son, Hannah's father, had been the only time when Dotty had become more reserved, unwilling to see people whilst she quietly went through the grieving process.

Now, she met her friends in the snug more often and yet she still wasn't the same. Perhaps you never were after the loss of a loved one, thought Hannah, knowing how much she missed her dad as well.

Dotty was still staring over at the garden. 'Of course, I only did a bit of weeding and digging,' she carried on. 'I'm not a florist. I leave that to your dear mother.'

'I definitely haven't inherited that talent,' said Hannah, with a grimace.

Dotty smiled at her granddaughter. 'But you're a brilliant baker, just like Faye. And lovely Molly too, come to think of it. See what a little success can do you for, my sweet girl,' she said, waving her hand at the busy tea garden.

If you have a supportive partner, thought Hannah as she considered Molly's words.

'Who's Molly's fiancé?' she asked.

'Logan,' replied Dotty. 'He makes the most amazing furniture. His shop's next to the tea room. But he also runs the watermill over there.'

'Oh!' exclaimed Hannah. 'I've used his flour for my bread. It's wonderful.'

Dotty nodded. 'Local businesses,' she said. 'It's great to support them.'

Hannah made a mental note to ensure that she sourced her ingredients as locally as she could. She could use the farms in the villages all around them for local fruits as well as dairy. She had heard about a new chocolate shop in Cranfield and also added that to the list of future places to visit.

'Seems like you're going to be busy over the next few weeks and months,' said Dotty in a wistful tone before looking cross. 'Unlike me. I need to get a move on.'

'With what?' asked Hannah, her eyebrows raised in surprise.

'Life, dear girl. Life,' said Dotty, looking more determined.

'And swimming. I enjoyed it so much when I went out with young Alex recently. I reckon my friends will love it too.'

'If not finding it a little cold.' Hannah shuddered, knowing that the water temperature would be at its most refreshing at the moment. 'Rather you than me.'

'It does wonders for the circulation,' said Dotty. 'And I've already broken my duck for this year. You know, I've swum in it every summer.' She paused before carrying on. 'Apart from last year, that is.'

Hannah reached out and squeezed her grandmother's hand.

Dotty sighed. 'It was quite a year and not in a good way. We lost your dad. And then Jane, of course. Such a dear friend. And then Maud became a widow. Suddenly our happy little group wasn't so happy.' She frowned to herself. 'I must get in contact with Maud. It's been too long since I saw her. Word on the street is that she's become something of a recluse.'

Hannah stayed quiet, she knew all about hiding away when you were feeling vulnerable and upset.

'Of course, old age is not so bad when you consider the alternative,' carried on her grandmother. 'Growing old is inevitable, if we're lucky. Growing up isn't a guarantee, thankfully.' Dotty frowned to herself. 'I feel that I need to gather my friends around me this summer. Last year, we had a lot of funerals to go to. It all became rather depressing and it gets you down after a while.' She suddenly turned her piercing gaze upon her granddaughter.

'And how are you doing, darling? We don't get much time to talk on our own these days.'

Hannah looked at her grandmother. 'I miss Dad,' she confessed.

'Of course you do,' said Dotty. 'But he would want you to live life to the full. And love too, come to think of it.' She broke into a wicked grin. 'Any handsome men in your life that I should know about?'

'Absolutely none,' said Hannah, blushing furiously as she thought briefly about kissing Alex.

'Well, that is indeed a travesty which we'll need to do something about,' said Dotty in a determined tone of voice.

Hannah decided to swiftly change the subject, unable to bear the thought of her own grandmother setting her up on a date.

'So you think you'll swim every week over the summer like you used to?' she asked.

'Absolutely,' said Dotty, bringing out her mobile. 'And no time like the present to get the gang back together again.'

She spoke out loud as she typed:

> Who's up for a wild swim tomorrow? 10 a.m. at Dragonfly Lake. Be there or be square.

Hannah grinned. 'Do you expect any replies?' she asked.

'Of course,' said Dotty. 'I'm always telling them that it's the swimming that's kept me looking this young and gorgeous!'

Hannah was still laughing when Dotty saw someone she knew who had just walked alongside the garden and went over to say hello. As her grandmother chatted over the low wall, Hannah watched her. How wonderful to go through life with that amount of confidence, she thought. How different her life would have been had she had an ounce of self-assurance. She wouldn't have got involved with Sean, that was for certain.

She thought about her grandmother asking about whether she had any handsome men in her life. The only single men she knew were Del. Not on your life, she mentally added immediately. And Jake, who was far too much of a ladies' man and anyway she thought of him like an elder brother.

So that left Alex. He too had been like an elder brother to her.

And yet recently, she had found herself letting her eyes remain on him for just a bit too long as she studied his wide shoulders and muscles. Her mind drifted to thinking about him more often than it had ever used to do. She even knew what it was like to kiss him although it was only a drunken, hazy memory.

She shook her head to herself. So he was handsome, so what? It was his personality that she liked. And anyway, they were just friends. Really good friends and nothing was going to ruin that.

Dotty returned to the table and told Hannah all the local gossip that she had just caught up on.

'You know, I'll take you up on that offer of help in the café if anyone turns up,' said Hannah.

Dotty looked delighted. 'Thank you, sweetheart. And of course they'll turn up. You just mark my words.'

They finished their drinks sitting in companiable silence, listening to the chatter around the garden. The whole garden seemed alive with conversation and the gentle clink of china.

Hannah wondered whether it would ever feel the same at the Boathouse Café. Surely it was too much for her to expect to enjoy making a living from her favourite thing in the whole world?

29

The following morning, Alex stood on the sandy beach as Dotty and her friends emerged from the hotel and began to walk towards him, giggling nervously in their excitement.

Nearby, Tiny snuffled at the sand and bounced around in giddy excitement. He was growing day by day and now his legs were longer than his body, giving him the stance of a gawky, awkward teenager. But there was no denying how big his head was, the dense fur of a Newfoundland who was going to grow to epic proportions.

Alex woke up each morning to find him sprawled across the bed, even though Tiny had silently promised that he would sleep in his dog bed each night. And yet it was hard to be cross with the puppy when his soulful eyes stared up at you.

In the meantime, Tiny was a great distraction. He gave Alex purpose in that he could focus on the dog training.

Training Tiny was just like his athletic training in the routine and purpose. Tiny was no different. Apart from the fact that he wasn't human. And he didn't always behave. But he was a stubborn, affectionate, gentle giant.

Alex had done thorough research on how to train him, as always telling himself that if he was going to do this, he would do it to the best of his ability. The training was coming along well though and despite a few puppy tantrums and tussles, Tiny could now walk to heel on his lead and come when called. Unless there were ducks nearby, of course, in which case he would bounce merrily into the water up to his ankles and try to get them to play with him, much to the ducks' horror.

Right now, the dog was watching the group of elderly women making their way towards them, wagging his tail in hopeful anticipation that they would have treats stashed away somewhere in the many layers of clothing they were wearing.

Dotty had told Alex over dinner the previous day that she had invited her friends to swim with her in the lake.

It was unfortunate that it was cloudy that day, thus reducing the warmth of late spring in the air. The water temperature had begun to increase but still, it would be a chilly dip for them all.

'Good morning, Alex and Tiny,' said Dotty, with a beam. 'Ladies, you all remember me talking about our hunky athlete, don't you? Well, here he is! Isn't he a marvellous specimen?'

Alex found himself blushing at Dotty's indiscreet way but found he couldn't be annoyed with her. She was such a force of life to be reckoned with.

'I thought that was me, Grandma,' said Ben, appearing from behind the group.

'Darling boy,' said Dotty, leaning up to give her grandson a kiss. 'You're welcome to join us.'

'Not on your life,' replied Ben with a shudder before wandering up to Alex. 'Well, we did want the lake to be utilised more often.'

Alex nodded but he was still a little concerned about the lack of safety features laid out across the lake, despite adding a couple of lifebuoys around the lake edge and on the jetty where they were standing.

'They really all ought to be wearing safety floats with lights on,' he said.

His years of experience of swimming across various treacherous waters in competitions meant that he was well versed in the safety measures put in place for the athletes.

'They're not in a race though,' Ben reminded him.

'I know,' he replied. 'But safety should always be the number one priority where water is concerned.'

Dotty overheard him and walked over to stand in front of Alex. She was so short he had to lower his head to look down at her.

'Young man, I've been swimming in this lake for fifty years,' she told him, putting her hands on her hips. 'I know what I'm doing.'

'Just humour me this one time and please stick to the shallows until we work out a better system if this is to be a regular occurrence,' he told her. 'You might be used to the cold water but your friends aren't.'

'Humph,' muttered Dotty. 'I'm really too old to be mollycoddled but I see your point, I suppose.'

She returned to walk with her friends to the nearby beach. Dotty's friends suddenly looked less keen on entering the water as without the sun, the lake looked grey and uninviting.

'We must be mad,' muttered someone.

'Come on, ladies,' hollered Dotty. 'Just remember, adventure before dementia!'

With that, Dotty slid off her tracksuit bottoms and sweatshirt to reveal a bright pink swimming costume. She then shucked off her Crocs and headed for the water.

'Go, Grandma!' came a nearby shout.

Alex spun around and saw Hannah waving at the group from the balcony of the boathouse. He was glad to see her smiling, despite the nerves that she had confessed about the opening of the café the following day.

Among the group, and far more slowly than Dotty, robes and jumpers were then stripped off and shoes removed.

Then someone yelled, 'Charge!'

With a collective groan, her friends followed suit, shivering across the sand towards the water's edge. On putting their feet in, there were squeals of shock as the icy water hit the ankles and the cold bit to the bone. From his years of experience, Alex knew exactly how that felt.

'Let's just get on and get it over,' muttered someone.

'Ten minutes only,' announced Alex. 'I'll be timing you all.'

'Can't you make it five?' asked Mavis, one of Dotty's least athletic friends.

He smiled at her. 'Just remember, you'll be at your coldest when you get out of the water so wrap up in your clothes as soon as you get out,' he told them.

'Come on, girls,' urged Dotty, already up to her knees in the water.

Accompanied by various squeals and screams in deference to the cold temperature of the water, the women finally went in.

As they paddled out, Alex could hear their chatter as they all moaned and groaned in solidarity in the freezing cold. He checked his watch and set the timer, determined to watch them all.

Once exactly ten minutes were up, Alex called across for them to come out of the water. He noticed that there wasn't too much resistance being made, and that included Dotty.

As they all waded back to shore, Alex kept an eye on each of the ladies to make sure that they didn't go into shock from the chilly temperature.

'Get dressed quickly, remember,' he told them.

'As if we're going to stand around in the freezing cold,' muttered someone.

Alex shot them a grin, just grateful that they were all safe and had survived their first icy-cold dip.

30

Hannah looked down from the boathouse veranda at her grandmother and friends shivering on the beach as the sun went back behind another cloud.

She immediately felt glad that she had already asked Dotty to invite them into the boathouse for some warm drinks.

In a way, it would be a trial run for any customers that appeared for the opening of the café the following day. She was torn between wanting it to be busy and successful and just wanting to hide behind the counter all day.

She felt a little nervous when the women came into the café but then noticed that, despite getting dressed, they were still shivering from the cold and decided that it was more important to get their temperatures back up to normal once more, given that none of them were under the age of seventy.

'Please sit down,' she told them. 'I'll bring you all some hot drinks.'

A new coffee machine had been delivered the previous day but the instructions might as well have been written in Mandarin for all the sense she had been able to make of them. She had already decided to ask Alex to help decipher them but as he was still chatting with Ben outside, she decided on heating up some milk on the stove for a mug of hot chocolate which would help warm them all up on the inside. Then she added tiny marshmallows and whipped cream on the top with chocolate flakes, all in an effort to make a good first impression. And this was her first dummy run.

She put all the mugs onto a tray and carefully carried them outside where the ladies had decided to sit to carry on enjoying the fresh air.

Despite their shivers and protestations about not enjoying it, Hannah was pleased to find that they were all laughing and chatting excitedly after their cold swim.

'It's been too many years since I did this,' said Mavis.

'Me too,' said another. 'And I did always so enjoy swimming outside. We're so lucky to have this on our doorstep.'

'Why ever did we stop?' asked the first lady.

'Fear and old age,' said Dotty with a grimace. 'Well, that's not going to hold us back any longer.'

Hannah placed a large plate piled with flapjacks and pastries onto the table alongside the drinks.

'How kind of you, dear,' said Mavis. 'My purse is back at the hotel but remind me to pay you later.'

Hannah shook her head. 'Oh, no,' she replied. 'It's on the house. You're my very first customers so it doesn't matter.'

'What a treat,' said Dotty, reaching out to squeeze her granddaughter's hand. 'I tell you, ladies, this place is going to be jumping come the afternoons when tea is served.'

'When's your first day?' asked one of the friends.

'Tomorrow,' said Hannah, trying to ignore the feeling of dread in her stomach.

'It looks lovely in there,' said another lady. 'I'll definitely be coming up here for afternoon tea.'

There was a general nodding of heads in agreement swiftly followed by murmurs of appreciation as they all took a mug of steaming hot drink and held it in their cold fingers.

'What about the mornings?' asked Mavis. 'Are you not going to be open then as well?'

Hannah shook her head. 'We weren't sure how many people would be around,' she told them.

'To be honest,' said one of the ladies, 'I can't see me surviving if I don't know that there's a hot drink at the end of the next swim.'

'And one of these flapjacks,' added another.

'Well, we will be back, won't we, ladies?' said Mavis, with a determined nod.

'Absolutely,' they all agreed.

'And I might even bring my great-niece Aimee along, if that's all right?' added Mavis.

'More the merrier! In fact, from now on, swim club will be every Tuesday and Thursday morning,' announced Dotty to a reluctant chorus of agreement. 'With coffee and cakes afterwards?'

'So you'll be opening up for us in the mornings?' asked Mavis, in a hopeful tone.

They all looked up at Hannah with red cheeks, glowing from the shock of going from cold to warm in a matter of moments.

'Yes, she will.'

Hannah spun around to find Alex standing behind her.

Hannah gave him a worried look but he merely laughed. 'I wouldn't be turning down any customers if I had a fledgling business,' he told her.

'Are you going to be keeping a watchful eye on us as well each time?' asked one of the women in a hopeful tone.

'Just try and stop me, ladies,' said Alex with a smile.

He really could be quite charming, thought Hannah, watching as the women all grinned at the thought of the handsome athlete looking out for them twice a week.

Whilst the ladies chatted on, Hannah walked away with Alex.

'Are you sure about this?' she asked. 'Can I afford to open up in the morning as well?'

'I think this could be the start of something big,' he told her.

She grimaced to which he laughed.

'You want it to be a failure?' he asked.

'It's not that,' she told him, giving him a playful shove with her hand. 'But what can one small group of Grandma's friends do?'

'I think a group like that could take on the whole world,' said Alex, in playful alarm.

'You know what I mean,' she muttered.

'And think how you'd be disappointing your grandmother if there wasn't somewhere to warm up immediately afterwards,' he told her. 'Let alone the worry about what the extreme temperature differences could do at their age.'

'That was below the belt,' she replied.

'But it's worked, eh?' he said, with a wink.

And so the decision was made to open up the Boathouse Café all day. She just hoped that there would be enough customers to fill it.

31

Later that afternoon, Hannah looked around the coffee shop and decided that she was about set for the opening.

Alex had shown her the complicated coffee machine which she was hoping would become easier in time. The fridge had been stocked and all she needed to do was get up early to complete the baking of the items on the menu.

She looked around the café, pleased despite her nerves at how great it looked. Each table was set and laid with a small glass of wildflowers, which her mum had provided. The cutlery on the table sparkled and the turquoise chairs were the pop of colour that she had imagined.

But no décor could match the amazing view as the lake sparkled in the May sunshine outside.

'So? Are you all set?'

She spun round to find Beth and Ella standing in the doorway.

'What are you doing here?' she asked, rushing over to give them a hug.

'You'd think we'd miss the grand opening?' asked Ella.

'We wouldn't miss it for the world,' added Beth.

Hannah was tearily grateful that her friends had decided to come and stay that weekend as a surprise.

'Besides, we have a surprise for you!' announced Lily with a flourish as she joined them.

Hannah looked past her friend to where the door to the Boathouse Café was wide open.

'A surprise?' she asked. 'An open door?'

Ella rolled her eyes. 'Come outside and see. We've been working hard on your secret project all morning.'

'You have?' Hannah was amazed that they had kept a secret from her.

So she followed them outside and was taken aback to see an old bicycle leant up against the back wall of the boathouse.

'Is this supposed to be part of the wellness stuff for the hotel because I'm not sure it's particularly road worthy,' she said, making a face.

The bike was full of rust, despite the pretty pale blue paint that appeared almost new. The basket on the front had been filled with flowers which did make it more attractive.

'You're not going to be riding it,' Beth told her.

'Then what?' asked Hannah, confused.

'Here it is,' announced Lily, with a flourish, bringing out a large blackboard which had been hidden around the corner out of sight.

Beth brought out some twine and after a short while, the sign was fixed on the side of the bicycle.

Hannah moved around to view what it said. 'The Boathouse Café. Come for the delicious cakes and tea, stay for the amazing views.'

She looked up at her friends. 'Who did this?' she asked, delighted.

'I designed it,' said Lily.

'I chose the colour,' added Beth.

'And I wrote the sign because I've got the neatest handwriting,' said Ella.

'Yes, and let us do the painting,' said Beth, holding up her fingers which were covered in blue paint.

'I like to view myself as more management material rather than a labourer,' said Ella with a grin.

'So?' asked Beth, turning to look at Hannah. 'What do you think?'

'I think it's lovely,' began Hannah. 'Thank you.'

'Why can I hear a "but" in that sentence?' asked Ella, frowning.

Hannah shrugged. 'It looks great. Honestly. I'm just a bit nervous, that's all. What if someone doesn't like one of my cakes?'

'Then so what?' asked Ella. 'You can't keep everyone happy 100 per cent of the time. Say someone doesn't like carrot cake. It doesn't mean that it's not a great carrot cake, just not for them. That's not a criticism. That's just a personal preference. Like the way that I don't like wearing pink. Just me. Nothing against Beth's skirt which looks great on you, by the way.'

'Isn't it fab?' asked Beth, looking down at her fuchsia miniskirt. 'Found it in a charity shop at the weekend.'

'You'll have to be careful when you sit down,' said Ella, with a grin. 'Unless of course you're looking for your next Mr Right Now, that is.'

'Oh, stop,' said Beth, blushing. 'I told you that Jeremy and I are made for each other.'

Beth had quickly moved on after her relationship with Brad had been as disastrous as all her other romances.

Lily grimaced. 'That guy from your work? He's a bit old for you, isn't he?'

Beth shook her head. 'Not at all,' she said briskly. 'Besides, he's so much more mature than my other boyfriends.'

'So mature he'll be needing a bus pass,' muttered Ella before holding up her hand. 'OK. I surrender. Go in peace with your old fella.'

Beth rolled her eyes.

'Anyway,' said Lily, looking back at Hannah. 'Back to the matter in hand. I know what it's like when someone criticises your work. It happened all the time when I was designing someone's interior. It doesn't mean that you're no good, just that they don't share the same taste as you.'

'Literally in this case,' added Beth.

'So you need to grow a rhinoceros skin,' said Ella.

'Not necessarily,' said Lily. 'Hannah can't change completely who she is.'

'I hate that you've got no confidence in yourself,' said Beth, coming over to give her a hug. 'Especially because you're so amazing.'

Hannah shrugged off the praise almost immediately. 'Yes, but...' she began.

'Listen, we all know that you can be overly sensitive at times,' said Lily, interrupting her. 'It makes you a great friend with empathy and compassion. You're loving and loyal.'

'But you take things too personally,' added Ella. 'Make some practical goals for yourself. Look at what you've achieved so far.' She held up her hand. 'And before you say that the business might fail, the summer season is only just beginning.'

'Exactly,' said Beth, nodding in agreement. 'This could be your best summer ever.'

'In the meantime, we've got your back and your front too,' said Lily, as they all came forward as one unit.

Enveloped in a group hug, Hannah found herself grateful for the support of her best friends, whatever happened in the future. She just hoped that they were right and that the café would be the success that everyone was hoping for.

32

'And so I declare this Boathouse Café open!'

With a flourish, Ben popped open the champagne and the group of family and friends all gathered around so that their empty glass flutes could be topped up.

Hannah looked around, enveloped in the warmth and support of everyone she loved. But there was no denying the nerves still rattled inside of her.

In actual fact, she was almost relieved to finally have the café ready and the wait was hopefully going to be worse than the actual opening. Or so she was really hoping.

'Cheers!' said Alex, clinking his glass against hers.

'Do we really need all this fuss?' she murmured, so that only he could hear.

'Yes,' he told her. 'Because it's an amazing thing that you're doing and it needs to be honoured.'

So Hannah fixed a smile on her face and let her loved ones celebrate the moment. She knew it was a big deal for the hotel to have an extra source of income and so everyone was in a hopeful mood.

'How many have you got booked in for afternoon tea later?' asked Ben, coming to join them.

'Four.' Hannah gave a shrug. 'It's not many but at least that'll help me iron out any kinks before it gets busier, I guess.' She was hoping that, with Lily's prompting from behind the reception desk, a full hotel at the weekend might mean they received a few more customers.

'I'm sure it'll go brilliantly,' said Alex, ever supportive.

As usual, Alex was right. The afternoon tea was a success and Hannah was pleased with the feedback from the hotel guests. They raved about the pretty chinaware and declared her cakes delicious. The relief she felt was immense and she actually went to sleep with a smile on her face that evening. Maybe she could do this after all, she told herself.

Her positive mood continued through the long weekend as a steady stream of guests popped in for coffee, enjoying the view and, from their feedback, all of her food as well.

The only trouble was that apart from the hotel guests, and the members of Dotty's swim club coming along to support her, the café stayed quiet for the rest of the weekend.

'I'm sorry we're leaving,' Ella told her on the bank holiday Monday as she and Beth came to say their goodbyes. 'We were hoping to help out with the rush.'

'What rush?' joked Hannah, forcing herself to sound more jolly than she felt. 'I dream of having a rush.'

'Things will pick up, I'm sure,' said Beth, giving her a hug.

'In the meantime, I've got a parting gift for you both,' Hannah told them.

So she packed off her friends with a box of leftover cakes which they were thrilled with.

'We get to take a little of Hannah home with us,' said Beth, with a smile.

'Don't worry,' murmured Ella, as she said goodbye. 'Business is always slow to begin with.'

The trouble was, thought Hannah, that it wasn't just slow. It was glacially slow. By Monday evening, many of the weekend hotel guests had left and so it was an extremely quiet day. So much for a successful business, she thought, beginning to get worried.

At least Tuesday would see some customers, she reminded herself. Because the swimming club was set for the morning and, to her amazement, four hotel guests had booked an afternoon tea as well.

So on Tuesday, she tried to find some positivity from somewhere. She looked around. At least it was all ready to go.

The tables all shone under the thankfully sunny skies outside. The glass jars filled with wildflower posies gleamed, as did the new patio doors. She had hung bunting across the oak frames, along with fairy lights and streams of fake flowers to give it an ethereal feel. It was perfect.

She felt the tears prick her eyes. Whatever happened in the future when, inevitably, it closed due to lack of customers, she had achieved her long-held dream and seen the idea that she had held on to so tightly as a dream come to fruition. Her life goal had been achieved. She had to remind herself of that, she decided.

Just after ten o'clock, Dotty's swim club staggered in, full of lively chatter and laughter about their exploits in the lake during the previous half an hour.

They insisted on sitting outside so as not to drip all over the floorboards, they told Hannah. She wondered whether she should set up a table and chairs on the beach by the lake but then realised that the place would remain completely empty and what was the point in that? At least it looked as if she had customers.

Mavis had brought along her great-niece Aimee as promised.

'That swim was amazing,' said Aimee, with a wide smile. 'I'm definitely going to try and make this a regular thing.'

'I knew you'd enjoy it,' replied Mavis.

Hannah smiled at Aimee, trying not to recall her knee-jerk reaction to Aimee flirting with Alex which had resulted in her drunkenly kissing him.

She also tried not to notice Aimee giving Alex a wide smile when he arrived as the group of swimmers, fuelled and warmed up by their coffees and cakes, were leaving.

She left them chatting and went to tidy up the table.

A little while later, when she and Alex were alone in the café, she crouched down to stroke Tiny and asked, 'How was your walk?'

'Great,' said Alex, nodding. 'A bit of pain here and there but another week and I'll be fighting fit again.'

He smiled at her and she realised that he had caught the sun over the past couple of weeks of good weather and his skin was beginning to turn a pale gold, meaning his blue eyes stood out even more. No wonder Aimee had been flirting with him again. He looked great.

She quickly looked away once she realised she was staring at him. 'Coffee?' she asked.

'Please.' Alex brought out his phone. 'I've had confirmation of all the public liability and food hygiene certificates,' he told her. 'I'll get them printed out for you later and put it in the business file behind the counter.'

'It's all gobbledegook to me but OK,' she said, shooting him a grin across the counter.

Hannah mentally crossed her fingers but, to her relief, the

afternoon tea was a success. The feedback she received from the customers that they would definitely be back.

'That's great news,' said Lily over dinner later that evening. 'You're going to need staff to help you before too long.'

Hannah laughed. 'I'm not so sure about that,' she told her friend.

Lily shook her head. 'Just wait and see,' she said, with a wink.

But, for once, Lily's optimism seemed a little misplaced. The longed-for customers never appeared and by Friday of that week, Hannah stared across the kitchen table at the vast amount of left-over cakes that she had brought back with her from the café. Some were two days old and were in danger of going to waste so she gave them to the family to enjoy.

'Wonderful,' said Walter, halfway through a large slice of chocolate cake.

Hannah had kept the menu short, full of her favourite bakes. But the leftovers only served to remind her that she was severely lacking customers.

'I'm sure it will pick up again now that the weekend is here,' Faye told her, giving her daughter a reassuring hug.

'Absolutely,' said Alex, who was sitting next to her. 'We have every faith in you.'

Hannah tried to smile at him but the truth was that her heart was breaking. The café had not been the success that everyone had hoped for. Perhaps she couldn't do this, no matter how much her friends and family tried to reassure her, she thought with a heavy sigh.

33

Alex looked at Hannah sitting next to him at the dinner table with concern and tried to cheer her up.

'This is great,' he told her, reaching for another slice of carrot cake.

It was true, he thought. The nutmeg and spices were an amazing contrast to the sharp but sweet icing.

Hannah smiled but he noticed that it failed to reach her blue eyes. 'Thankfully there's plenty to go around,' she said, gesturing at the couple of cakes that she had brought in for dessert after dinner that evening.

He had caught her heavy sigh and wished that he some kind of magic wand to conjure up a whole load of new customers for the café to make it a success.

'Is this my second?' asked Ben, reaching out to take a brownie.

'Third,' said Lily, taking the brownie out of his hand. 'This will be my second.'

Ben looked at his sister. 'They'll come, you know,' he told

Hannah. 'The customers, I mean. It just takes time. Look at the hotel when we reopened it last year.'

Hannah nodded but didn't look as if she believed him.

Alex wondered how he could take the pain away for her.

'Any more of this and I won't be fitting into my shorts this summer,' said Lily, with a grimace. 'No matter how delicious your cakes are,' she added, reaching out to squeeze Hannah's arm.

'Well, you've got the perfect place to walk it off,' said Walter, who had almost finished his chocolate cake.

'Or swim,' added Dotty, licking some icing off her finger and looking at Lily. 'I think we're up to seven people next week with Aimee again. Want to make it an even eight?'

Lily wrinkled up her nose. 'I'm not that strong a swimmer,' she replied.

'At least they're regular customers at the café,' said Hannah.

'So we need to fill up the café with elderly swimmers?' said Ben, with a grin.

'Excuse me?' Dotty pretended to look affronted. 'Who are you calling elderly?'

'It's certainly an idea,' said Alex, his mind racing as he thought through the possibilities of bringing in more customers.

'I'm not sure I've got that many friends, dear,' said Dotty.

'What I'm saying is that perhaps you should be utilising the lake a bit more,' Alex found himself saying, thinking about the opportunities around Maple Tree Lodge and what that would mean for the success of the Boathouse Café.

Everyone turned to look at him.

'What I mean is,' he carried on, 'I know how much I'm enjoying my morning swim. The setting is incredible. Seems a shame not to have more people using it.'

'How?' asked Ben, looking at Walter. 'I suppose we've got those couple of boats.'

'They're hardly stable,' Walter told him, making a face. 'And one of them leaks.'

'Anyway, I thought Del was bringing you some paddleboards. Isn't that the latest fad these days?' said Frankie.

'It is,' Alex told her, suddenly feeling inspired. 'Actually, that's a great idea. You'd probably need some safe areas, away from Dotty's swim club,' he added. 'You know, you could even have classes for hotel guests.'

'Are we talking about swimming or paddleboards?' asked Hannah.

'Both,' Alex told her. 'Why not utilise the water more?'

'But why have it for just the guests?' asked Faye. 'I'm sure some local people would enjoy coming here. There always seems to be somebody on the river when I drive over it on the way to the supermarket.'

'We could advertise locally,' said Lily, looking at Ben.

'So we're going to have like a water sports centre?' asked Frankie, looking confused.

Ben nodded. 'Sounds a great idea but we just don't have the money to invest in anything else. That's why I thought about Del and his cheap paddleboards which was a mistake. We need proper equipment including wetsuits and all the other paraphernalia.' He sighed. 'The trouble is that all costs money we haven't got. We've ploughed everything into the hotel and Boathouse Café. Even the lodges will have to wait until we've got some more money as well.'

The idea for lots more customers at the café suddenly dissolved and Alex caught the sudden downswing in the mood around the table. It was such a shame, he thought. The Jackson family had always been so kind to him, especially these past five weeks when he'd been recuperating. How could he help them out?

And then he realised he knew exactly what the answer was.

'I'll do it,' Alex found himself blurting out.

'Do what?' asked Ben.

'I'll be your not-so-silent partner,' Alex told his best friend with a grin. 'I've wanted to invest in something worthwhile for a long time.'

It was true. He had been considering various investments but had never come across a project that he felt passionate about until that moment.

'Do you have that kind of money?' asked Ben, frowning.

Alex nodded. 'I've been sensible over the years so yeah, I have enough to invest in this. I reckon it's right up my street with the health opportunities for everyone.'

Ben looked delighted and the family burst into life once more with excited chatter.

'Oh, yes, this could be really amazing!' said Lily, clapping her hands together in glee.

However, Alex noticed that Walter wasn't smiling and was actually shaking his head.

He held up his hand to quieten everyone down. 'I'm not so sure about this,' he said. 'It'll disturb the guests for one thing. They come here for the peace and quiet, not all of that messing about.'

'Grandad, I understand your concerns but we need this from a business point of view this summer,' said Ben, looking serious. 'You know how tight things still are for us all.'

Alex blanched at the honesty of his friend.

Grandfather and grandson exchanged a long look before Walter finally nodded.

'OK. I trust you, Ben, to get it right,' said Walter, still not looking pleased. 'But I don't want the place ruined. Folks should be able to eat their breakfast in peace in our hotel, not overlooking Piccadilly Circus out there.'

'I understand,' said Ben, frowning. 'So how do we keep everyone happy?'

'Why don't you have all the swimming at the other end of the lake beyond the boathouse?' suggested Dotty. 'There's that smaller beach there and it would be more private for the swimmers too. Not all ladies feel confident swanning about in their swimsuits, you know.'

'Good idea,' said Ben, nodding. 'And there's a clearing over there that we can use as a car park instead of the hotel one. That way it doesn't impact the hotel guests.'

'So what are we talking about?' asked Alex. 'Paddleboards and more swimming clubs?'

'Absolutely,' replied Ben. 'With you running it, that is!'

Alex laughed. 'I'm not qualified as either a lifeguard or a teacher,' he told his friend.

But Ben didn't look put off. 'But you'd be free, right?' he said, with a grin.

Alex was still smiling. 'Is that my only criteria?'

'Nonsense,' said Faye. 'I think you'd be an excellent teacher. You're very patient.'

'And you're always harping on about the health and safety to me and my friends,' added Dotty, with a wink.

'But I've never even used a paddleboard,' Alex told them. 'I only know how to swim, run and cycle.'

'Well, you can't do that without some level of fitness,' joked Walter.

'And I'll have to find some kind of lifeguard course,' carried on Alex.

'There must be some online that we can look up,' said Lily.

'So what do you say?' asked Ben. 'The job's yours, mate, if you want it. Just for those summer months that you were struggling to fill, if I remember.'

'And the weather's going to be amazing, according to the papers,' added Frankie.

Everyone turned to look at Alex.

'There's a lot to sort out,' he told them before stealing a quick glance at Hannah but even she was nodding thoughtfully.

'It might just bring in a few more people to the hotel and the café,' she said quietly.

Alex looked at her and found himself saying, 'Well, if it helps the café,' he began.

There was a general whooping around the table as everyone began to talk at once excitedly.

He was somewhat surprised at himself. It was another impetuous decision. But as he felt Tiny settle down next to his feet, he realised that the dog had been another impulse choice and had worked out for the best. Perhaps he'd been sensible for so long that it was time for a change.

'This is great,' said Ben, getting up and coming around the table to clap him on the shoulder. 'Thanks for the support. I think it's a cracking idea. And who knows where it will lead?'

Alex glanced across at Hannah once more. Who knows, he thought, and found himself smiling back at his friend.

34

Hannah stood on the beach and looked down at the paddleboard that Alex had just inflated.

'This looks good quality actually,' she said.

'Let's hope Dodgy Del has finally delivered something decent,' he replied. 'Otherwise we'll both end up in the water sooner than we'd envisaged.'

It was only two days after the idea for the swim and paddleboard club but Alex had already got to work on buying some of the equipment needed. As the Boathouse Café was still extremely quiet, Hannah had offered to close the café early to give him a hand.

'Have you used one before?' asked Hannah, as she tested out the firmness of the other board that he had already inflated.

Alex straightened up. 'No. But how hard can it be?' he asked.

'It depends on your sense on balance,' she told him, smiling. She looked across the lake. 'Well, at least the sun's out.'

The weather had turned for the better in the past week or so and finally the warm sun was shining down on them, warming up both the air and more importantly the water temperature as well.

Not that Tiny seemed to mind as he dashed in and out of the water nearby, his long black coat growing wetter and darker.

Deciding it was now or never, Hannah stripped down to her swimming costume and picked up the paddleboard before taking it into the water. The cool temperature made her gasp briefly before she continued to head into the water up to her knees.

Then she turned around, wondering where Alex was. She watched as he played around with Tiny at the shoreline.

'Come on,' she teased him. 'You can't put it off any longer.'

Already in his swimming shorts, he picked up his own paddleboard and strode into the water, as confident as always.

'So,' she said. 'How do we go about this then, teacher?' she asked, looking down at the paddleboard she had placed to float next to her.

'No idea,' said Alex, with a grin. 'But how hard can it be, right?'

He steadied the paddleboard on the water next to him and then carefully stepped onto it. But he was too quick and almost immediately the board flipped over, causing him to crash into the water.

Because they were standing in such shallow water, his bottom bounced off the sandy base of the lake and he sat up, spluttering.

Hannah burst into laughter, whilst managing to hold on to both of their boards and the oars as well. She couldn't believe that he had fallen in!

He stood up, looking a little embarrassed. 'OK. So that wasn't good for a first try,' he muttered.

She grinned at him. 'I've got to say,' she told him, 'I wish I'd had my phone on me.'

'If you think it's so easy, you give it a go,' he replied. 'Go on. I dare you.'

She shrugged her shoulders. 'OK.'

Figuring that she couldn't be as bad as Alex had been, she carefully knelt onto the top of the board, steadying herself with the oar. Then, once she had her balance, she looked at him with raised eyebrows.

'Show off,' he muttered. 'OK. Second time lucky.'

Once more, he went too fast and went over the front of the board that time and not the side.

Hannah had only just stopped laughing when he had surfaced in the shallow water once more.

Meanwhile, Tiny thought it the best game that he had ever seen and was barking joyfully as he bounced around in the water, splashing them both.

From his prone position sitting down on the sandy bottom, Alex looked up at Hannah, who was floating nearby.

'Well, it's obviously not as simple as it looks,' he said, with a sheepish grin. 'Let's be honest, you've taken the easy route.'

'Have I?' she teased him, feeling more confident about her chances by the minute, compared to his disastrous efforts. 'How do you get to that conclusion?'

'Because you're kneeling down which is the safest way and therefore your balance threshold is nearest the board,' he told her.

'I see.'

She shot him another smile before she clutched onto each side of the board with her hands and drew herself up into a standing position. She then picked up the oar and slowly spun the board around in the water to face him.

'How are you doing that?' he spluttered, looking amazed.

'Have we actually found something that the great Alex Grant

can't do? A sport that he isn't good at?' Hannah laughed. 'Oh, this wonderful. How does it feel to be just like us other mere mortals?'

He grinned at her teasing before he stood up and grabbed hold of the board.

'I can do this,' she heard him muttering to himself. 'I can.'

'Can you?' she teased him before deciding that he actually needed her help, for once. 'OK. I can't be mean to you after all the kindness you've shown me. So here's what you're going to do. Take it slow. And by slow, I mean slooooow.'

Step by step, she told him exactly what to do and finally, although still looking somewhat unsteady, he was kneeling on the paddleboard.

'There!' said Hannah, clapping. 'That's it! You're off and running now.'

'Am I?' asked Alex, pulling the oar around him and looking unsure. 'So why do I feel like I'm still going to fall off?'

'You'll be fine,' she told him. 'You really have no gift of balance, do you?'

'I've never needed it before now,' he replied, clutching onto the board as a ripple threatened to unseat him once more.

'You rode a bike in every race,' she reminded him.

'Yes, but that had wheels and nice flat tarmac,' he told her. 'This is a whole different matter. Much harder on water, it turns out.'

'Then how come I have mastered it first time?' she asked, with a wide smile.

'Well, I guess you're just special,' he told her, shooting her a grin.

She blushed at his words. 'Come on,' she said. 'How are you going to run a water sports centre looking like that?'

He was clutching onto the side of the board for dear life and, after a moment, reluctantly let go, looking unsteady once more.

'I'm going to practise every evening when there's nobody about,' he told her. 'I've never yet come across a sport I can't master.'

She laughed. 'Well, just remember that in this particular sport I beat you fair and square.'

'Oh, I'll definitely remember that,' he told her, grinning. 'Now, what about standing up?'

'You'll be fine now you've got your centre of balance,' she replied, coming over to stand on her board nearby. 'Just take it nice and slow.'

She watched as he carefully began to move into a standing position. It seemed to take forever and with every wobble of the board, she was convinced that he was going to land in the water again. But finally and with a tremendous look of satisfaction, he was up and standing on the paddleboard.

'I've done it!' he shouted, delighted with himself.

'Well done,' replied Hannah.

Unfortunately his exuberance had attracted the interest of Tiny who, until that point, had been happily bouncing around in the shallow waters. With a bark of delight, the puppy began to wade out towards where the paddleboards were.

Then, to Alex's and Hannah's amazement, Tiny then began to paddle in the water towards them.

'He can swim!' said Hannah.

Alex nodded. 'They're supposed to be good in the water but I had no idea it would come so naturally to him. Good boy, Tiny!'

Tiny ploughed on with his doggy paddle towards them, his front paws propelling him ever forwards until he was next to Alex's board.

'What a good boy!' he told the dog, as he smiled down at him.

Tiny was so pleased with himself that he decided that his next trick would be learning to paddleboard and suddenly placed his front paws onto the board.

'No,' said Alex, shaking his head. 'No. No. No!'

But Hannah realised that it was too late. With the weight of the enormous and somewhat heavy puppy leaning on the side of the board, there was only ever going to be one outcome. The board immediately tipped over and Alex went headfirst into the water once more.

As he surfaced, spluttering, Tiny swam around him in delight that he finally had a playmate to mess around with in the water.

Alex looked up at her as she stared down at them both, still laughing.

'Maybe Tiny could teach the paddleboarding instead,' she said, still giggling.

'Maybe,' he said, swimming towards her with ease across the water with Tiny in hot pursuit.

'What are you doing?' she asked, suddenly feeling nervous at his mischievous smile.

'Just didn't want you to feel left out,' he told her, before turning around to look for Tiny. He called the dog over. 'Tiny! Where's Hannah? Go and find Hannah!'

Hannah's face dropped as the dog began to swim towards her.

'Wait a minute,' she began.

But Alex had been using a familiar phrase whereby he normally rushed over to find Hannah when he came into the café and just because they were on the water, it didn't appear to make any difference to his obeying the instructions.

So as the dog reached the paddleboard, he placed his paws on the edge and Hannah crouched down to settle it. 'Hang on,' she urged the dog.

But it was too late. He was desperately trying to climb up to see her and with one flip of the board, Hannah was now in the water as well.

She came up to the surface, spluttering, and found Alex laughing at her.

'You rotten...' she began, spraying him water as her hand skimmed the surface.

'Hey, I'm already wet,' he reminded her.

Eventually, they lay on their stomachs and paddled back to the shore using their hands with Tiny at the front of Alex's board, looking like a ship's proud bust at the front of a galleon.

Alex may have completely failed at his first attempt at paddleboarding but Hannah knew that he wouldn't give up that easily.

And she found herself hoping that perhaps he wouldn't give up on her either. Because despite telling him otherwise, her feelings for him were growing stronger by the day.

35

Alex found to his surprise that he was really excited about the idea of running a water sports centre over the summer at Maple Tree Lodge.

It was something completely different to get stuck into, he realised. Something new. A feeling that he hadn't experienced in so very long. His life had consisted of work and competitions over and over, week after week, year after year. Only his intermittent dating life had been any different but even there, he hadn't felt particularly energised. He had been a polite, interested date and yet there hadn't been a spark with anyone.

Except Claire, of course. And look how that had turned out. Trust was still a bit of an issue for him. He had trusted his parents, his dad, and they had almost rejected him because of his decision to step away from the competitions. But he was thirty-four now. He wanted a life of his own. And perhaps the water sports centre might just be the start of that.

But before he could almost start to relax and enjoy himself, there was an awful lot of work to set it all up.

First and most important was the practical side of things to work out. Alex sat down with the family to brainstorm.

'First off, we'll need an official lifeguard,' began Alex. 'Which will be me, of course. I'll position myself on the jetty where I'll have the best vantage point.'

'I can lend you my binoculars,' said Walter. 'And then there's always the boat which can be used to get to anyone quickly.'

Alex was glad that Walter was offering to help, considering he still had reservations as to the lake being utilised so much that summer.

'Excellent,' replied Alex. 'But if things go well then I may just need some assistance with that.'

'Well, I can help with that too,' said Walter.

Everyone turned to look at the octogenarian in surprise.

'What?' he snapped. 'I can make a call and get help, can't I? I'm not completely feeble and useless.'

'Nobody said you were, Grandad,' said Ben in a reassuring tone. 'But how can you make a call when there's no signal out there?'

'Walkie-talkies,' said Frankie, nodding. 'That'll do the trick.'

'Good idea,' said Alex, making a note on his phone. 'OK, Walter. If we're a runaway success, you'll be my number two lifeguard.'

Walter smiled and nodded, looking smug. Everyone else looked a little alarmed but Alex tried not to worry about that for the time being.

'I think the best way to monitor everyone safely is to set up some strict timings for being in the water,' carried on Alex. 'At least if anyone is swimming laps of the lake, that is. Say, give an hour or two per session.'

'I agree,' said Dotty. 'If they're all going in at different times, how do you keep track if anyone gets into difficulties?'

'Exactly,' said Alex, with a nod. 'So I suggest some kind of morning swimming session, say 8–10 a.m. Then a lunchtime one from 11–1 p.m. Then the afternoon can be for the paddleboards, say, until four o'clock. Finally one last swimming session from 4–5 p.m.'

'You think that many?' asked Faye, looking surprised.

'I agree, actually.' Ben shrugged his shoulders. 'I guess we should try to attract as many people as we can, by giving them as much choice as we're able to do.'

'But we make sure that it's all done and dusted by 5 p.m.,' said Walter, with a firm nod. 'Then we get the peace and tranquillity back for us and our guests.'

'Talking of hotel guests,' said Lily. 'They should be able to swim free, I think. As part of the perk of staying here.'

'But outsiders will have to pay a fee,' added Ben.

'If we're going to do this properly, we'll need some kind of check-in system,' said Alex. 'Especially if it's not just going to be restricted to hotel guests.'

'Ella's working on a local Facebook page,' said Lily, checking her phone. 'Maple Tree Lodge Water Sports Centre. It's already got over 100 followers and she only started it two days ago.'

'That's great,' said Hannah. 'She's a star, isn't she?'

'How will we monitor everyone and get their payment?' asked Frankie.

'What about a separate reception area?' said Faye.

'We don't want everyone trudging through the hotel reception in their swimming costumes,' said Ben, making a face.

'What about that old storage barn?' said Walter. 'The one just outside of the boathouse and next to the clearing we're going to use as a car park.'

'Barn?' asked Alex, trying to recall if he'd seen anything that big in the location.

Ben shook his head. 'We call it that but it's more an old woodshed but that's a good idea, Grandad. It'll catch everyone arriving so nobody gets missed. It's also weatherproof for whoever is manning the reception.'

'I'm happy to muck in,' said Frankie.

'Me too,' added Faye.

'I'd also like to add a couple more safety rules,' said Alex, who had been mulling everything over and researching online for the past few days.

'Yes, teacher,' murmured Ben, giving his friend a wink to bely his teasing.

Alex ignored him. 'Thinking back to my triathlon days, everyone always wears a swimming cap.'

The ladies all began to protest but he shook his head.

'The reason behind that was that it was easier to see if anyone got into difficulties in the water,' he carried on.

The protests faded as quickly as they had begun.

'Well, at least it'll keep my hair dry,' said Dotty, with a shrug. 'Perhaps I can go for shocking pink!'

'Also, I've seen floats used as well,' said Alex. 'Fluorescent ones which can be used to keep people's car keys safe and dry, as well as a buoyancy aid if the swimmer gets tired.'

There was a general murmur of assent around the kitchen table.

'Better that we're safe rather than get the wrong kind of publicity if someone gets into trouble,' said Walter.

'I agree,' said Faye, biting her lip. 'It would be terrible if someone got hurt. After all, this is our land. It's our responsibility to keep everyone safe.'

Alex nodded. 'Absolutely.'

'Does it all seem a bit professional though?' asked Frankie, looking concerned. 'You know, not for the likes of, well, us, I mean?'

Alex shook his head. 'The idea is that there is no judgement on anyone going in the water,' he told her. 'We want to invite all abilities who can go as little or as far as they want. But they need to be safe.'

'Fair enough, I guess,' replied Frankie.

As the family all agreed with the ideas, Alex felt pleased that they were being so positive about the water sports centre and just hoped that it would be the success that everyone was praying it could be.

36

As another week went by, business continued to remain slow at the Boathouse Café, much to Hannah's dismay.

She tried to be positive, especially with the idea that the new water sports centre might bring in some much-needed customers, but it was hard.

She found herself confessing as much to Alex one morning when he was out on the beach watching Dotty's swim club in the water.

'I'd better get ready for when the ladies are finished,' she told him. 'They might be my only customers today.'

'I'm sure things will turn around,' he told her.

Hannah nodded, although she still wasn't sure.

'In the meantime, whilst I'm out, can you take care of Tiny for me during the day?' asked Alex. 'I probably won't be back until late each evening.'

Alex had announced that he had managed to book a three-day course that week which would give him the open-water qualification to act as an official lifeguard when the lake opened for the swimming and paddleboard sessions.

'Of course,' said Hannah, glancing over to where the dog was standing at the shore, wagging his tail at the swimmers further out in the water. 'He always behaves himself with me.'

'That would be a first,' said Alex. Although Hannah knew that thanks to his training, Tiny was actually pretty obedient considering his young age.

'Are you looking forward to the course?' she asked.

He nodded. 'In a way, it'll be good to start using my brain again. Apparently, as well as the lifesaving skills, they also cover some first-aid basics and even CPR. Which hopefully I'll never get to use.'

Hannah nodded. 'Hopefully not. Unless you attempt paddle-boarding again,' she added with a grin.

Alex laughed. 'Actually I've been practising for a couple of hours every day and I can now stand up without even a wobble.'

Hannah found that she was still smiling when she headed back to the café, thinking back to Alex's dreadful first attempts at paddleboarding.

As she brought out a tray of biscuits to be decorated, she thought that it was nice that they could laugh together and she could relax around him. For all of her embarrassment about the drunken kiss all those weeks ago, he was still Alex. Safe, reliable, trustworthy Alex.

And yet she couldn't stop her gaze lingering a few times on his supremely fit body when he was dressed in just shorts each morning when he went out for his early swim. Of course, he had an incredible body. But it was the whole package that she found appealing.

She looked down at the biscuits she was supposed to be decorating and found that an enormous lump of blue icing had fallen over three of the biscuits, and quickly wiped it away.

Why was she so distracted lately? Was it because she was bored because business was so slow?

Or, she was beginning to think, had she been too hasty to dismiss Alex after she had kissed him? She kept trying to go over in her mind when she had apologised to him. There had been a moment when he had flirted with her, seemingly wanting more from her and she had almost run off, so scared was she of commitment. But as she grew to know and trust Alex even more, she couldn't help but wonder if perhaps she was beginning to change her mind.

As Dotty's swim club came into the café in a bubble of laughter and merriment, she couldn't help but glance at him as Alex followed them inside.

She had always thought that she knew where she was in her relationship with Alex. He was her big brother's best friend. That was all. Except ever since his accident and he was around all the time, she was noticing so much more about him. His blond eyelashes. The way his smile was slightly crooked. And the way her heart raced a little when he smiled at her.

Of course, she had tried to convince herself that nothing had changed between them. She had drunkenly kissed him and then apologised. That should be the end of the matter. She had told him so.

And yet, for some reason, she couldn't seem to move on. And a tiny part of her wondered whether he wanted more from her as well.

As she began to take everyone's orders, she became aware of Alex chatting with Aimee on the other side of the bar. Despite her reservations about Aimee's flirtation with Alex, Hannah had to concede that she was a nice person.

'You'll have to tell me about the first-aid stuff you learn on your course,' she heard Aimee say. 'I should probably do something like that for my yoga classes.'

'Sure,' said Alex. 'I'll be back this weekend if you wanted to chat it through.'

There was a small pause before Hannah heard Aimee speak again.

'Actually I was going to watch a great band playing in the Black Swan in Cranbridge this weekend,' she said. 'They have live music in the beer garden once a month.'

'Sounds great,' replied Alex.

But as Hannah turned to pour out the next coffee order, she heard Aimee say, 'Maybe we could go for a drink and have a chat then?'

Hannah took the cocoa powder shaker down from the shelf in a daze as she completed the cappuccino order and found she was holding her breath.

'That would be great,' she then heard Alex reply.

Hannah made up the rest of the orders and carried them across to the table where Dotty and her friends were now sitting.

Alex was going on a date with Aimee, she thought to herself in shock. Alex? Her Alex?

Except he wasn't hers, she reminded herself. She had kissed him and then backed off fast, pretending that it had been all about the alcohol and not the feelings she had for him.

And with sudden clarity, she realised that she did like him that way after all. But now that he was going out with Aimee, she had left it too late.

37

Despite the band playing at the other end of the pub garden, Alex couldn't help but suppress a yawn from Aimee as they watched them from one of the many full tables in the Black Swan Inn that evening.

It had been an unexpectedly busy week. At the last minute, he had found a lifeguard course which was specific to open-water swimming which was ideal for the lake. So he had suddenly had three days away from Maple Tree Lodge and that meant that he was behind in his preparation for the grand opening of the water sports centre the following weekend.

He also hadn't considered the knock-on effect that being away would have on Tiny. Having been warned early on when he was a puppy that Newfoundlands suffer with separation anxiety, the family had told him that the dog had sulked for three days and no amount of cajoling would bring him out of his sad mood. Then, after his initial delight when Alex returned home each evening, Tiny had become been very clingy and wouldn't leave him alone for a second.

All in all, it had been somewhat stressful and Alex would

have actually preferred a quiet night at home. And yet here he was out on a date.

He had been aware of Aimee flirting with him over the past few weeks but hadn't really thought about it until she asked him out. She seemed a nice enough lady, he thought, looking across the table.

Of course, she wasn't Hannah but so much had changed after she had kissed him. That kiss had changed everything. He knew what it felt like to have her in his arms. He knew how her lips felt. His dream had come true and yet it had almost instantly dissolved after coming to fruition.

Out of respect for her wishes, when Hannah had made it plainly clear that she wanted nothing more than to be friends, he had made a determined effort to back off.

And it had worked. Almost.

Except he still saw her every day. Still found himself catching his breath sometimes when she smiled at him.

But the crush that he had harboured for over a decade now felt like the chase of a gold medal. Something perhaps to be kept in the past. It was over and he was going to have to force himself to move on.

After all, this summer was supposed to be about moving on in every aspect of his life. So when Aimee had asked him out, he had found himself saying yes.

And yet, despite them having fitness and well-being in common, there was an awkwardness to their conversation, he was finding. He wasn't as relaxed as he normally felt. It felt pressured and unnatural and he couldn't work out why. He had almost been grateful when the music had been so loud that it had precluded any more talking between them.

The setting, though, couldn't be more perfect for a date. He and Aimee were sitting on comfortable chairs in the garden which was mainly laid to lawn with a white picket fence running along one side. On the other side of the fence, he could see the river through the gaps, the evening sun dappled on the crystal-clear water. The garden was filled with many beautiful hanging baskets and pots of overflowing colourful flowers. Fairy lights twinkled in the warm evening air and the garden was almost full of people watching the popular band.

As the band finished their set, Alex joined in with the applause and then looked at Aimee.

'They were great, you were right,' he told her.

She nodded. 'Told you so,' she replied.

An awkward silence stretched out between them as Alex tried to think of something else to say.

Eventually though, Aimee beat him to it.

'Listen, Alex, this has been really nice,' she said.

'It has,' he lied, nodding his head in fake agreement.

'But perhaps we'll just forget about any more dates,' she added briskly. 'Because to be honest, I've realised that you're not my type and I'm pretty certain now that I'm not yours.'

Alex looked at her for a second and gave a shocked laugh.

'Sorry,' she told him, with a grin. 'I'm always brutally honest when things don't work out.'

'Yes, you are,' he replied.

In a way it was quite a revelation, he thought, finding himself smiling at her.

'But I'm still interested in running a couple of sunrise yoga sessions by the lake,' she carried on.

Alex was surprised. 'Won't it be awkward?' he asked. 'I mean, between us.'

Aimee raised her eyebrows at him. 'Alex, we've had one drink together. We're grown-ups. I think you're safe from me making a pass at you in the future.'

He laughed. 'Sorry. I've had awkward break-ups in the past.'

In fact, Claire hadn't let go when he had tried to break up with her even though she had been the one to cheat on him. So Aimee's honesty was refreshing in many ways.

Free from the feeling that any romance between them had felt forced, Alex finally began to relax and they spent the remainder of the evening discussing timing and the right position to hold the yoga sessions. It was a positive outcome for a somewhat disastrous date, he thought as he drove home.

Aimee was pretty and fun to be around. And so he knew the problem with their date was all him and not her at all. The problem was that he still felt the same way about Hannah and, if anything, the date that evening had confirmed it.

He knew that before the summer was over, he was going to have to tell her how he felt. Because the ache in his heart was just too strong for him to be getting over.

He just hoped he didn't ruin their friendship because of it.

38

Hannah spent the rest of the week trying to hide how upset she was about Alex's date with Aimee the following weekend.

Thankfully, luck was on her side as he was away on his lifeguard course during the day so she didn't have to bump into him at the café as usual. And when he returned, Hannah made sure that she had already eaten dinner and made out that she was going to have an early night in her room.

But she couldn't fool everyone, it seemed. Especially when she made herself scarce before Alex went out on his date.

That Saturday night, Lily came into her bedroom and held up her phone so that she could continue her group call with Beth and Ella.

'I was having a quiet night,' moaned Hannah, who was sitting in her bed in her pyjamas.

'So?' said Beth. 'Lily's worried about you so we wanted to make sure that you're OK.'

'Why are you worried about me?' asked Hannah, looking at Lily as she sat down next to her on top of the covers.

'Because you've been extra quiet this week,' replied Lily. 'And I'm worried that this café business is too much stress for you.'

'It's fine,' said Hannah, quickly. 'Anyway, everyone keeps telling me that it'll get better as soon as the water sports centre opens in a week's time. Hopefully they're right.'

'Of course we're right,' said Ella.

'So what else is the matter if it's not the café?' asked Beth, looking concerned.

Hannah sighed. 'It's nothing,' she told them.

'I think I know,' said Lily, in a triumphant tone.

'What?' chorused Beth and Ella together.

'She missed Alex this week,' announced Lily with a flourish.

Hannah looked at her friend with her mouth open in shock. How did she know?

'Alex?' repeated Ella, goggle-eyed.

'What's wrong with Alex?' asked Beth, looking confused.

'Nothing, actually. He's one of the good guys and believe me they're few and far between,' said Ella.

'Of course he is,' said Lily. 'He's a great guy.'

'Exactly,' said Beth, nodding. 'He's decent, you know? Trustworthy.'

And so sexy. The thought popped into Hannah's head before she could stop it.

Lily leant her head to one side as she studied her friend. 'Why are you blushing?' she asked.

'I'm not,' protested Hannah.

'Liar. You've got the most colour that I've seen you have all week,' said Lily.

'I know! I reckon it's because she likes Alex,' said Beth, looking delighted.

Ella frowned. 'Everyone likes Alex. You can't not. It would be like hating Tiny.'

'No, Beth means that Hannah *really* likes Alex,' said Lily, with a gleam in her eyes.

They all stared at Hannah whilst she shuffled in the bed, feeling awkward under their gaze. In the end though, they were her best friends. She couldn't hide the truth from them any longer.

So she gave them a small nod in response, hoping her silence would encourage her friends to change topics. But her prayers weren't answered.

'Well, I don't know how I feel about this considering it's come out of the blue,' said Ella. 'Let's check the list.'

'OK. We like him,' began Lily, counting on her fingers.

'He's got bigger shoulders than we have,' added Beth.

'Ben trusts him and says he's a good guy,' said Lily.

'Ben's also known him for a long time so no scary secrets to be discovered,' said Ella.

'And the man sure looks good in swimming shorts,' said Beth with a cheeky grin.

Hannah nodded, thinking back to the previous week when she had watched him come out of the water, the droplets dripping down his bare chest. She gulped and remembered that she had almost dropped the tea pot.

She blinked back to life and found her friends watching her, all of them wearing a smile.

'What?' she snapped.

'You're not disagreeing that the man sure looks mighty fine,' said Lily.

'I'm not blind,' said Hannah, throwing off the duvet and getting up to go over to the dressing table to brush her hair.

'The question is how much does he like Hannah in return?' asked Beth.

'Oh, I know the answer to that one,' announced Lily. 'My

radar is always right.'

Hannah spun around to look down at her friend in shock.

'Go on,' urged Beth.

'He's been giving Hannah some serious side-eye pretty much since I met him last year,' she said, with a grin.

'Excellent,' said Beth, clapping her hands.

'No, it's not,' muttered Hannah. 'It's all nonsense. I mean, look at him! He would never be interested in someone like me.'

'First off, you're mad,' said Lily.

'Because you're gorgeous,' added Beth.

'Exactly,' said Ella. 'You're kind, and beautiful and generous.'

'And I think he feels the same way about you,' said Lily, with a knowing smile.

'Does Ben know?' asked Beth.

Lily shook her head. 'Men do tend to be clueless about this sort of thing, let's be honest. And I wanted to make sure what was best for Hannah first before I let him in on the little secret. It's best us women take charge, I reckon.'

Hannah shook her head, not able to believe any of her friends' words.

'Yes, but you're forgetting one thing, aren't you?' she said, putting her hands on her hips. 'If he likes me that much, why is he out on a date with Aimee tonight?'

'On a date?' stammered Beth.

'Tonight?' asked Ella.

'With Aimee?' said Lily, looking aghast. 'How? When?'

'She asked him the other day,' said Hannah, coming back to the bed to sit down and slump against the pillows. 'So I guess your radar is way off, for once.'

Her friends were silent for a moment after hearing her shaky voice and she could feel Beth and Ella's sympathy even through the phone screen.

Lily, though, immediately drew her into a hug and Hannah couldn't help but let a stray tear fall as she finally admitted to herself how upset she really was over Alex.

How long had she been lying to herself that her feelings for him were purely friendly? How long had she been harbouring a secret crush on him?

She had tried so hard not to give in to her feelings. And yet it seemed as if they were stronger than ever.

But with Alex out on a date with someone else, she had no choice but to just remain friends.

39

The water sports centre opened on the following Saturday morning.

Alex was hoping that the lack of hype surrounding the opening meant that there were no expectations on the place to succeed. Obviously he was desperate for it to flourish for the family's sake. Ben had already impressed on him the need for the summer takings to be up on the previous summer.

'They couldn't be much worse,' Ben had told him a few days previously, with a grimace.

But the hotel had been in the middle of extensive renovations at that time. Now it was open and a steady trickle of guests were ensuring that the rooms were at seventy-five per cent capacity each weekend.

The problem was encouraging new guests along during the week. However, Ella had done a sterling job in creating some hype around the opening of the hotel and so had made a similar effort with the water sports centre, such as a new Facebook page and advertising on the local community online hub.

'They'll come,' announced Dotty that morning over breakfast. 'How could they possibly stay away?'

Alex nodded, hoping that sheer willpower and prayer alone would help achieve that particular goal.

As it happened, when he headed past the hotel lobby after breakfast and went to nervously check on the noticeboard, he was amazed. There had been a blank list placed there the previous evening asking for any parties interested in renting out the paddleboards on the lake. To his surprise, all eight paddleboards had been reserved.

'Looks like you're in for a busy morning,' said Ben, coming out of the hotel office and nodding at the noticeboard.

Alex nodded. 'I can't believe it,' he replied.

Ben grinned at him. 'Why not? They all heard that there was an experienced triathlete ready to hand over his expertise.'

Alex raised his eyebrows at his best friend. 'And how did they hear that?' he asked.

'You know what?' replied Ben, laughing. 'I honestly can't remember.'

As he headed outside, Alex felt a little embarrassed. Ever since the disastrous charity run where he had ended up breaking his foot and becoming somewhat of a local joke overnight, the thought of trading on his relatively infamous name had filled him with horror.

But it seemed that the hotel needed to capitalise on his infamy and, reluctantly, he had to agree with them. Especially if it brought in more people into the area.

So when the eight eager paddleboarders arrived for their lesson that afternoon, he fixed a smile on his face and graciously granted them all a selfie before he began to run through the health and safety rules.

He was somewhat grateful that he had been able to practise

extensively on his own paddleboard up to that point so he too didn't look like a complete novice. He had even begun using it whilst on lifeguard duty for Dotty's swim club.

That morning, the first of the advertised swimming sessions had been an eye-opener. As it was the Whitsun bank holiday weekend and the weather was glorious, at least twenty people had arrived for the 11 a.m. opening and he had been grateful that Faye and Frankie had joined him to help organise everyone's arrival.

He was grateful for all the preparations they had put in place beforehand. The signs to the additional car park for the swimming clubs had been put in place, keeping the hotel car park free for guests. In addition, there was now a reception hut where the swimmers could pay for their sessions and pick up their floats and swimming caps, if they hadn't brought their own.

He was thankful that he had insisted on floats and swimming caps for everyone participating as there were far more people than he had anticipated and needed to keep an eye on everyone.

Despite still having doubts about the use of the lake, Walter had offered to keep watch on the other side with his walkie-talkie but thankfully there were no dramas that would need their lifesaving endeavours.

However, the first session did at least show Alex where some adjustments still needed to be made and he discussed it with Walter when it was over.

'I did notice a few people struggling to get changed afterwards because there was nowhere to sit down apart from those couple of deck chairs that we brought over from the bigger beach,' Alex told him.

Walter nodded thoughtfully. 'That's no use,' he said, looking across to where people were sitting on the grass, relaxing after their swim. 'I can make up a few picnic benches, if you like.'

'That would be great,' said Alex, although he was anxious not to upset Walter any further. 'If it's not too much trouble.'

'It's not like we haven't got enough wood,' said Walter, gesturing at the surrounding forest before he walked away.

Watching some people nervously test the water with their toes before going in led Alex to make a note to put up a notice-board near the beach on which he could post the daily water cleanliness test results and temperature of the water. He also looked up a number of health and safety rules for guidance which he would also post on a laminated sheet alongside.

But he had been pleased with how smoothly it had gone and thankfully he was still smiling during the paddleboard class as well.

The group that had hired boards had included a number of relative beginners and, as such, he was able to tell them how hopeless he had been at the beginning. Especially when they were frustrated with their frequent dunkings in the water.

But Tiny always helped bring a smile to people's faces, especially when he swam out to greet anyone who had just fallen into the water for the umpteenth time.

Alex was grateful for his many hours of practice which meant that he was able to stand on his own paddleboard for the whole session. He might not ever feel as graceful as Hannah had looked on a paddleboard, but at least he could pretend and not make a total fool of himself any more, he reckoned.

As the session finished later in the afternoon, the paddle-boarders were all full of enthusiasm and lively chatter as they discussed their varying levels of ability. Even better, as far as Alex was concerned, was that as soon as they had gotten changed out of their wetsuits, they headed into the Boathouse Café for a drink which then extended into a busier afternoon session than during the week. Whilst he tidied up, he spotted Hannah rushing around on the veranda serving all the new customers and was thrilled for her.

Once he had packed away all the equipment, and with no more activities booked for that day, Alex headed into the café to check on her own success.

'I thought you'd need this,' she told him, placing a cold drink and slice of lemon drizzle cake on the table on the veranda.

The café had become quiet at last so he invited her to join him.

'Sit down for a minute,' he told her. 'I could see how busy you were today as well.'

She nodded as she sat down. 'Wasn't it amazing?' she asked, a smile lighting up her pretty face.

'Absolutely,' he told her, mesmerised once more by her eyes.

'How did you find your first paddleboard session?' she asked. 'Did you enjoy it?'

'You know what?' he replied. 'I did.' He thought for a moment. 'I think that all these years it was all about me, me, me. How fast I could run. How fit I was. The diet. The training. It was exhausting.'

She nodded. 'You were always on the go,' she told him.

'Plus I'm not sure it's that healthy, mentally speaking, to be so wrapped up in myself,' he carried on. 'So this afternoon, teaching that guy who kept falling in how to stand upright was really satisfying. Like I had some knowledge to pass on. Pay it forward, I guess.'

She smiled. '*Your* knowledge of paddleboarding?' she said, teasing him.

He laughed. 'OK. So I should give you all the credit for me not falling in any more.'

'Absolutely,' she told him, standing up. 'Listen, you sit there and relax after your busy day. It'll do you some good.'

He found that he couldn't disagree with her. He had been so used to running around, training and competing. For the first time, he had had to embrace a slower pace of life. And he was loving it. He enjoyed the downtime. A beer at sunset without worrying that it would affect his strict diet. Cake. Sunshine. The good weather.

As Hannah headed back to the kitchen, he thought how much stronger she sounded. As if she were starting to feel more confident in herself.

He wondered how many more changes there would be for both of them by the end of the summer.

40

Hannah was both amazed and overjoyed at the almost overnight success in the water sports centre. Alex had worked so hard and it was great to see that hard work pay off.

A week after opening and the bookings were still flooding in for the paddleboarding from hotel guests.

The biggest success, however, was the swim club. Word had spread and there were at least a dozen people for each of the timed sessions throughout the day. The first morning session was the most popular and was already up to twenty people every day of the week. It seemed that everyone wanted to start their day with a swim, especially when the temperature began to rise and summer arrived with hot sunny days.

Equally as joyful to her was that the Boathouse Café had a surge of interest as the swimmers began to use it after their session. Suddenly word of mouth had spread and Hannah was flat-out every day.

The only small blot of cloud on the horizon was that Aimee was now running a couple of sunrise yoga sessions on the beach throughout the week. Hannah had never dared asked Alex how the date went and managed to steer clear of that subject completely. She wasn't that good an actress, she knew. Ben didn't get any feedback either, according to Lily when Hannah had plucked up the courage to ask. Alex was a private person. It was one of the many reasons she liked him so much.

But if Alex was happy, then she was happy, she told herself.

And the yoga was certainly garnering great feedback as well so it was all good for the future of Maple Tree Lodge too.

'I sooo needed that,' said Lily, coming into the café after an early-morning sunrise yoga session and leaning against the counter. 'I feel so zen right now.'

'Are you stressed?' asked Hannah, looking up from her pastry and concerned for her friend.

'Oh, no,' replied Lily, with a dreamy smile. 'Business is doing great. We've had loads of interest from people hearing about the water sports centre. I just feel so relaxed right now.' She rolled her shoulders a couple of times. 'You should join us sometime. It's great for de-stressing.'

'I don't feel stressed,' Hannah told her quickly.

She was pleased that Alex and Aimee were dating but that didn't mean that she wanted to spend every minute with her.

And actually, as she thought on, she realised she had told the truth to Lily. Somewhere along the way, the fear and stress of running her own business had begun to fade.

The business had picked up quickly alongside the water sports centre as people had begun to visit the café afterwards for refreshments. She was receiving so much positive feedback regarding her bakes that she could feel herself getting stronger mentally.

She was also enjoying baking every day and, she had to admit, she was enjoying being her own boss as well. Of course, it was only for the summer. The temporary licence would be up on 21 September when British Summertime ended, and then what?

She tried not to think about it. What would she do when the café closed? No baking each day. No customers. And no water sports centre either. Which would mean no Alex, presumably, as well. She had gotten so used to seeing him every day as well. Having him in her life had felt life changing, even though they'd only exchanged one silly drunken kiss.

'Who are you thinking of?' murmured Lily, watching her.

'No one,' said Hannah quickly, feeling the blushes spread across her cheeks.

Lily grinned. 'Yeah, right,' she said sarcastically. 'Anyway, Aimee was saying that she might put on a self-defence class soon if she has enough takers. Shall I put our names down for it?'

'Self-defence?' asked Hannah, a little shocked. 'Is my brother that scary?'

Lily laughed. 'No, but I just feel every woman should have some idea as to self-defence. In case of an emergency.'

'Can't I be your knight in shining armour instead?' asked Ben, coming into the café and obviously having overheard the conversation.

Lily reached up to kiss him on the lips. 'You are that anyway,' she said, between kisses. 'But I just like to be prepared. I mean, look at this muscle!' She held up her arm and flexed a non-existent bicep.

Ben laughed. 'Maybe you should take up paddleboarding,' he told her. 'My arms were killing me when I tried it a few days ago.'

'You're so unfit,' Hannah told him, shaking her head. 'I was fine afterwards.'

'You obviously didn't work as hard as I did,' teased Ben.

'Maybe Alex let her off for good behaviour,' said Lily in a knowing tone, flashing Hannah a grin before leaving the café.

Hannah blushed once more and tried to concentrate on making her pastry.

'You OK?' asked Ben, noting her blushes. 'You look like you're overheating.'

'I'm fine,' Hannah told him. 'Actually, I wanted to run something past you. A lot of the swimmers have been requesting that they take their drinks outside so I was going to order some takeout cups. Reusable ones, if I can, as they're so much better for the environment. Plates too, if I can source them. What do you think?'

Ben's eyebrows shot up. 'I think that's a great idea. You know, you don't need to run everything past me. You're the boss here, not me.'

'OK,' said Hannah with a nod. 'Alex said he'll get me a good bargain on the cups and plates.'

'Good lad,' said Ben, but he was still frowning. 'I guess you wanted someone else to double check your numbers and him being an accountant was the obvious choice.'

Was her brother put out? She couldn't quite tell.

'Alex offered,' she told him. 'You know that I'm no good at numbers.'

'Yeah, and I'm no good at baking, sis,' said Ben. 'We each have our plus and negative things. What's your point?'

He was teasing her and yet she suddenly found that she didn't want to joke around with him.

'I could never compete with you,' she said simply.

Ben's face instantly dropped. 'And I don't want you to,' he said quickly. 'We're not in competition. We never were.'

Hannah sighed. 'I know. It's just…' She hesitated briefly. 'It's just that you're so good at everything.'

It was true. Her brother had made school and his career look so effortless, whereas her life had been somewhat harder, a struggle, for so long.

Ben studied her for a moment. 'Is that what you think?' he asked her softly.

'You just make everything seem so easy,' she told him. 'I'm glad for you, obviously. But I just wish some of that confidence had rubbed off on me, that's all.'

He nodded thoughtfully. 'You know, not all of it was easy. When I was in London running the architect firm, I hated it most days.'

Hannah was shocked. 'You never said anything,' she told him. She was shocked that he too had faced difficulties of which she hadn't had a clue.

'There was lots of other stuff going on,' he said. 'And I didn't want to admit that the path I'd taken was completely the wrong one.'

'I had no idea.' She shook her head.

'Nobody did,' he told her. 'Not until I told Lily.'

Hannah smiled, grateful that he had someone to confide in. 'You really love her,' she stated.

He nodded. 'Yup. I do. And talking of which, you'd better be prepared for a bridesmaid dress at some point down the line.'

Hannah gave a little squeal of joy. 'And it'll be my best day ever.' She stepped forward to give him a hug. As she held him close, she said, 'I wish you'd told me you were struggling.'

'You were here looking after Mum, Dad and our grandparents,' he said against her shoulder as he held her tight. 'That's more important than any job or career misery. And makes you a far better person than I am.'

She stepped back and looked at him. 'It's not a competition,' she said.

He nodded. 'Which is exactly what I'm trying to tell you, sis.'

He frowned as if to himself. 'I've been a decent big brother, haven't I?' he asked. 'Supported you whenever I could? Done my best?'

'The very best,' she told him.

He sagged with relief. 'Good. You know, I'm happy now,' he replied. 'And that's all I've ever wanted for my baby sister as well. To be happy.'

'I'm getting there,' she told him, with a smile.

'I can tell,' he said. 'Something's changed this summer.'

She blushed once more.

'Alex is so positive all the time, some of it must have rubbed off,' she told him, with a shrug.

'Glad to hear it,' he said, grinning. 'And let him help you with the numbers, if you want. He's always liked all that boring number stuff.'

Hannah could describe Alex ad infinitum and yet the word she could never use for him was boring. He was clever, funny, kind and strong. All wrapped up in the most perfect face and body she had ever seen.

But he was dating Aimee so for now she would just have to be grateful for the success of the café, not her love life.

41

Towards the end of June, the heat began to ratchet up with the longer days.

'Told you folks would want to cool off in our lovely lake,' said Walter, as he stood next to Alex on the small beach.

Alex smiled his agreement but didn't feel like reminding Walter of his objections to the water sports centre. In fact, the pensioner seemed to positively revel in the daily activities.

Walter was a secondary lifeguard in the mornings, keeping watch on the busiest swimming sessions from his position on the jetty. Then, in the afternoons, he would keep busy in his workshop.

More picnic tables and even a couple of benches had appeared over the past couple of weeks and all the swimmers were taking advantage of a sit down after their dip in the water.

'I was thinking that perhaps we could add some sort of low shelving unit over there,' carried on Walter, turning around to point at an empty spot near the water's edge. 'I've been watching and some people want a place to pop their bags and shoes in.'

'That sounds great,' replied Alex, grateful for both the fresh ideas and the support.

In fact, all the Jackson family were revelling in the success of the water sports. Faye and Frankie were taking turns to man the reception booth. Word had also spread about the snug and Frankie had been telling Alex the previous evening that the weekend had been their busiest nights since opening. Meanwhile, Ben and Lily had both mentioned the uptick in bookings as word had spread about the hotel from visitors.

Then there was the queen of the swim club, Dotty. She was a positive life force, always around during the swimming sessions to encourage any nervous newcomers, both young and old.

All in all, the water sports centre had turned out to be a huge success and it had given him a sense of fulfilment that he had never imagined. He found that he garnered the most pleasure from the more reluctant swimmers.

'There's no rush,' he would tell them. 'Go at your own pace. You can be as slow or as fast as you like. Just take your time and enjoy yourself.'

Over the days and weeks, Alex watched with pride as the hesitant swimmers' confidence began to soar.

'It's my favourite part of the day,' one elderly gentleman told him. 'Gets me out of the house, to be honest.'

'I've always felt a bit vulnerable because of my size,' one larger lady had said. 'Now I don't give two hoots what I look like. I'm just enjoying it too much to care what other people think of me.'

'Work is so stressful,' a younger man told him. 'This just takes me away from all that and I just focus on swimming and being in the here and now.'

Alex had been both amazed and thrilled with all the positive reactions. Everyone felt differently about their experiences in the water but the sense of satisfaction and overall well-being was the same for each person. He was beginning to realise just how much the swimming clubs meant to them and how much enjoyment that in turn gave him as well.

Alex placed the paddleboard in the water and looked down at Tiny.

'So are you coming with me?' he asked.

The puppy recognised the familiar words and threw himself at the paddleboard, landing far more gracefully than his bulky weight suggested or indeed Alex would have thought.

'You're getting better at this than I am,' Alex told him.

But he couldn't help but smile at the dog as he too climbed onto the paddleboard from the jetty. He was really enjoying having a dog. The company was nice but also the dog was benefitting from all the training and commands and was growing into a delightful companion. He was a gentle soon-to-be giant with both young and old. Children delighted him with their shrieks of laughter as he bounded in and out of the water and older, more cautious hotel guests found themselves unable to stop patting him or stroking his thick fur when he was sprawled out in the middle of the entrance hall.

'Morning, Alex, morning, Tiny,' said Maud, who had only just arrived for her second week of swimming club.

'Morning, Maud,' said Alex. 'How are you today?'

'Battling on,' said Maud, with a smile.

She was at least seventy years old and Alex knew that she had a number of health issues. And yet she had already told him that she had slept better after last week's swim out on the lake than she had done in years.

Dotty had also told him that Maud had been widowed the previous summer and had become somewhat of a recluse in her grief. With Dotty's gentle encouragement, Maud had finally joined what they had named 'The Old Girls' Swimming Club' and was promising to keep coming twice a week.

'Water looks perfect,' she told him.

'A balmy 22 degrees,' he replied.

'And clean as a whistle too,' she said, peering down at her feet in the water.

As Maud waded into the lake, Alex steadied himself with the paddle and, with Tiny sprawled on the front of the board as a fluffy mast, they headed out.

It really was a glorious day, thought Alex. He had the headspace now to be able to enjoy it and not think about timings and training and all the pressures that had smothered him when he had been competing.

He had had no idea how tense he must have been all those years. But day by day, he could feel how relaxed he had become. How much he was enjoying each and every day. How much time he had to take for himself.

He paddled out past the shallow water and on to deeper depths where the water became a little bit darker. He wanted to check the rope line to ensure that both the paddleboarders and swimmers were safe and kept separate.

A few swimmers had already completed a couple of laps, their bright swimming caps and floats highlighting where they were. Alex knew them and that they were more than competent but still he kept an eye on both them and Maud as she began a more gentle circuit.

Noting some rope had become tangled with a bit of weed, he paddled over and bent down to correct it. Carefully standing back up again, he thought back to how unsteady he had been in those first early practices and how much Hannah had laughed with him.

He was still enjoying her company and yet there seemed to be a distance between them that he couldn't understand.

He was still puzzling over what might have happened when Tiny suddenly barked and sat up, almost unbalancing Alex, who just about kept his balance to stay standing on the board.

Imagining it was a duck or goose nearby, Alex glanced around. But Tiny barked again and all of Alex's attention was focused on Maud, who Tiny was barking at.

Instantly Alex could see her struggling to breathe and paddled quickly over to where she was splashing around in the water, looking panicked. He jumped in next to her, reaching for the lifebuoy that he had placed on the back of the paddleboard and placing it over her.

'Hang on,' he said, letting go of the board and holding on to both the buoy and Maud to start to take her towards the shore.

'Can't breathe,' she gasped.

'It's OK,' he told her, gently turning her onto her back and pulling her back quickly across the water towards the beach.

On the beach, he could see Dotty and some other swimmers had gathered by the shore in a group and were looking concerned.

When his feet finally reached the sandy bottom, Alex continued to pull Maud out of the water.

'What is it?' asked Dotty, as Alex removed the lifebuoy from her to lay her gently on the sand.

'Inhaler,' gasped Maud, lifting a finger to point at a bag nearby.

'She's got asthma,' said Dotty, rushing over to feel around in the bag.

When the inhaler was produced, they gently sat Maud up a little, with her leaning on Alex, and she took a couple of puffs from the inhaler.

As Maud held up a thumbs-up to say that she was beginning to feel better, Alex suddenly realised that he had abandoned Tiny on the paddleboard.

He looked back at the lake to check the dog was OK, figuring that he would still be cast adrift where he had left him.

But to his amazement, Tiny was in the water and had the long lead of the paddleboard in his mouth and was gently pulling it back to the beach.

'Well, I'll be a monkey's uncle,' muttered Walter, who had just joined them and had noticed Tiny as well.

As Tiny reached the beach, he let go of the paddleboard, which one of the other swimmers brought ashore.

After a dramatic shaking of his coat, Tiny padded over and slumped next to where Alex was still kneeling on the ground.

'Sorry about that,' said Maud, looking up at him and still looking a little red in the face. 'Haven't had an attack for ages.'

'It's fine,' said Alex. 'Let's just sit here quietly for a little while whilst you get your breath back.'

'And he means literally,' added Dotty, with a grin. Although she was looking somewhat relieved. 'Think we'll need something stronger in our post-swim coffee this morning,' she said to Hannah as she rushed up to them, looking concerned.

'What's happened?' she asked. 'I heard Tiny barking and then saw everyone gathered here.'

'Maud had an asthma attack in the water,' Dotty told her granddaughter. 'Alex saved her.'

'I think "save" is perhaps an over-dramatic way of saying that I helped her to shore,' said Alex. 'And actually the hero of the day was Tiny. He barked when he saw Maud in distress.'

'Good boy,' murmured Maud, reaching out to stroke the dog's wet head.

'Extra treats for Tiny later,' said Dotty.

The dog's ears perked up at his favourite word and his tongue lolled out in anticipation.

'Well, as long as you're both all right,' said Hannah, looking from Maud to Alex.

He nodded at her to say that he was fine.

He was a little shaken after the dramatic encounter in the past half an hour and yet grateful that he had insisted on all the safety measures that he had put in place. Also that he had been studying the lifeguard practices for saving and helping people in distress in the water. It had been worth all the reading and studying to be able to help Maud that morning.

When she was ready, they gently helped Maud to her feet and took her into the Boathouse Café for a reviving drink.

Finally, Alex could relax and leant against his lifeguard chair with a heavy sigh of relief.

'Are you OK?'

He looked up to see Hannah nearby and realised that she had stayed behind, concerned about him.

'A little shaken,' he told her. 'But I was just grateful that I was there to help.'

'So are we,' she replied.

She hesitated before stepping forward to give him a hug.

'And you are a hero,' he heard her murmur into his shoulder before stepping back. 'No matter what you say.'

She appeared to hesitate before she leaned forward and kissed him on the cheek before walking away towards the boathouse. And that was the greatest prize of all, he realised.

42

The heatwave rolled on. And so did the success of the water sports centre which meant that the whole family were busy as July arrived and the heat showed no signs of abating.

Hannah found that her days were getting busier and busier. The delivery of takeout cups meant that the swimmers could have their drinks outside on Walter's picnic benches and were able to enjoy their cakes and treats too.

After Alex had rescued Maud, word of her asthma attack whilst in the water had spread and even brought the local newspaper to write up the story, which in turn had meant even more free marketing for both the swimming club and the café.

With the upsurge in customers, Hannah had realised that not everyone wanted cake, some customers wanted savoury items on the menu as well so she had begun to experiment once more with the summer flavours, now confident in her abilities to choose her own bakes. So to the menu she added frittata with feta cheese and red peppers. Salads full of fresh ingredients, with the addition of fresh basil and chicken, or pasta with olives. Tasty crudites and a salmon quiche. Even cold cucumber soup and gazpacho, both of which were easily made, flew off the menu, along with freshly baked crusty bread.

She'd even begun to make home-made ice cream lollies full of fresh summer flavours which were a huge hit in the intense heat. Furthermore, she had another idea.

'We need to order some doggy ice cream,' she told Ben, before glancing down at a panting Tiny one hot afternoon as she placed a water bowl next to him.

'Seriously?' Ben's eyebrows shot up as he leant against the bar. 'I'm not sure.'

'I am.' Hannah was enthused with assertiveness about the business now. 'Trust me.'

Thankfully he did and the ice cream for dogs was a huge success with everyone who brought their canine family members with them to cool off in the lake.

Life began to slow down under the intense heat of the day and everyone was eager to escape the heat of the towns and cities to the cool waters of Dragonfly Lake.

That included Beth and Ella, who joined them one weekend in early July.

As it had been her busiest day so far that summer, Hannah felt weary but pleased with the success.

She just wanted a quiet drink with her friends that evening to relax. However, the snug was packed with all the people who had been enjoying the beach and lake throughout the day and had decided to prolong their journeys home and enjoy one of Frankie's delicious cocktails first.

It meant that when the four friends arrived, there wasn't a single seat left either in the bar or outside on the veranda.

'I thought we would have got some kind of reserved seating as we're pretty much family,' said Ella, frowning as she stared down at the picnic blanket that Hannah had just brought out to lay on the grass. 'Do I have to go on that? I'm wearing white shorts.'

'You'll survive,' said Lily, carefully sinking to the rug so as not to spill her drink.

'Enjoy being outdoors,' said Beth. 'I spent all day yesterday in a room without air conditioning and then a packed train where I had to stand up the whole way. Right now I'm thinking about stripping off and running straight into the lake.'

'Well, that would get the customers out of the snug,' said Ella. 'Maybe I'll let you do it so we can grab a seat whilst they're ogling you.'

Beth rolled her eyes. 'Cocktail first,' she said, taking a sip. 'Mmm, that's amazing.'

'Frankie's latest creation,' said Lily. 'Summer Dream, I think she's called it.'

Hannah took a sip. The fresh mango and strawberries plus a hint of rum made it feel as if she were on holiday.

'I needed this,' she said, before taking another sip. She could feel the rum relaxing her shoulders and sank back on the rug.

'It's great that everyone's so busy,' said Ella.

'You're doing so well,' said Beth to Hannah.

'Isn't she?' said Lily. 'The café's been a huge success.'

'Absolutely,' said Ella, before looking at Beth. 'Go on. I'll let you streak into the lake in just your underwear. Maybe that'll bring in even more customers.'

They all laughed and continued to enjoy their cocktail and gossip as they lay by the beach until the sun had gone down, watching the bright blue dragonflies making the most of the long, warm rays as they fizzed above the water like fairy aeroplanes.

Much later on, and feeling relaxed due to Frankie's delicious cocktails, the girls were finally able to find a comfortable sofa in the snug after all the customers had left and it was only the family in the bar.

'What a day,' said Frankie, with a sigh.

Faye, who was sitting on a barstool nearby, looked at her, concerned. 'Is it getting too much for you?' she asked.

'You know me, I like to keep busy,' replied Frankie. 'But some customers left without even ordering a drink because there weren't any spare seats.'

'Such a shame,' said Dotty. 'Can we put some extra chairs out? On the beach perhaps.'

Alex grimaced. 'That might be a bit risky with any early swimmers, especially if they're taking glass out there.'

'I agree,' added Faye. 'The beach should be kept clear.'

'Well, we can't go on like this,' said Dotty. 'This run of good weather is set to last so it's only going to get busier, not quieter.'

'Excellent,' said Walter. 'It's doing wonders for our profits!'

Frankie, who was massaging her feet, shot him a look. 'Good. You can pay for my spa treatment when this rush is over.'

'We just need to spread the customers out a bit,' said Lily, who suddenly began to smile as if she had had a brilliant idea. 'They need to go somewhere that's already set up for catering so nobody ends up with any extra work.'

'Somewhere with a kitchen,' said Ben, looking at his girlfriend as he too broke into a smile.

'And an amazing view,' added Lily, grinning back at him.

'Where are you two talking about?' asked Faye, looking bemused.

'The Boathouse Café, of course!' said Ben.

Everyone turned to look at Hannah.

'But we're closed in the evenings,' she told them.

'So?' laughed Frankie. 'Keep the café open instead! Oh, it's perfect.'

'It is!' said Beth. 'It can be a cocktail bar in the evening at the weekends. Just imagine a few fairy lights twinkling and the view over there at sunset. You'll be inundated with customers.'

Hannah bit her lip. It would mean a lot of extra work, if only for a short while. But could she do it? She wasn't sure.

But for once, as everyone looked at her, and knowing that Frankie desperately needed some kind of break with all the customers, she decided to take heart from everything she had achieved so far and found herself saying, 'Oh, why not?' instead.

As a whoop of approval ran around her family and friends, she found herself looking at Alex for reassurance. But he was smiling and nodding at her as well. And if he thought it was a good idea then it must be, she told herself.

43

Early the next morning, eager to set up before the heat built and the crowds came to cool off, Hannah raced around the café. It was her usual routine and she had it down pretty quickly these days.

So when she was all set, with the cakes in the oven, she allowed herself a few thoughts as to how the cocktail bar could work.

Thankfully Frankie came along after breakfast and had a few ideas. 'Ben's getting some signs printed up,' she said. 'About the cocktail bar.'

'Are you sure you don't mind?' asked Hannah. 'The snug has been such a success.'

'Can we have too much success after the many previous years of failure?' drawled Frankie, before laughing.

'Yes, but you're the cocktail guru, not me,' said Hannah.

'Listen, I've been thinking it over ever since my second espresso this morning,' began Frankie. 'And here's how it's going to play.'

Frankie then handed over a short list of cocktails, most of

which Hannah had helped her make whenever she had given her a hand behind the bar. They were mostly simple and ones that she was used to making. Rhubarb and ginger cocktail. Mojitos – mint, rum, ice and soda water. Home-made pink lemonade. Frozen strawberry daiquiri – strawberries, rum, sugar and lime. Gin, elderflower and cucumber cooler.

Then there was the idea for the ice cubes. Ice trays sprinkled with edible pansies, violets and rose petals before freezing. They looked enchanting when sitting in the tall cocktail glasses. They even made ice-cold water look glamorous.

Ben had already applied for an alcohol licence, although because it came under the hotel grounds he thought they would be OK anyway so pretty much everything had been thought of.

Hannah's nerves were still rattling though.

'What if I can't do it?' she said, confessing her worst fears to Alex when they had a private moment later that day.

'You're always so quick to write yourself off,' he told her. 'Have faith in yourself.'

'That's easy for you to say,' she said.

'Actually, it is,' he replied. 'It's part of my athletic training. To win. To succeed. Determination.'

'I know,' she told him. 'But like I said. It's easy for you. You win at everything.'

He looked at her intently. 'Not everything,' he said.

She looked at him, wondering what he was talking about before Frankie interrupted them to give them her box of spare cocktail shakers.

As Alex and Frankie chatted away, Hannah glanced around the café. During the day it was lovely but she had to admit that when she had been tidying up in the early days when it had just been her, with the fairy lights twinkling in the fading light and with the view of the sparkling lake beyond, it had felt really special.

She was excited to share it with any customers, if they came, she reminded herself.

But in the end, her fears weren't justified. The following Saturday, the beach and lake were packed once more as the sun rose high in the sky and the temperatures matched it. People came into the café for cold drinks and lunch, then later on, when the heat of the day was still intense, people stayed for cocktail hour as well.

With the help of Faye and Lily assisting behind the coffee bar and in the kitchen, they were able to serve all of the cocktails and the café was packed with people looking for a little shade but also that incredible view of the water.

It ended up being a really fun evening. Everyone's excitement at trying out something completely new in turn fed off the enjoyment of the guests and it was long into the evening before the last customer finally left and they could all relax at last.

'What a night,' said Faye, taking off her shoes and rubbing her feet.

'Did you hear everyone asking when we were next open?' asked Lily, her eyes shining.

Hannah nodded, also hearing her refer to the café as 'we', which pleased her immensely.

'So is this where all the people went this evening?' asked Ben, coming into the café and looking around at all the used glasses piled up on the counter.

'It was brilliant,' said Lily, suppressing a yawn. 'I'm that excited but equally absolutely shattered.'

Everyone agreed that it had worked it for the best and began to make their weary way back to the hotel to their rooms.

Hannah found that she couldn't relax and insisted that she

was only going to spend five minutes tidying up. Half an hour later, when Alex came in through the front door, she was still there.

'Thought I'd find you in here,' he said, as Tiny rushed up to sit on her feet with a heavy lump of weight. 'Everyone else has gone to bed.'

'I was still buzzing,' she told him.

'You look like you enjoyed yourself,' he said, smiling at her.

She nodded. 'I thought I wouldn't be able to cope but then I remembered what you'd said about being positive and all that and also that I'd already been a relative success with the café and thought, why not?'

'That's the spirit,' he said, laughing.

She was about to contradict herself when she stopped. She was OK, she decided. She had done it and succeeded. She had to keep doing it over and over but now that she had done it once, she would be all right, she told herself.

And with the success of the new cocktail bar, she wondered what else she could succeed at.

44

The date of the Commonwealth Games had always been on Alex's radar but he had tried to push it to one side.

But on the Thursday night of the triathlon, knowing that it was taking place on the other side of the world, the temptation to watch it live was too great. So he made his excuses to the family about having a headache and went back to the apartment to settle down on the bed.

Hannah had told him that she would take care of Tiny as they had only just finished dinner so he was all alone as he lay on the covers, staring at the images on his phone.

He thought that he would be OK. He thought that he would be relieved to watch the race and not be taking part.

But he didn't feel like that at all. The hurt and guilt over the fractured relationship with his dad came rushing back, along with all the pain he had tried to hide, even from himself.

He watched the triathletes swim across the water, trying to remind himself how much he enjoyed swimming in the lake these days. And yet he could feel the tears rolling down his cheeks as he stared at the screen.

He barely registered the sound of paws and footsteps on the stairs until it was too late and Tiny was rushing across the room towards him, followed by Hannah.

'I hope you don't mind,' she began to say. 'I brought some pills for your headache...'

But her words were swiftly replaced with a gasp as she stared at him, noting his tears. 'What's the matter?' she asked, rushing across the room to sit down next to him.

He couldn't speak and merely held the phone out for Hannah to look at the screen.

'Is it the race? Today?' she asked softly.

He nodded.

She appeared to hesitate before suddenly swinging her legs onto the bed to lie down next to him, resting her head on his shoulder.

He was instantly comforted by her support, knowing that he wasn't alone, and laid his head on hers.

'Johnny's in the lead,' he muttered.

'Your friend?' she asked.

'He's a good guy. He should win easily.'

They watched in silence as the runners headed around Sydney Harbour before coming to the finish along by the water. Huge crowds were cheering them along and he couldn't help but wonder what would have happened if it had been him winning instead.

The race finished with his friend winning the gold medal easily. They watched the celebrations in silence before Alex switched off his phone.

Hannah finally lifted her head to look at him.

'Do you miss it?' she asked. 'The competitions? The training?'

He nodded. 'I didn't think I would. I thought I was ready to step away. And I was. But...'

She took his hand with hers and gave it a squeeze and at once the pain was shared.

'They all called and texted when they heard that I was out of the competition,' he told her, gulping to clear his thick throat. 'I was even invited to go over and do some coaching. Moral support and all that.'

'Why didn't you go?'

He sighed. 'I could lie to you and say that I was too busy here and needed to recover.' He gave her a sad smile. 'But I never can seem to lie to you.'

'So why are you here and not out there in Australia?' she asked.

He took a deep breath. 'Because, truth be told, I couldn't bear to be there and not race. To be a part of all of it but only on the outside. It wouldn't be the same.'

'Have you heard from your dad since you saw him?'

He shook his head.

'I'm so sorry,' she told him.

'But I'm not.' He looked down at her hand still resting on top of his and squeezed it. 'Just call me confused. Because I was desperately unhappy towards the end. And I think that perhaps I've found my way forward. Here. With you.'

The silence stretched out and he sensed her still holding back from him.

'And Tiny and your family,' he added quickly.

She nodded slowly. 'Well, Tiny is very important and needs a steady home life,' she said, with a smile.

'He does.'

'And for what it's worth, we all want you here too.' She appeared to take a deep breath. '*I* want you here.'

'You do?' He stared at her in wonder, reaching out to smooth down a lock of hair that had escaped from her ponytail.

She grabbed hold of his hand before he could pull it back and they locked eyes once more. His breathing quickened and yet neither of them made a move for a moment. It was if they were locked in time, in their own private moment.

Finally he couldn't bear it any longer. So he leant forward to close the gap between them and kissed her gently on the lips.

He felt her start before her hand moved around behind his head and drew him even closer to her. The kiss was nothing like he had ever felt before. Passion, desire, love all rushed forward into his consciousness as the kiss went on and on, deeper and deeper.

Finally, she pulled back to look at him with wide eyes.

'I was supposed to be cheering you up,' she told him, breathless.

He smiled slowly at her. 'Well, you've certainly done that,' he replied.

They looked at each other for a long time before Tiny suddenly leapt onto the bed to join them, breaking their eye contact and also the moment.

They both laughed as he ran round and round chasing his tail before finally settling down.

'Well, I'd better let you boys settle down,' said Hannah, getting up from the bed.

Still reeling from their unexpected kiss, Alex looked up at her. She was looking a little confused, a tiny crease appearing on her forehead as she too processed what had just happened.

He didn't want to pressure her and so said the first thing that came into his mind. 'I'll watch the medal ceremony, I think.'

She puffed out a sigh of relief and he realised that he had been right not to push her about the kiss.

So they shared a knowing smile and said goodnight before Hannah turned around and headed downstairs.

Alex lay back on the bed and stared up at the ceiling, wondering how the very worst of times could quickly become the best of them as well. And despite still being upset about the race, he went to sleep with a smile on his face.

45

It had been two weeks since the cocktail bar in the boathouse had been opened and on Friday night it was even busier.

It had also been two days since Hannah and Alex had kissed. Seeing him so upset when watching the Commonwealth Games where he should have won a medal had been hard. So hard that she had ended up kissing him as a way to comfort him. Except she couldn't stop reliving that kiss, the way he had kissed her back.

And she still felt guilty. As much as she had relished being in his arms, she couldn't ignore the tiny voice inside reminding her that he was probably still dating Aimee. But Alex wasn't a cheater and nor was she.

Neither of them had referred to the kiss since then and she was grateful just to be friends with him, friends who were comfortable with each other. Friends who had shared one amazing kiss.

Thankfully Ella and Beth had come back to help out in the cocktail bar that weekend and were proving just the distraction that she needed.

'That was a great idea,' said Beth, flexing her biceps after the self-defence class which they had just finished early on Saturday morning.

Ella rolled her eyes. 'I can do more damage with my stiletto than my hands,' she said.

'I think those false nails could be your biggest weapon, to be honest,' said Hannah.

Ella gave a fake roar and raked her French tips through the air as if they were claws.

It had been Aimee's tentative idea to Alex about self-defence classes that had triggered their interest. Aimee was unsure about a new direction so Alex had suggested that she teach the girls first to see how she got on.

Despite her guilt over kissing Alex and jealousy over their dating, Hannah had begun to like Aimee. She was kind and funny and was a really good teacher as well.

'Those self-defence tips were amazing,' said Hannah as they sat down afterwards for a coffee. She had decided to not open up the café until 10 a.m., just to give herself a bit of breathing space.

They all breathed a sigh of satisfaction before looking out across the lake from the veranda.

'What a lovely day,' said Lily. 'But you know what, I feel more empowered thanks to Aimee.'

'Absolutely,' said Beth. 'If anyone ever tries it on with me on the tube, then I'm going to try out that trick with the fingers.'

'Or you could just wear slightly longer skirts,' murmured Ella.

Beth laughed. 'It's not my fault that my favourite vintage style is from the sixties,' she said. 'I love those miniskirts.'

'And you've got the amazing legs to go with them,' Lily told her.

But Hannah couldn't get over what Ella had just said. 'Look, I know you've got a classic style which is gorgeous, by the way,' she said to Ella. 'But why should Beth change whatever she wears just to placate some weirdo on the tube? She should be able to wear what she likes whenever she likes and not be hassled because of it.'

All three friends turned to look at her with surprised looks on their faces.

'I don't think I've ever heard you speak like that,' said Lily.

Ella nodded. 'And I absolutely agree with your sentiment, by the way. Who'd have thought? Hannah Jackman embodying the spirit of girl power.'

Hannah giggled. 'I did just sound like someone else, didn't I?' she said, now feeling a little embarrassed.

'Oh, no, you can't take it back now,' said Ella, shaking her head. 'The mouse has started roaring and we love you even more for it.'

'What's changed?' asked Lily.

Her friends waited whilst Hannah tried to find the right words to explain to them how she was feeling. 'I guess it was this place,' she said, gesturing around the café. 'I had to be brave at long last and yes, it totally took me out of my comfort zone and yet I'm proud of myself,' she said, before slumping back in her chair in amazement. 'I've never said that before.'

'Well, it's long overdue,' said Lily, smiling at her.

But Hannah couldn't find her own smile. Instead, she was thinking back to the worst of times in her life. 'Actually, it's ten years overdue,' she said in a soft tone.

There was a short silence whilst her friends exchanged concerned looks.

'Since Sean,' prompted Beth, gently.

Hannah hesitated before finally nodding. Would her friends judge her for being with him in the first place?

'You know, you've never told us what happened all those years ago.' Ella reached out and took Hannah's spare hand to squeeze it in hers. 'We will never ever judge you,' she said, as if reading her friend's mind.

And that what good friends did, thought Hannah. But despite trusting them implicitly, she had kept a secret from them. The fallout from her relationship with Sean had been her burden alone to carry. She had never shared quite how bad it had been with him, although her friends knew that it hadn't been good. But now, she finally felt strong enough to tell them the truth.

Hannah took a deep breath. 'He frightened me.'

She heard her friends breathe in sharply.

'Did he ever hurt you?' asked Lily, frowning.

Hannah shook her head. 'Not physically, no. But mentally? Absolutely. He used to criticise me over and over, making me think that every little fault that I had was of my own making. Whatever I did, however hard I tried, I was never good enough. Then one night, he shouted at me and he was so angry. So very angry.' She shivered and Lily leant across to wrap her arm around her.

'Tell us,' said Beth, coming over to kneel in front of her. She squeezed Hannah's knee with her hand and then her friends waited.

'He pushed me over one evening, shouting over and over at me. Afterwards I lay there in bed that night shaking with fear,' said Hannah. 'He was asleep and I just prayed that he didn't wake up. It was the longest night of my life. I was so worried. I honestly thought that he was going to hurt me. So, after he'd left for work the next day, I quickly packed up my stuff and somehow made it home on the train. I ran away.'

'And there's no shame in that,' said Ella. Despite her firm nod, there were tears glittering in her eyes. 'You left him and you were safe, that was the main thing.'

'Thank goodness,' said Beth, shaking her head and looking upset.

'We knew it was bad,' said Lily, squeezing her even tighter. 'Of course we did, but we never knew how bad.'

'So he's the reason that you've never dated anyone since then,' said Ella.

'Well, Maple Tree Lodge hasn't exactly been overflowing with available men,' said Hannah, with a small smile.

'And even if it had been?' prompted Beth.

Hannah shook her head. 'I've never been comfortable with anyone to feel that way,' she said.

'Except Alex,' said Lily.

Hannah was about to deny it but then she realised that she couldn't deny it any longer, to herself or to her friends. So instead she nodded. 'Except Alex,' she muttered.

'So don't reject Alex just because he's a man,' Ella told her. 'Although I admit the majority of them are pretty hopeless,' she added with a grin. 'Learn from Sean and build a better more honest relationship with Alex who's a good guy.'

'Except he's already in a relationship,' Hannah reminded them. 'With Aimee.'

'Actually, that might not be true,' said Beth, frowning. 'Aimee was just telling me about her hot date tonight with some drummer from a band. Definitely not Alex.'

Hannah stared at her. 'You mean they might not be going out any more?'

'Doesn't sound like it.'

Hannah drew in a sharp breath. Could it be true? Was Alex available?

She looked out from the veranda and watched him wade out

of the water after his morning swim. Looking at his perfect body half-naked in the water, she wondered how she'd ever managed to walk away after their kiss. His body was perfect. His personality was too.

She frowned to herself. Actually, he was too perfect a gentleman. Too polite. No searing looks since. No flirting. No hint or suggestion of any impropriety at all. It was completely infuriating and she was being slowly driven crazy with desire for him.

As she contemplated how on earth she could move things forward between them, she slowly became aware that her friends had gone quiet.

She turned her head and found them all watching her with smiles on their faces.

'What?' she asked.

'Do you need to jump in the lake to cool off?' teased Ella.

'I know the perfect lifeguard to save you if you want to drown,' added Beth, with a grin.

Hannah huffed out a sigh. 'You lot are impossible, you know? Nothing's happening between us.'

'But you'd like it to,' said Lily, raising her eyebrows in question.

Hannah couldn't think up a slick enough answer, leading to a flurry of more exchanged grins.

'Oh, this is so exciting,' cooed Beth who liked to see the romance in everything.

They all glanced over to where Alex was now sitting on the paddleboard. Hannah couldn't stop herself looking at his skin glistening with drops of water and gulped.

'Yes, but you know what they say,' carried on Beth. 'Good on paper or paddleboard, bad kisser.'

'Actually, he's a great kisser,' murmured Hannah, lost in her own world of memory.

'Yes, but you were drunk that doesn't count,' Ella reminded her. 'You could have imagined he was a good kisser.'

Hannah shook her head. 'I've kissed him twice actually.'

'And you didn't tell us?' asked Lily agog.

Beth rolled her eyes. 'Yes, the first thing she should have done upon being kissed by Alex is get on the phone to us all.'

'Let her speak,' said Lily, hushing her friends.

So Hannah explained how upset he'd been on viewing the triathlon event at the Commonwealth Games and how her support had somehow ended up with them kissing.

'So now what?' asked Beth.

'I honestly don't know,' replied Hannah.

'But you want something more, don't you?' asked Lily. 'Now you know he's single.'

'He's so lovely,' she told them. 'He's kind and funny and so supportive.'

'So what's the problem?' asked Ella.

'I've kissed him twice and he hasn't said anything about it,' moaned Hannah, burying her face in her hands. 'I made a total fool of myself and he doesn't feel the same way.'

'Well, this doesn't sound like the new Hannah Jackson, does it?' said Lily. 'Be brave. You've been through so much. And who knows what you might get from all this positivity and success you've had recently?'

Hannah found herself wondering what it would be like to date someone like Alex, someone true and trustworthy. She just didn't know if he felt the same way.

But her friends were right. Maybe it was time to find out.

Because she had moved on at last, she realised. And now it was about finding the true happiness that she knew she deserved.

46

It had been another busy weekend at the water sports centre and Alex had ended up working late to get everything packed away.

He had noticed how busy the Boathouse Café had been as well and by the time they had both finished work, the sun had already set beyond the horizon.

'What a day,' Hannah told him as she switched on the dishwasher in the café kitchen. 'I don't think I've even had a chance to get any fresh air today.'

'I was just about to take Tiny around the lake to stretch his legs if you want to join us,' said Alex.

She looked delighted. 'I'd love to,' she told him. 'Let me just put these cakes away and then I'll be ready.'

As he waited outside for her, Alex was pleased that they were both still able to relax around each other. Neither of them had said anything about the kiss two nights ago. But it had been on his mind the whole time ever since.

They enjoyed a leisurely walk along the track around the lake with Tiny who enjoyed racing in and out of the water at every opportunity.

The heatwave had been building for many weeks now and the grass either side of the hardened track was parched and yellow.

'I wish we could do this every night,' said Hannah, as they walked along. 'Take the time to enjoy the extra light whilst we can.'

'You're not enjoying the cocktail evenings?' asked Alex, concerned. 'Listen, if it's too much pressure on you then I'll have a word with Ben.'

'Thanks,' she told him. 'If it was then I could certainly have a word with my big brother, don't worry.'

He smiled at her as they crossed the narrow bridge on the furthest point from the hotel.

'But what I meant was that this is nice being together,' carried on Hannah. 'I mean, just the two of us for once.'

Alex's feet faltered as he registered what she had just told him.

So he stopped to lean against the wooden railing of the bridge to look at her as Hannah came to stand next to him.

About to speak, he was interrupted by Tiny coming towards them as he raced out of the water once more.

'Don't you mean just the three of us?' asked Alex, laughing. But his laughter was short-lived as Tiny came to a halt. 'No, wait!' said Alex in a warning tone.

But it was too late. Tiny started to shake his fur free of water which covered them both in hundreds of droplets, causing them both to flinch and, in Hannah's case, shriek.

Content that he was much drier now, Tiny sauntered away to sit on the other end of the bridge and study the ducks which were paddling nearby.

Alex glanced down at his now wet shirt, still laughing. 'I seem to spend my entire day being wet,' he said.

He looked up and found Hannah looking at him with a nervous look in her eyes.

'I need to ask you something,' she said, biting her lip.

'What is it?' he asked, going up to stand in front of her. 'Are you OK?'

'I'm fine,' she replied. 'But it's personal. About you, I mean.'

'OK,' he said slowly.

She took a deep breath. 'Are you still going out with Aimee?'

Alex was startled by the unexpected question and shook his head. 'No. We just went out that one time.'

'Once?' Hannah stared at him with wide eyes.

'I mean, she's lovely but we're not very suited, as it turns out,' he carried on.

'Just *once*?' she repeated.

Alex nodded, wondering why she was asking and hoping that he knew the reason why.

To his amazement, Hannah suddenly burst out laughing. 'I don't believe this!' she said, shaking her head. 'I thought you were with her.'

'I'm not,' Alex told her, taking a step forward. 'I'm here. With you.'

And Hannah's laughter faded as she looked up at him before clearing her throat. 'Wow, this is really hard for me even though it's you,' she began. 'Right. OK. Well, I've kissed you twice now.'

Alex's mouth fell open in shock at her words and found he couldn't speak. She sounded like a whole new Hannah, assured and confident.

'And I was drunk the first time, of course,' she carried on.

He nodded.

'But then we had that second kiss two nights ago.'

He nodded again, feeling like a dummy but unable to form

any kind of words. Was this really happening at last? Or was she about to reject him?

'Listen, I think it's admirable that you've been such a gentleman with me,' she told him. 'But you've been so perfect and so nice to me,' she carried on, giving him a soft smile. 'The trouble is, well, it's not very flattering. Makes a girl think that perhaps you're not into her after all. That perhaps you wish those kisses had never happened.'

'Nothing could be further from the truth,' he said, finally finding his voice. He took a step forward to take her hands in his. 'I've waited so long to kiss you properly and then you get drunk and steal my thunder.' He reached out to stroke her face. 'And then you kiss me when I'm upset and it still isn't the right moment. But here, now, this is finally the right time to tell you that I am completely and utterly crazy about you.'

Hannah was staring up at him with her beautiful blue eyes and he still couldn't quite believe that they were finally having this conversation.

He took a shaky breath and ran a hand through his hair. 'This is ridiculous. I'm actually nervous,' he said, with a small laugh of disbelief.

Hannah grinned up at him. 'Well, that's not very good, is it? If we're both this nervous then nothing's ever going to happen between us.'

He looked at her and smiled, suddenly relaxing. It was Hannah, beautiful, kind, gentle Hannah who he knew so well.

He reached out and drew her near as he wrapped his arms around her.

'Oh, nothing is a terrible word,' he told her, pulling her close so that their bodies touched. 'We should definitely work against that.'

'We should,' she murmured, reaching up with her hands to draw them up to his chest.

He wondered if she could feel his heart thumping under his shirt. Suddenly their heads were leaning towards each other at the same time and their lips met.

It was a kiss of desire, of passion and of familiarity as well. He lost all track of time, only aware of Hannah and nothing else as he held her close at last.

Much later, when he was looking down at her pretty face in wonder, she said, 'Perhaps we should get going before anyone misses us.'

But at that moment, Tiny came over and sat on their feet, his heavy weight pushing Hannah further into Alex's arms.

He laughed. 'Good boy,' he told Tiny, before grinning at Hannah. 'Tiny has spoken. He says we should stay here for a while longer yet.'

'Thank goodness for Tiny,' she murmured as he bent down to kiss her once more.

47

The following day, Hannah found she couldn't stop smiling at everyone and everything.

Finally she had been brave and told Alex how she felt. She still couldn't believe he felt the same way, although his many kisses had begun to make her feel that perhaps he was telling the truth.

That night, when the café was closed and it was just them alone in the boathouse, they kissed once more. The stolen kisses continued over the next few weeks and she began to feel confident in her own emotions as well as his.

He wouldn't hurt her. It was Alex and the trust she felt for him meant that she could relax and be herself with him.

Of course, Lily noticed Hannah's change of mood and it wasn't too long before she received excited calls from both Beth and Ella, anxious to hear all about her new romance. Faye too had noticed the change in her daughter and would give her a knowing smile whenever she found Hannah humming to herself as she baked.

Hannah was still nervous about telling Ben, however. She

knew how protective he could be and didn't want to ruin the close friendship that he and Alex had enjoyed for so long.

'I think he'll be fine,' Alex told her one night, as he held her close. 'We should tell him tomorrow.'

'Just a little while longer,' said Hannah, stopping his protests with her kisses until they were lost in each other once more.

She felt so much confidence in their relationship, felt whole and completely and utterly safe. It was the happiest time she had ever known, both personally and also professionally as well.

As she was serving a table one morning, she realised that it was a familiar face.

'Hi,' said Molly, who Hannah recognised from her visit to the Cranbridge tea room. 'I was just saying to my friend Lucy here how amazing this place looks.'

'Thanks,' replied Hannah, smiling at them both. 'It's so kind of you to visit. And thank you once again for your advice all those weeks ago. It really helped.'

'I'm so glad,' said Molly.

'And you're obviously doing really well,' added her friend Lucy. 'We struggled to get a spare table.'

Hannah nodded. 'I'm rushed off my feet most days. Now, what would you like? It's on the house.'

'How kind,' Molly told her. She and her friend left later with the promise of returning for a cocktail the following weekend.

Slowly Hannah could feel herself transitioning into the role of hostess as well as business owner. Her smile was genuine as she rushed around. In fact, she was getting too rushed and had begun to discuss with Alex the possibility of hiring a waitress to keep on top of all the customers.

The summer would be drawing to a close soon but Ben had already renewed the contract for the café to make it a more permanent addition to Maple Tree Lodge. Hannah was aware that the busy summer days would become more quiet as the seasons changed and yet she had already begun to make plans to ensure that the business continued throughout autumn and winter as well.

'I was thinking of maybe asking some groups if they wanted to utilise the café during the week in the colder months,' she told Alex one evening as she tidied up the kitchen.

'Great idea,' he murmured, putting his arms around her as she stood next to the counter and pressed his lips against the back of her neck. 'What about book groups?'

She couldn't stop herself from leaning back into his strong arms. 'Crafting classes,' she said.

'Art classes,' he whispered, drawing his lips slowly up to nibble on her ear.

'Mmm,' she said, starting to lose her train of thought. 'You're distracting me from vital business decisions.'

'It's your fault,' he told her, gently spinning her around so that she was looking up at him. 'I can't seem to keep my hands off you.'

'And how is that my fault?' she asked, laughing as she drew his head down to hers.

He kissed her and she lost track of how long they had been standing there until they finally drew apart.

'Have dinner with me,' he murmured against her lips.

'Of course,' she replied. 'Your place or mine?'

It was a running joke between them. They would sit at the dinner table with the family, from the outside as if nothing had changed, all the while brushing their hands against each other's under the table and wishing the time away until they were alone again.

'I could always cook here one evening,' she told him.

But Alex shook his head. 'I mean, let's go out one night,' he told her, kissing her on the nose.

Her eyebrows shot up. 'Out like a date?' she asked.

'Not *like* a date,' he said, smiling down at her. 'I mean, an actual date.'

'Oh.'

'What's the problem?' he asked. 'We have dinner all the time.'

She nodded. 'We do.'

'With your family,' he added. 'This time I want it to be just you and me. And I need to talk to your brother. I want to make this official, let the whole world know. Is that OK with you?'

She loved that he respected her feelings and was so patient with her.

'So?' he prompted her. 'What do you think?'

'It feels like pressure having a date,' she confessed, biting her lip.

He drew her close so she felt safe and warm once more. 'It won't feel like pressure because you'll be with me. And I'll be with you. It's just us.'

She began to relax once more as he held her.

'And if you feel nervous, just remember that because it's a date, there'll be an awful lot of kissing going on,' he added, with a gleam in his eyes.

She laughed and reached up to kiss him once more.

And as they kissed again, she found herself thinking, what harm could one date do?

48

Alex felt as if he were riding on cloud nine.

Almost all the stars had aligned and he felt as if he were floating most of the time. Somehow, and he still couldn't work out how it had finally happened, he had ended up with Hannah in his arms at long last. They were kissing, and enjoying each other's company, and it felt as if it were a dream. He couldn't stop smiling. She cared for him and he cared for her. It felt natural and uncomplicated.

He was in serious danger of losing his heart to her and he didn't care. She wasn't Claire. She was more amazing, more beautiful, more kind, more generous in spirit. She was, in short, fast becoming the love of his life.

And yet the sadness that he still didn't have his parents' support of his new life weighed over him a little. But he knew that by taking a stand he had found happiness, not only in his personal life but in his professional life as well.

He was taking huge satisfaction from his work each day. People with no paddleboarding abilities or confidence in swimming were leaving each day stronger and more motivated towards getting fit. They were more confident in their abilities and happier too. He had seen it at close hand with the swimming club. He had so many ideas that he was buzzing as to what the future might hold. New clubs, new training and teaching opportunities all waited for him in the coming months.

But all that had to wait.

Because before he and Hannah had a future, there was one more hurdle to get across. And it was a big one.

Ben had always been her protective big brother. That much he knew from over the years. He had always declared that nobody was good enough for his little sister. So where did that leave Alex?

He decided to tell him when they were relaxed and having Jake there would help, he knew. So he waited patiently for a few weeks until Jake was able to visit them again. Then, one Sunday night when the bar was relatively quiet, he invited Ben and Jake to a game of snooker in the snug.

'I can't get over how popular that swim club has become,' said Jake, lining up the triangle of balls.

'It really is,' said Ben, chalking the end of the snooker cue before looking at Alex. 'I owe you.'

Alex found himself at a loss for words, not really concentrating on the conversation as he tried to think of how to find the words that came next.

'It's not like you to be silently modest,' said Jake, teeing off. 'Oh, no, wait, that's me.'

'Modest?' Ben laughed. 'As if.'

Alex stepped up to take his shot.

'OK. So I'm the playboy and Alex is the good guy,' said Jake.

Was he a good guy? Alex sincerely hoped so. Even so, he misjudged the ball so badly it flew off and nearly hit Frankie as she came in.

'Howzat?' she asked, catching it in one hand. 'Thought the game was snooker, not cricket.'

She placed the ball on the table and carried on to the bar.

'You OK?' asked Jake, looking at Alex with concern.

'Yeah, what's going on?' asked Ben, frowning. 'I've never seen you play so badly.'

'You're making even me look good and I'm the worst player out of the three of us,' said Jake, with a grin.

'Nothing,' said Alex quickly, deciding that honesty perhaps wasn't the best policy. Perhaps he and Hannah were best staying in a private relationship after all. But then again, he hated having secrets from his best friends.

'It's definitely something rather than nothing,' said Jake, studying him. 'I'm trying to work out your lapse of concentration with this game. Business is great. So it must be personal.'

Jake and Ben looked at him with raised eyebrows.

'I'm fine,' replied Alex automatically.

'No, you're not,' said Ben. 'Let's see if another beer helps loosen your tongue a bit. I'll get them in.'

He wandered away and up to the bar to ask Frankie for another round.

'Is it Hannah?' asked Jake softly.

Alex looked at him and nodded.

'At last,' replied Jake, with a grin. 'Is it serious?'

'The most serious relationship of my life,' Alex told him.

Jake looked delighted, however Ben returned before he had a chance to reply.

'So what did you find out?' asked Ben, looking between them. 'And who is she?'

Alex and Jake exchanged a look.

'Well, she's beautiful, lovely and incredibly gifted,' Jake told him.

'Blimey,' said Ben, amazed. 'So come on. Where did you meet this goddess?'

Alex took a deep breath. 'Right here,' he said, finally deciding to come clean.

Ben's eyebrows shot up. 'Here? Is she a guest?'

Alex found that the words wouldn't come and looked at Jake for help.

'Actually, it was just after we'd graduated,' Jake told Ben. 'When he and I first visited Maple Tree Lodge.'

Ben was still looking confused. 'But that was years ago!'

Jake took a deep breath. 'True. But that was also the first time that he met your sister.'

His words rang out in the almost empty bar. Ben stared across at Alex in wide-eyed shock.

There was a short silence before anyone spoke.

'You know, I haven't caught up with Frankie for a long time and I suddenly feel like that's long overdue,' said Jake, before excusing himself.

Alone by the snooker table, Ben looked down and took his shot which bounced off the side and slid into the pocket. Meanwhile Alex stood nearby and waited for whatever came next. He just hoped it wasn't the end of their friendship.

'How long has it been going on?' asked Ben.

'We've been together about three weeks,' Alex told him. 'I've asked her out on a proper date but I didn't want to keep it from you. Neither of us did.'

'And she's happy?' asked Ben.

'I think so,' replied Alex, before nodding. 'Yes. She is.'

'And you?'

'Ecstatic,' Alex told him. 'I've been in love with her for a very long time. Not that she knew anything about that.'

Ben looked at him. 'Neither did I,' he said, frowning.

'There was never the right time and besides, I didn't think she felt the same way,' said Alex.

'But she does?' asked Ben, looking concerned.

'I hope so.' Alex attempted a smile but could feel the nerves spread across his face as he tried. 'At least, that's what she tells me.'

'You're my best friend and I trust you,' said Ben. 'But hurt her and...'

'I would never do that,' Alex told him fiercely. 'You have to believe me.'

'Oh, I do,' said Ben, breaking into a grin. 'I was just teasing you. You've got to give me something as the protective older brother here.'

Alex puffed out a sigh of relief just as Jake returned.

'So, is it pistols at dawn, or do I need to choose one of you in the divorce?' he asked.

'Neither,' said Ben. 'Unlike you, Alex is the perfect gentleman where women are concerned.'

Jake shook his head. 'I don't see how he can be so perfect when he's had so little experience with women compared to me,' he said.

'My point exactly,' said Ben.

Alex felt relieved and grateful to have Ben's blessing in what was beginning to feel like the most important relationship of his life. Finally he could relax and make it official by taking Hannah out on their very first date.

49

Hannah had spent the whole day in a bit of a muddled mess. She was equally nervous and yet excited about her date with Alex later on.

'Where are you taking me?' she asked him when he popped in for a coffee later in the morning.

But he shook his head in reply. 'It's a secret. But as it's our first date, it's also got to be special.' He finished his coffee and stood up. 'Anyway, I'll see you later when I pick you up at four.'

Hannah was shocked. 'Four o'clock in the afternoon?' she asked, with a shocked laugh. 'What kind of a date is it?'

He smiled at her. 'A special one. I'll see you then.'

'Wait, what about the café?' she asked. 'We don't shut until five o'clock today.'

He winked at her. 'It's all in hand,' he told her with a mysterious smile before he left.

Hannah was then rushed off her feet for the remainder of the day until at half past three, Lily and Faye arrived.

'What are you doing here?' asked Hannah.

'Taking over so that you can enjoy your hot date,' said Lily, with a grin. 'So quickly show us the ropes and then get out of here,' she added.

Once the temporary staff had their orders, Faye gave her a daughter a huge hug and told her to enjoy herself.

Hannah then headed back to the lodge to quickly shower and get changed. Not knowing where they were going, she decided on a knee-length skirt, T-shirt, small cardigan and wedge heels. Hopefully it was just the right amount of smart and casual to cover whatever situation and setting she would find herself in.

When she headed downstairs at five minutes to four, she found Ben at the reception desk. He looked her up and down and told her, 'You look nice.'

'Thanks,' she said.

They actually hadn't spoken at all about her dating Alex and she glanced at him nervously.

'For the record, I approve,' said her big brother.

Hannah found herself smiling. 'For the record, I don't need your approval,' she replied before reaching over to give him a kiss on the cheek. 'But I'm happy to have it all the same, thanks, bro.'

Ben shot her a grin just as Alex appeared in the entrance hall.

'You kids have fun,' she heard Ben joke as they walked out of the hotel together.

'So where are we going?' asked Hannah once Alex was driving her through the forest and out to the main road.

It was a glorious summer's afternoon and she wound down the window to let in the warm air.

'We're going to the Willow Tree Hall summer fete,' he told her.

'Oh, how lovely,' said Hannah, in delight. 'I went to one a couple of years ago, after it was renovated. What a great idea.'

He smiled. 'Good. I'm glad you approve.'

Hannah found herself relaxing. Willow Tree Hall was a

stately home on the other side of the village of Cranley. In recent years, they had resurrected the annual summer fete and she had completely forgotten that it was being held that day.

Thankfully the weather was glorious and it was the perfect day for an English summer fete.

She directed Alex the right way and soon they were turning into a long driveway. Flanked by fields either side, in the distance was Willow Tree Hall. It was only two storeys high but stretched wide instead. She had always thought it looked like a miniature version of Buckingham Palace. Large sash windows spread evenly across the pale brick front. The centrepiece was a huge red double front door, framed by tall pillars of the same warm-coloured stone.

On the left-hand side, in one of the large fields that lay in front of the great house, was the setting for the fete.

Surrounding the large willow tree from which the hall had received its name were a number of small marquees and gazebos covered in pretty pastel-coloured bunting and a huge crowd of people. As they parked the car in an opposite field and got out, all Hannah could hear was conversation and laughter.

'This was a great idea,' she said, as they began to walk towards the entrance gate to pay their fee to go in.

'Glad you think so,' replied Alex.

She gave a start as she felt his hand slip into hers. For a second, she almost pulled away in a panic, but then she remembered that it was Alex and relaxed once more, giving his hand a squeeze.

They paid the small entrance fee and then wandered around the many stalls, enjoying the convivial atmosphere.

As she noticed a number of families enjoying a picnic in the shade of some nearby oak trees, Hannah groaned.

'I should have brought a picnic,' she complained.

But Alex shook his head. 'As much as I love your baking,' he told her, 'there's no cooking for you tonight. This is downtime. Our chance to relax.'

She smiled up at him. 'OK,' she replied. 'But I'll buy the ice creams.'

'Deal,' he said, drawing his arm around her.

Relishing the feel of his strong arm against her back, she leaned into him. She felt so relaxed and confident around Alex that she realised that there had been no need for nerves after all. With him she could just be herself.

'This is the perfect date,' she told him, leaning her head on his shoulder. 'Thank you.'

'It's perfect because I'm here with you,' he replied, dropping a kiss on her top of her head.

As they carried on walking across the grass, Hannah realised that over the course of the long hot summer, she had begun to fall in love with Alex. And where before that thought would have horrified her, now it only brought her the deepest joy as to what the future might hold for them both.

She couldn't wait to find out.

50

Alex was delighted that Hannah was enjoying their first date.

He had racked his brains to try and think of somewhere where she might feel at home and when Faye had suggested the fete, he thought that it would be a relaxed enough setting.

He knew she hadn't dated much and perhaps might even be nervous. So they needed to do something fun and the fete fitted the bill perfectly. Even so, he had felt a little nervous when he had picked her up in the entrance hall, despite Ben's mock-stern grin at him.

But now that it was just the two of them walking hand in hand amongst the stalls and small arena, he couldn't imagine taking her anywhere else for their first date.

The huge front lawn was filled with people from every walk of life in the village. Everyone was either walking around like themselves, chatting, or lounging on picnic rugs.

There were plenty of stalls catering for children where they could enjoy having their faces painted or trying their luck at a raffle. The main arena hosted a number of competitions including tug of war, croquet, as well as a dog show where a dog named Dylan had just won Most Waggy Tail.

When they began to get hungry, Hannah led Alex over to the main stalls where home-made produce was piled high on checked tablecloths fluttering in a gentle breeze. There was so much choice but they eventually decided on a couple of glasses of Pimm's, as well as a large quiche and side dishes such as a bowl of olives and a fresh baguette.

They took their goodies and sat down on the grass under the shade of a tree, enjoying the atmosphere.

'This is delicious,' said Hannah, looking down at her quiche. 'I haven't thought of using chorizo. I must remember this flavour.'

Alex was pleased to see her buzzing with ideas for future bakes, full of renewed faith in her abilities compared to the Hannah that he had always known. She had grown in confidence over the summer and he was pleased for her.

They had just finished a delicious elderflower ice cream when a glamorous-looking lady wandered over to where they lay.

'Hannah? Is that you?' she asked, in a very aristocratic tone of voice.

'Rose!' said Hannah, leaping up, to give her a hug. 'How lovely to see you.'

'I'm so glad you came to our little shindig,' said Rose, turning to look at Alex as he stood up to greet the elderly lady. 'My word. What a handsome fella you've found yourself.'

Hannah smiled. 'Alex, this is Rose Harris. She's the Earl of Cranley's sister.'

'Younger sister,' said Rose, with a wicked grin. 'Much younger, in fact.'

Alex had a feeling that Rose was a whole bundle of both fun and trouble.

Rose turned to look at Hannah. 'Your Boathouse Café sounds

marvellous, sweetheart. I will swing by soon, I promise. And Dotty has been telling me all about her swimming club,' she said. 'Such fun. I must come and see it in action.'

'Alex is the lifeguard and he runs the swimming club too,' said Hannah, with a proud tone in her voice which made Alex smile.

'Is he?' Rose ran a studied eye up and down Alex which almost made him blush. 'Look at all those muscles! You're worth almost drowning for.'

Alex laughed. 'As long as it's only "almost",' he replied.

'Please forgive my aunt,' said a dark-haired man coming to stand next to Rose. 'I hope you're not easily embarrassed. I'm Sam Harris.'

Alex remembered the name as Faye had told him that Sam was the future Earl of Cranley and had taken over the daily running of the stately home.

'I'm always on the naughty step,' said Rose, with a giggle. 'Now, you must have some champagne, darlings. Not Annie, of course. Did you hear the news? Baby number two is on the way for our future countess.'

'Oh, congratulations,' said Hannah, in a delighted tone.

'Thanks,' said Sam. 'We're delighted to be getting a little brother or sister for Eddie. I hope you're both able to stay for the evening entertainment. There'll be live music later.'

'Toodle-oo, darlings,' said Rose, blowing Hannah a kiss before Sam took her by the arm and led her away.

'That Rose! What a character,' said Alex.

'Oh, you don't know the half of it,' said Hannah, laughing as they settled back onto the ground.

They chatted for a while about the Harris family before Alex became aware that the afternoon was slowly turning into early evening as the sun had begun to sink below the horizon of trees surrounding the estate.

'So what do you think?' he asked. 'Would you like to stay here for the evening or go on somewhere else?'

'I'd like to stay, if that's OK,' she replied.

Alex was pleased, also in no rush to leave the beautiful surroundings and break the magical spell of the date so far.

As dusk arrived, the tree above them as well as many others were suddenly lit up with fairy lights. Tea lights and candles in jam jars were lit everywhere else and the whole setting began to turn even more dreamy under the soft lighting in the semi-darkness.

A makeshift stage had been set up nearby and later on, Arthur, the Earl of Cranley, stood up to announce how much money they had raised for a local stroke charity. A huge cheer went up at the large amount of money, followed by an even louder cheer as Tommy Starr came onto the stage.

Tommy was a global superstar in his own right, a hugely popular singer-songwriter who had taken a step back in recent years when he had got engaged and started a family. He now lived in the old forge in Cranley but had close connections to Willow Tree Hall, apparently.

Tommy sang many of his most popular songs by himself, just him and his guitar, and it gave the whole evening an even more laid-back feel.

It couldn't have felt more romantic, thought Alex. And then Hannah leant her head on his shoulder and snuggled in closer to him and his heart leapt. He put his arm around her and couldn't stop himself from kissing her on the lips.

After a long time, she drew her head back slightly to look up at him with a soft smile. 'This has been the most wonderful first date,' she murmured.

'Good,' he replied.

'I can't seem to stop myself from kissing you,' she told him.

'Well, don't think that I'm going to stop you,' he said, his eyes gleaming.

He wanted to tell how he was falling in love with her. How much she meant to him. And yet, as she brought him closer for another kiss, the words were lost on his lips. Soon, he told himself, before he lost all coherent thought. Soon he would tell her just how much he loved her.

But for now, he was happy to lose himself in her delicious kisses.

51

With the beginning of September heralding the end of the summer season, it had been decided to celebrate the end of the long lighter days with another triathlon.

'As the first one didn't pan out quite as expected,' Ben had said to Alex, with a wink.

Alex found that he was happy to organise it and felt the most relaxed he had ever been before a competition as he held on to his stopwatch by the starting line.

Perhaps because he wasn't actually competing. He felt a small pang as he watched the competitors lining up but it soon disappeared. He was so much more relaxed away from the circuit of training and competing, he realised.

He glanced over to the Boathouse Café where the veranda was already packed with people watching from the vantage point.

Hannah was the main reason that he was happy, he knew. Their date had been special, wonderful and the kisses they had shared had been the icing on the cake as far as he was concerned.

The family had all given their approval and life was good. The best it had ever been, in fact.

He shook his head, trying to dismiss her sweet lips from his mind and tried to concentrate on the matter in hand.

But as he looked across the crowds standing on the path around the lake, as well as in front of the hotel, two very familiar faces stood out to him.

'I'll be back in a minute,' he told Ben, walking quickly over to where his parents were standing.

'Hi,' he said, standing in front of them, feeling a little nervous.

He and his mum moved at the same time for a kiss and hug.

As he stepped back, Alex and his dad exchanged an awkward nod.

'What are you both doing here?' he asked.

His mum looked from her husband to her son before rolling her eyes, seemingly at them both. After all, they hadn't seen or spoken to each other for four months. It felt like a lifetime for Alex.

'We wanted to come and see you,' said his mum. 'So we booked a night at the hotel. Or rather *I* booked us a night here. I must say, we've only just arrived but it's the most delightful place. The receptionist told us all about the charity run and I thought you must be involved somehow.'

Alex nodded. 'I organised it,' he told her. 'The idea came from one of my regulars at the swimming club.' He glanced at his watch. 'I'm sorry but I'm needed at the start line.'

'Of course,' said his mum, reaching out to squeeze his arm. 'We'll still be here when you're finished, won't we, Tom?'

Alex looked at his dad, who nodded silently before looking away once more.

Alex gave his mum a small smile before dashing back to the start line.

The race went smoothly with no lifesaving heroics needed from either Alex or Tiny, he was grateful to see. Once the winners' medals had been handed out and the photographs had been taken, Alex looked around to try and find his parents.

'They've gone to the boathouse for a drink,' said Jake, standing nearby, as he cooked up a storm on the barbeque for all the visitors.

Alex nodded and, feeling nervous once more, set off towards the café.

The café was packed and he had trouble getting through, such was the number of people who were greeting him. He realised that he had become a local without realising it and was part of a community now.

Finally he made his way through the crowd to the kitchen.

'They're on the veranda,' Hannah told him, coming around holding a tray of drinks. But that didn't stop her from reaching up to give him a kiss on his cheek. 'Go on. You'll be fine,' she added.

Despite his nerves, he couldn't be anything but proud of how much stronger she sounded. At that moment, he was grateful for her newfound strength, worried about the conversation about to take place.

He found his parents on the veranda, sharing a pot of tea and two plates of Hannah's cakes. He grabbed the last spare chair from a nearby table and sat down.

As if by magic, Hannah placed his favourite cold drink, a strawberry iced tea, and carrot cake in front of him before disappearing once more. But not before he felt her gently squeeze his shoulder.

'These cakes are delicious,' said his mum, glancing at Hannah as she headed away. Alex was certain that she had spotted Hannah's hand on his shoulder. 'Does Hannah make them all herself?'

Alex nodded. 'She's done so well.'

'It certainly seems to be the case. This place is very popular,' replied his mum, glancing around. 'And she's Ben's younger sister, I understand.'

'You've met him too?' he asked.

'At last, after all these years. In fact, we've met all the family,' said his mum, with a smile. 'I must say, it's a lovely place. The hotel is charming and our room looks amazing.' She looked out across the lake. 'What a beautiful setting. I can see why you'd want to stay here for the summer.'

Alex glanced across at his dad, who had stayed silent until that time.

But after receiving a stern glance from his wife, he cleared his throat and finally spoke. 'The race went well,' he said. 'Close finish.'

Alex nodded. 'They're pretty competitive when it comes to a small trophy,' he said, with a grin. 'But they've raised hundreds for a local charity today, which is good.'

'And these are people that you've been teaching to swim apparently,' said his dad.

'Ben's mother told us all about the swimming club,' added his mum.

Alex went on to tell them about the various clubs and even found himself relaxing enough to laugh about his paddle-boarding failure in the early days. Perhaps they could get through this first meeting after all, he thought.

During the conversation, Tiny headed over to slump next to his feet.

'And who's this?' asked his mum.

'He's my dog,' replied Alex. 'He was a stray but I'm adopting him, officially. He's one of my fellow lifeguards out here on the lake.'

He reached down to stroke the enormous head of Tiny.

'So you're staying here.' It was a statement from his dad, not a question, Alex realised.

He nodded. 'Yes. I am,' he replied. 'I like being part of something bigger than competitions. I like being part of a team, of a community. I've helped people that have been widowed, scared, depressed, all of which a small swimming club in the middle of nowhere has been able to help them face up to another day.'

'We were told earlier that you saved someone's life,' said his dad.

Alex raised his eyebrows and guessed that it must have been Hannah. 'It sounds more dramatic than it actually was,' he replied, with a shrug of his shoulders. 'Besides, Tiny here did most of the saving.'

'Tiny?' His parents both laughed.

Alex smiled, grateful to see their faces light up in amusement and break the awkward atmosphere. 'Yeah, I know,' he told them. 'Not my choice of name. But he's a good boy.'

Tiny looked up expectantly at the familiar words and was given a small piece of carrot cake which he looked extremely pleased about as he settled back down under the table.

His mum excused herself to pop to the bathroom, leaving Alex alone with his dad. He found himself nervous once more but forced himself to speak into the silence that had suddenly appeared.

'How are you?' he asked.

His dad turned to look at him. 'Busy. I've joined a golf club and I've also been enjoying the garden this summer. I've grown some vegetables, which I've never had time to do before now. Your mother's pleased. We've had a couple of lunches out and I've taken some time to just sit and literally watch the flowers, or rather the tomatoes, grow.'

Alex raised his eyebrows in surprise but couldn't think what to say in reply.

His dad studied his son. 'I understand it now,' he carried on. 'The pressure that I put on both of us. How unhealthy it had become.' He hesitated before going on. 'I'm proud of you. I never said that before and I reckon it's long overdue. I'm proud of what you accomplished competing but also of what you've achieved here. You're encouraging people to try out new things, help them, using exercise and fresh air. Nothing better, I reckon. This is a good thing you've done, son.'

'Thank you,' said Alex, feeling grateful and touched by his father's unexpected words. 'But I'm also so proud of all *we* achieved, Dad. All those medals. All those competitions.'

His dad grinned. 'We were formidable, weren't we, son?'

Alex nodded. 'We were. Hopefully we still are!'

'I reckon so.'

His mum returned to the table and looked surprised to see her husband and son smiling at each other.

'Is everything OK?' she asked, sitting down.

His dad looked at Alex. 'Of course it is,' he said. 'Never better.'

She smiled. 'So does this mean we can have some more delicious cake?' she asked.

Alex nodded. 'Absolutely,' he replied. 'Let me find Hannah. I want you to meet her properly.' He hesitated before carrying on. 'She's someone very important to me.'

'I'm not surprised,' said his dad. 'She's quite formidable.'

Alex was amazed. 'Formidable? Hannah?'

He thought of her kindness, her goodness and her inner strength but formidable was something entirely new.

'She gave me a right ticking off when I came to see you after the race,' said his dad, looking a little sheepish.

Alex was goggle-eyed. 'She did?'

His dad nodded. 'She got very cross with me about how I'd treated you.'

Something deep inside of Alex melted at the thought of Hannah defending him.

'She's got spirit. I like that,' carried on his dad.

'Then perhaps we could have a drink with Hannah later when she's not so busy,' said his mum.

'We'll make the time,' said Alex, standing up. 'I'll get you some more tea and cake.'

As he headed back across the café, he stopped and chatted to a couple of the swimmers whom he knew. He was starting to become a local and he was enjoying being part of a community. He had roots at Maple Tree Lodge and Cranley, the village beyond.

Now that the relationship with his parents was beginning to mend, he wondered whether it was a home he could live in forever. Hopefully with Hannah by his side.

52

After the triathlon, Hannah had been thrilled to be properly introduced to Alex's parents. It felt like another piece in their relationship and she was so pleased that he was getting along with his dad, knowing how much of a family man he was.

All in all, everything was perfect. Apart from one awful thing.

Hannah had received another text from Sean using a different number again. It had arrived just as she had been falling asleep the previous night and suddenly the old feelings of inadequacy appeared and she had lain awake all night terrified. What if she mucked everything up? What if she couldn't do this and upset Alex just like she used to upset Sean? What if it all went wrong and she lost him?

The following morning, she could feel herself beginning to hold Alex at arm's length, the old fears rushing in from out of nowhere. It was no good. Maybe Sean would be the first and only one ever to put up with her. Nobody else would. Perhaps Alex would grow bored of her. What did he even see in her anyway? He was special and gifted and bright and she was none of those things.

She was so on edge that she couldn't even concentrate on her baking the following morning.

Alex came rushing down the stairs at the sound of the smoke alarm. Hannah stared down at the burnt scones that she had just taken out of the oven whilst he switched off the alarm.

Having opened the doors to let out the acrid smell, Alex walked back across the floor to stand in front of her.

'OK,' he said. 'What's going on?'

She took off her oven mitts. 'Nothing,' she told him quickly.

'Honey, you're so tense you can't even bake,' he said.

She gulped. She hated that she couldn't talk to him. Hated to keep secrets from him.

'Are you stressed?' he asked.

She nodded, unable to speak.

'What about?' he asked.

She shook her head as he drew her close, not daring herself to speak. How could she even begin to tell him everything?

'Right. Well, for a start, what can we do to make things better?' He looked down at her. 'What do you normally do when you're stressed?'

She couldn't stop herself from smiling at the irony. 'I bake.'

'Oh.'

He drew her back into a hug and she leant against him. He was so good. So reliable. She willed herself to find the strength to tell him what was going on.

He stepped back to look down at her. 'You can always trust me,' he told her.

She nodded. 'I know.'

'I love you.'

She stared up at him in wonder. It had been the words she had been longing to hear for so very long. And she felt bolted to the floor in stiff agony. She couldn't think about any of it, about love, about any kind of future with Alex. Not until she had dealt with the issue of Sean.

Suddenly aware of the long silence, she realised that she had to say something.

'Thank you,' she finally blurted out.

It was all she could think of to say and he raised his eyebrows at her in surprise. 'OK,' he said slowly.

At that moment, the door opened and they both stepped backwards.

She looked at Alex in despair. She could feel him beginning to pull away from her emotionally. After all, he had his own heart to protect.

Wanting to talk to him more, she glanced over to see who had come into the café and whether she could turn them away.

To her shock, Sean was standing in the doorway.

'Hey, babe, I thought you would be in here,' he said, in a pleasant tone.

His eyes flickered over Alex as he stepped away from Hannah, looking at her with hurt in his eyes.

Hannah stared in amazement at Sean. It had been ten years since she had last seen him but her stomach suddenly knotted in tension just like it had done whenever she was around him all that time ago.

She didn't know what to do, but in the end, she blurted out, 'Sean, this is my, er, friend, Alex.'

'Hi,' said Sean, all smiles and charm as he came over to shake Alex's hand.

Alex scowled down at him and took Sean's hand in his, giving it such a firm grip that she saw Sean wince.

'Well, this is quite a place,' said Sean. 'Are you going to give me the tour as I've heard so much about it?'

Despite registering how easy it was for him to lie, Hannah

still couldn't quite believe that Sean was here after all these years. She drew a deep breath, making a swift decision. She didn't want Sean to know about Alex. She didn't want him anywhere near Alex. He was too good for Sean. It was too precious a relationship for Sean to ruin with his toxicity.

Above all, she wanted to protect Alex, so she said, 'I'll see you later. OK?' to him, in a dismissive tone. Then she turned to Sean and added, 'Come and see the view outside.'

But as she walked out of the boathouse, she couldn't stop herself from checking on Alex over her shoulder. His face registered the shock that she was walking away from him. His eyes were full of hurt and she almost ran to him to reassure him that it would all be OK. That she still cared deeply for him.

But she had to deal with Sean first. She just hoped she didn't lose Alex in the meantime.

53

Alex stood on his own in the Boathouse Café and felt as if he was in shock. He couldn't believe it. Had Hannah been cheating on him all this time with Sean? Did he mean nothing to her? Perhaps not. Perhaps she had never felt the same way as he did.

But her kisses had been real, hadn't they? He was so confused and hurt. And if she didn't love him after all, then that was it. He would have to leave. He loved both her and Maple Tree Lodge but they were so entwined and it was her home that he had to be the one to go.

Not that anywhere would feel like home again. No woman would ever make him feel the way she did.

He was so deep in both thought and misery that he didn't hear Ben and Jake come into the café until they were almost upon him.

Anxious to leave, he went to side-step his friends. He didn't even want to talk to them at that moment. But Ben stood in his way and didn't budge.

'What's the matter?' he asked sharply. 'You look upset.'

'Is it your folks?' asked Jake. 'I thought you were getting on alright with them.'

Alex shook his head. 'Sean has returned.'

His words came out at a croak, hoarse with emotion.

Ben and Jake looked shocked.

'What? Why?' asked Jake.

'I have no idea,' said Alex, feeling as if he had been run over. He was all out of emotion – rage or jealousy were so far removed from the numbness he was currently feeling. 'I think they've been texting each other.'

'I'll kill him,' said Jake, scowling.

Alex shook his head. 'It doesn't matter if it's who she wants.'

'OK, I'm confused,' said Ben, running a hand through his hair. 'Talk me through it and quickly.'

'One minute I was telling her that I love her,' mumbled Alex. 'The next, he came in. She didn't seem shocked to see him.'

'You love her?' asked Ben.

Alex nodded.

'Oh, mate, that's amazing,' said Jake, before he frowned. 'Wait a minute, if you do love her, then what are you doing in here on your own? Why aren't you with Hannah?'

'She went outside with Sean,' Alex told them, shrugging his shoulders. 'I don't know. Maybe I just imagined the whole thing. The whole damn relationship. I've got to go and think.'

He turned around and walked out of the boathouse. Away from his friends, away from Hannah and the place where they had been so happy. His feet moved and he had no idea where he was going. He just hoped his heart didn't hurt as much when he got there.

54

Hannah walked along the jetty with Sean and checked that they were alone before she turned to look at him.

'What are you doing here?' she asked.

'Didn't you get my texts?' he asked.

'I blocked your number,' she told him.

'Thought you were a bit quiet,' he said, smiling. As if he wasn't listening to a word she was saying. 'Then it was the funniest thing. I googled your name, to see if you showed up anywhere on social media and this place came up. People raving about your cakes. And what a great baker you are. That was news to me, of course so I figured I'd come here and see for myself.'

She stared at him, barely registering his words. How had she never seen how small he looked? His greasy skin? His crumpled clothes. He was a stark contrast to Alex who was always brimming with good health.

She took a deep breath. 'I don't want you here,' she told him.

He just smiled at her. 'That doesn't matter. I've decided that I want you back. That we should be together again. You're a success apparently, although not as large as mine back in

London, of course. So perhaps you're good enough for me after all.'

'I said that I don't want you here,' said Hannah, hearing how shaky her voice was. 'I don't want you full stop.'

'Don't be ridiculous,' snapped Sean. 'I've told you that I want you. You're coming home with me.'

'You never listen to me,' she said, becoming annoyed and glaring at him. 'You don't care about me. You never did. It was always about what *you* wanted. What *you* needed. What about me? Where do I fit in? You just kept me around to make you feel bigger and to keep me feeling small and worthless.'

'Aren't you?' he asked, with a smug smile.

'No!' she shouted at him, beginning to feel angry. 'I'm not worthless! I'm strong, talented, and people love me. You're done frightening me!'

Why had she never seen before how weak he looked? Compared to Alex, Sean was a tiny man-child and he made her skin crawl.

Sean's smooth smile dropped into a familiar scowl. He walked up to her, his eyes glaring at her with barely controlled temper.

In the past Hannah would have cowered from him. But not any more. Somewhere along the years he had lost his power over her, she suddenly realised.

'Now listen,' he hissed. 'You're coming with me.'

Then he made the mistake of taking her arm in a firm grip. She recoiled briefly before recalling the self-defence training that Aimee had taught her. In a swift move, she took his arm and quickly pinned him to the ground, face down. Then she sat on top of him and twisted his arm behind his back.

She felt Sean trying to wrestle himself out from under her but she was too strong for him. All that paddleboarding and baking, she figured, had made her arms strong and firm.

'Now listen up,' she told him as he lay beneath her, half his face hidden by the deck. 'You're nothing, do you hear me? You were and still are a horrible bully, but you no longer have any power over me. We were done a long time ago. You know it and so do I.'

Sean mumbled something but she cut him off.

'If you ever, ever come back again, I'll break your arm in half, do you hear me?' she found herself shouting at him.

'And then I'll break the rest of your bones.'

She looked up to see who had spoken. It was her brother. Ben and Jake were both racing up the jetty towards them with Tiny trotting alongside.

'Are you OK?' asked Jake, his voice filled with concern as they stood next to her.

Hannah nodded.

'Let me at him,' snarled Ben, scowling down at the prone figure beneath her.

Hannah shook her head, feeling stronger than she had ever done before in her life. 'I've got this,' she told them, leaping off Sean.

He quickly stood up, brushing himself down before glaring at her.

'One day, when you're alone...' he began, his top lip curling in anger as he pointed his finger at her.

But this time Hannah felt nothing but strength. 'If you ever find me alone, I will do exactly what I just did all over again,' she said, walking towards him. Sean began to back away, looking a little afraid. 'Because you're nothing but small and weak. You're not a real man.'

Not like Alex, she thought. He was the strong one. A good listener, someone to lean on, someone to laugh with. Gentle, kind. And seriously hot too.

'I'm not afraid of you any more,' she carried on, feeling the strength surging through her veins.

Sean was looking a little unsure of the situation he had found himself in, although he still took a tentative step forward towards her. But Hannah knew better now and stood her ground. He was trying to threaten her but she no longer feared him. She would never fear him ever again.

However Tiny definitely felt some kind of threat towards Hannah and stepped in front of her to bark a loud and very deep woof.

Shocked, Sean staggered backwards in fear of the large dog and fell back over the edge of the jetty and into the water.

There was a loud splash beneath them and they all rushed to look over the edge to where Sean was flailing around in the lake.

'Can he swim?' asked Ben.

'I don't know. I think so,' said Hannah, not caring either way.

'Shame,' said Jake, picking up a lifebuoy and throwing it over the side next to Sean, who took it gratefully before they all turned away from him.

Hannah felt nothing but relief in that moment. She didn't care for Sean. Had she ever? Was he just the wrong person at the wrong time?

Suddenly the adrenaline wore off and she sagged against her brother.

'Are you OK?' asked Ben, holding her up. 'Did he hurt you?'

'I'm fine,' she replied. 'He didn't touch me. I'm just a little light-headed, I guess.'

'You were incredible,' said Jake, giving her hair an affectionate rub.

'I know, right?' said Ben in amazement. 'My baby sister just turned into Wonder Woman and I can't believe it.'

Jake laughed. 'Yeah and we normally leave all the superhero stuff to Alex.'

'Alex!' she gasped. Hannah took a swift intake of breath at the memory of his hurt expression.

He had told her that he loved her and she hadn't said anything. What must he think of her?

'Do you love him?' asked Ben.

She nodded. 'Yes, I love him! I love him so much!'

'Have you told him?' asked Jake, looking concerned.

She shook her head.

'He's not Sean,' Ben told her, taking her by the arms and looking into her eyes. 'He's a truly good guy.'

'I know,' replied Hannah. 'I trust him, body and soul.'

As she spoke out loud, she realised that it was true. She'd trusted Alex with so many things that she'd never told anyone. And yet she had held back regarding her relationship with Sean. But now she knew that she could rely on him completely. He would never judge her or hurt her.

He was the love of her life. She knew that now. She just had to make him trust her in return. She just hoped it wasn't too late.

'Where is he?' she asked, beginning to feel anxious.

Ben glanced across the water, scouring the edge with his eyes. 'Over there,' he told her, pointing to the other side of the lake.

Hannah took one last glance at Sean, as he floundered back to shore nearby before dismissing him from her mind. She no longer cared about him or what he thought of her.

Finally she was ready to move on with someone a million times better.

Then she rushed off the jetty and went to find Alex. She needed to tell him the truth about how she felt and she was desperately hoping that he would still want to listen to her.

55

It wasn't until she was rushing out onto the lakeside track that Hannah realised that Tiny was running alongside her.

'Find him, Tiny,' she said to the dog, picking up speed. 'Find Alex.'

Her mind ran with the possibility that he thought she had rejected him. That he didn't think that she loved him when it was the complete opposite. What if he had given up on her already?

Tiny raced ahead of her, barking as he went. She hoped it was a good sign as she hurtled around a corner and, to her relief, found Alex standing on one of the small bridges, looking out across the lake.

Tiny barked in joy at seeing his master and ran up to Alex in a joyful mood.

Hannah found her steps faltering as she reached him and crashed to a halt. She realised it was the bridge where they had shared their first kiss. The first time she had told him how she truly felt about him.

'Hey,' she said, almost out of breath. 'I'm so glad we found you.'

He nodded but didn't reply, merely looking out across the lake.

She took a deep breath, still trying to reduce her rapid pulse and then went onto the bridge to stand next to him.

She looked out across the lake, just in time to see Sean stagger out of the water before being frogmarched off the beach by Ben and Jake. They led him around the hotel and presumably to the car park before disappearing out of sight. Good riddance, thought Hannah. She would never see him again.

'So he's back.'

It was the first time Alex had spoken and she turned to look at him.

'Briefly,' she replied, deciding it was time to tell him the complete truth. 'He sent me a couple of texts over the years and each time I blocked the number, hoping it was the last time. Yesterday he got back in touch after a long time. I had no idea that he would track me down here.' She exhaled a long breath. 'He's a bully. He's always been a bully, even when we were together. But he doesn't frighten me any more.'

Alex immediately looked concerned. 'He frightened you?' he asked, his eyes running over her. 'Did he hurt you?'

'Not today but in the past, yes, he did,' she confessed, with a sigh. 'He destroyed what little self-confidence I had, making me feel small and worthless. That was bad enough until one evening he shoved me to the floor. That was when I walked out for good on our relationship and came home.' She looked up at Alex. 'I should have told you the truth about him before now but I wanted him to stay in the past where he belongs.'

'I'll kill him for hurting you,' he said, his eyes narrowing.

She held up her hand. 'He won't get that opportunity. Not any more. When we went outside, he began to threaten me so I threw him to the floor.'

Alex looked at her in open-mouthed astonishment.

'It turns out that Aimee is a really good self-defence teacher,' carried on Hannah with a grin. 'Seriously. We need to hold some regular classes.'

Alex ran a hand through his hair, looking confused. 'You threw him to the floor?' he asked. 'And then you threw him in the lake?'

She laughed. 'No, that was Tiny. Turns out his bark really is worse than his bite.'

Alex let out a shaky breath. 'I should have been there,' he said, frowning. 'I shouldn't have let you leave with him.'

Hannah reached out and took his hand in hers. 'You were there every other time I needed you,' she told him. 'When I needed confidence and had none. When I needed support and your friendship too. You gave me strength that I never knew I had.'

She could still feel him holding back. Still not sure of her feelings towards him when he had declared his so openly.

So she took his other hand in hers and held them tight. 'And I need you now,' she carried on. 'I want you in my life every single day for now and always. I need your big, generous heart. Those oh-so sexy muscles. And your love. Most of all your love. I want it all.' She took a shaky breath, suddenly nervous that he might not forgive her. 'If you'll have me.'

'If I'll have you?' His voice trailed off as he looked at her in disbelief.

'I love you,' she told him. 'I love you so very much. I'll make sure I tell you how much I love you each and every day until you believe me. I know I hurt you by not telling you that earlier and I'm truly sorry. I'll spend forever trying not to hurt you again, I promise.'

'Don't apologise,' he told her, pulling her close with a groan.

He wrapped his strong arms around her and looked down at her, his face almost touching hers. 'I should have given you more space. My timing was way off.'

'No, it wasn't,' she said, reaching up to stroke his face. 'Can we start over again, please?'

He nodded. 'I love you.'

'And I love you,' she told him.

'You're the love of my life,' he said. 'I knew from the first moment I ever saw you that there would never be anyone else for me. I promise to never make you feel anything other than the wonderful, beautiful and talented woman that you are. I promise to be your biggest fan each and every day. I will be there for you today and always.' He took her cheek in his large hand and smiled down at her. 'Every day these past few weeks has felt like a dream come true just being able to take you in my arms and kiss you.'

'Then let's not stop now,' she murmured.

They both moved into the kiss at the same time and it was as sweet, perhaps even more so, as all the other kisses they had ever shared. Because this time Hannah knew that it was forever and that nothing would keep them apart ever again.

56

Alex watched as a couple of golden leaves fluttered onto the surface of the lake.

Despite the sun shining down on him, all around the signs of autumn were beginning to appear.

It had been an incredible summer, he thought, looking out at the swimmers making their way around the lake in front of him at the end of the late-afternoon session.

The water sports centre had been more of a success than he or the Jackson family could have ever dreamt of. The swimming sessions were still hugely popular, even though it was the middle of September already.

Of course, some swimmers would disappear when the colder months appeared. But he and Ben had come up with a plan to keep the centre open. Alex had an idea to add a sauna to help everyone warm up when the water temperature dipped. He had been reading about the Nordic trend of adding a sauna session to a cold-water plunge. They already had some tentative ideas about using one on wheels so that it could be moved on and off the beach for the changing seasons.

In addition, Dotty had had the idea to add a few special sessions to the normal schedule. So as well as a night-time swim for the next full moon, they were going to add a night-time Halloween swim with everyone decorating their swimming hats. The event was proving to be so popular already that there was a waiting list and Alex was contemplating adding an additional session to the evening.

Everyone remained enthusiastic for all the different sports on and in the lake and for that, he was hugely grateful.

Success had also filtered through to the hotel where more rooms were becoming booked throughout the week with so many more people discovering Maple Tree Lodge after visiting either the café or the water sports centre.

Good news had also arrived with planning permission granted for the individual lodges to be built on the other side of the lake and Alex was looking forward to helping Ben and Walter build them over the quieter months ahead.

His tentative relationship with his parents was also making huge strides forward. They were planning to come back and stay at the hotel in the autumn, with the idea to go out for dinner with both him and Hannah.

As always, the thought of Hannah made him smile. He belonged somewhere and with someone now. The family were more than happy for Hannah to move into the apartment above the Boathouse Café with him, thrilled that their relationship was going so well. In turn, he loved that he had his surrogate family and friends living on his doorstep.

But he had made new friends too. He was part of something bigger now. A community of all ages and abilities with the water sports centre. He felt as if he were finally able to share and give back after his successes and it made life all the sweeter.

And he had Tiny too. He loved owning a dog and Tiny

revelled in both the attention from all the people visiting Maple Tree Lodge and the lake. He was the first port of call for most of the swimmers to greet as they had learnt to love the gentle giant sitting patiently at the water's edge watching them all. Walking Tiny around the lake each day had meant that Alex had finally been able to slow down and enjoy taking his time to enjoy nature in its most beautiful surroundings.

But best of all he had Hannah. The depth of her love continued to surprise and amaze him, along with the quiet strength of her support for him. She was the love of his life and the apartment in the boathouse was a happy home for them both and Tiny too. Each morning he woke up to find her snuggled into his arms, starting each day with as many of her soft kisses as they could make time for. He trusted her wholeheartedly and couldn't believe how lucky he was to be planning a future with her.

He smiled as he looked across the lake as the next session of swimmers waded in. He had the life he had always dreamt of and every dream he had always wanted had come true. He couldn't believe how lucky he was.

* * *

Hannah had just finished tidying up the café and glanced around one last time before heading outside.

Even though summer was at an end, the café continued to be extremely popular, especially over the weekends. She revelled in the success of the place, trying to remind herself that the accomplishment was all the sweeter because so much of it was hers alone. With a little help from her family and friends, of course. But these days she believed in herself more than she had ever done and was proud of all she had achieved over the summer.

In fact, it was so busy she had already hired a part-time waitress to help out with the hectic times such as the weekends.

For the quieter weekdays, Lily had suggested building it up as a venue for various clubs. So there was already a schedule for an art club, a book club and even a menopause club. It was a place for people to come together and it gave her joy to see friends being made, which she felt was so important to people in dealing with their isolation and loneliness.

She glanced at the new autumnal menu that she had just placed on the counter. She was more confident now in her abilities. She believed in herself. She could try out new flavours whenever she wanted to. If they didn't work then she didn't take it personally, just moved on and tried something else. She was strong in both mind and spirit and she loved feeling that way about herself.

The permanent licence for the Boathouse Café had been granted earlier that week. Hannah loved the café but it also gave her a life away from the family lodge. Maple Tree Lodge was Ben and Lily's domain and she was happy for them. But it was nice to have her own separate home, her own separate life with Alex.

At the thought of Alex, she smiled to herself and went outside to find him. She loved him, body and soul. Best of all, it was a partnership built on trust and friendship. When he was low, she picked him up and vice versa. They had each other's backs and she felt stronger for his support each and every day. She and Alex were equal partners in life but also love. She knew that he loved her as much as she loved him and that their future would be a long and happy one together.

She had finally moved on from Sean. She had not heard from him since he had fallen off the jetty and she didn't care. He would never impact her life nor her happiness ever again. He was nothing to her now, whereas Alex was absolutely everything.

Alex was on the jetty, keeping a careful eye on the swimmers. Smiling at those familiar wide shoulders, Hannah knew that he was every bit the hero that she had always dreamt of, both emotionally and physically. Alex had taught her that she was special and that she deserved his love just as much as he deserved hers.

Tiny looked up at her as she walked up the jetty towards them both, wagging his tail in delight as usual. They were a little family, the three of them, and she had loved making the apartment above the café a happy home for them all.

Once she had reached the end of the jetty, she stroked Tiny before she wrapped her arms around Alex and held him close, looking around him at the swimmers still ploughing up and down.

'Mmm,' he murmured as she reached up to kiss the back of his neck. 'There's a law against distracting lifeguards, you know.'

'Then you'd better come find me when you're finished up here,' she told him.

But she didn't let go. She stood there, holding him close, feeling his hand cover hers as they both looked out across the lake.

Nearby she spotted a dragonfly, its jewel-like colour glinting in the sun as it hovered over the reeds. Her grandad had told her that dragonflies don't live long so have to make the most of their limited time.

Hannah felt as if she too was making up for lost time. She had spent so many years hiding away, daydreaming of being in a loving, fulfilled relationship and over the summer her life had changed in the best possible way.

She smiled to herself, thinking that perhaps if you believed hard enough, dreams really will come true after all.

* * *

MORE FROM ALISON SHERLOCK

Another book from Alison Sherlock, *Starry Nights at Dragonfly Lake*, is available to order now here:

https://mybook.to/StarryNights

ACKNOWLEDGEMENTS

Thank you to my lovely editor Caroline Ridding for her continuing patience and encouragement with each new book.

Thank you to everyone at Boldwood Books for all their hard work behind the scenes on all my books.

Thank you to all the readers and bloggers for their enthusiasm and reviews, which are important to so many authors, myself included.

Thank you to my lovely author friends, most especially my fellow Team Boldwood authors and the wonderful Surrey Buddies whose good cheer makes the hard task of writing a book so much more fun!

Thanks as always to my friends, especially my best friend Jo Botelle for sharing with me her wisdom and experience in the joy of wild swimming.

Huge thanks to my wonderful family for all their continued support, especially Gill, Simon, Louise, Ross, Lee, Cara and Sian.

Special thanks to my husband Dave for showing his expertise – or rather the lack of it! – on a paddleboard which brought the family such amusement this past summer holiday! As always, this book could have never been written without your love, support and the many cups of tea you make for me.

ABOUT THE AUTHOR

Alison Sherlock is the author of the bestselling *Willow Tree Hall* books. Alison enjoyed reading and writing stories from an early age and gave up office life to follow her dream. Her series for Boldwood is set in a fictional Cotswold village.

Download your exclusive bonus content from Alison Sherlock here:

Follow Alison on social media:

facebook.com/alison.sherlock.73

x.com/AlisonSherlock

ALSO BY ALISON SHERLOCK

The Riverside Lane Series

The Village Shop for Lonely Hearts

The Village of Lost and Found

The Village Inn of Secret Dreams

The Village of Happy Ever Afters

The Railway Lane Series

Heading Home to Lavender Cottage

New Beginnings on Railway Lane

Sunrise over Strawberry Hill Farm

Winter Magic on Railway Lane

The Maple Tree Lodge Hotel Series

Coming Home to Maple Tree Lodge

Daydreaming at the Boathouse Cafe

Starry Nights at Dragonfly Lake

Printed in Dunstable, United Kingdom

81206670R00184